TRIANGLE
OF
FIRE

by

JOSEPH TOMLINSON

For Bonehead

ACKNOWLEDGMENTS

I WOULD LIKE TO THANK Mark Linane, Tony Duprey and Valdo Calvert for showing what accountability, honor, and leadership look like. Your steadfast example set a standard to strive for and instilled in me fundamental principles that have guided and made a tremendous impact on my life.

Thanks also to John Armstrong, Mike Klinger, Nate Messer, Mark von Tillow, Robert Angulo, Mike Byers, Mark Calhoun, Corey Stowe, Ron Bollier, Chris Childers and every current and past LP Hotshot. I respect you more than anything. After winning a championship, athletes often say that no one can ever take the feeling of achievement away. That's the way I feel about my time on the crew.

Many more thanks to Richard Marek, Dan Lundin, and David Holland for the editing insight, Kyle Miller for the cover photo, and Dan DeBardeleben, without your help this book would have remained eight pages collecting dust in a drawer of my desk. Jamie McElvain, Patrick Conner and especially Chris Johnson, thank you for the friendship and inspiration for the second novel of this trilogy.

Heartfelt thanks and immeasurable love go to my Mom and Dad, my Grandma and Grandpa, Antoinette and Frank Almaguer, Gilbert and Rita Gallegos and everyone who ever called me Pepe.

Lastly, I wish to acknowledge the four most important people in my life- my wife Christine, who encouraged and supported me when I wanted to take the time to write this book, and our children, the T-3s, my trifecta winners- Aidan, Evan and Sean. You are my reason for being and fill my heart to overflowing.

NOTE FROM THE AUTHOR:

Someone once said the best lies are wrapped in truth.
Although certain characters may resemble historical figures,
this is a work of fiction and a product of my imagination. As
they said on *Dragnet*, the names were changed to protect the
innocent.

CHAPTER

1

1991

Guitars start softly, melodic and clear. The rhythm builds, gaining momentum. Like an alarm bell of power chords, bass and drums, the energy of the Cult's song "Fire Woman" roused us from a trance.

I have no idea where we were going, which seems to be the story of my life, only that we were driving south from the Sierras past 29 Palms into Joshua Tree National Monument. The Supe barreled ahead in his green Forest Service pumper truck with the two lumbering crew trucks keeping pace behind. Sitting in the rear seat of the second crew buggy, I was playing Rummy 500 with Corndog, listening to music from the boom box. I played well but Corndog still crushed me. Originally from Montana, he must have played cards throughout their long, cold winters. The guy was a shark. The rest of the squad sprawled across seats, reading magazines and well worn paperback novels or stared out the windows, quietly watching the miles blow past.

I started chewing Red Man tobacco a couple hours earlier to keep from nodding off and now had a sharp edge going- that juice in my blood and head feeling. The music played from a compilation cassette tape I made that winter and had a solid blend of rock classics, as well as more progressive hard charging punk anthems. Picking tunes that'd appeal to the diverse group on the crew was not easy. In my opinion the mix did nicely covering the bases.

For the past week we were on a large timber fire at the edge of Yosemite National Park. Because of the Park Service's "let burn" policy, no one fought the fire until it crossed over the boundary onto National Forest lands. By then the fire intensified exponentially and burnt thousands of acres of resplendent timber forest before we were able to secure containment with a line around it. Fortunately we got the call down to Joshua Tree this morning, or we'd have been stuck doing mop-up for at least a week. This was shaping up to be one doozy of a fire season.

"Look at that country. There is nothing to burn."

After the high timber with mammoth Ponderosa Pine and even more impressive and majestic Redwoods, the desert did not look like much. Dusty sand sprinkled with lonely sagebrush, more sand, random cactus and occasional Yucca plants every fifteen feet or so. The ten man crew buggies were without air conditioning. We drove with sliding windows open. Instead of cooling us, the unremitting flow of dry, hot air only worsened the oven effect. Waves of heat rose from gray pavement where drifts of sand did not cover the road. The waves created a trippy optical effect, shimmering and shaking, dancing like spirits, distorting the landscape.

"What a God forsaken, nowhere land. We ought to let this hellhole burn."

Looking across the desolate plain, I tended to agree with Lupe's sentiments.

"Hey Nathan, turn that music down," Killer yelled over his shoulder into the cab. He sat in the front passenger seat, talking with the Supe over the radio. Corndog turned off the boom box, then stood and manually flipped the intercom at the front of the cabin to "on", so we could hear the discussion.

"Yeah, I copy, Supe. We'll keep a sharp eye on the winds."

Foreman on squad Four- A, Killer started with the hotshots years ago. Until recently he led the Arroyo Grande helitac crew. His angular face was lean with a full, sweeping black mustache and bronze features dark from the sun. He had the tall, rangy but strong frame of an endurance athlete. The nickname came from years ago after a drunken rant or maybe because he liked to blow things up. He was a good fireman.

"Okay, you heard the Supe. Gear up. We're hiking from here. Cracker, we won't need three saws, bring an extra shovel. Metlox and Gus, grab some combie tools. You won't be pulling much today. The local ranger says there've been fifteen and twenty-five mile an hour gusts from the west. Keep a lookout for wind shifts!"

Everyone piled from the truck. Even on flat ground, I threw the chock block behind the rear tire. The crew loaded on packs and hard hats, then grabbed tools from a side compartment. The Supe had already busted ahead with the Park Ranger. We formed a line behind Stew, the foreman on squad Four-B then started hiking to the east.

At one-thirty in the afternoon, the temperature was 110 degrees. After driving six hours straight, the legs were stiff. Stew's death march pace soon worked the kinks out. After a mile your legs practically hiked on their own.

Tramping the dusty path of coarse gray sand, visible ahead, the fire drove forward, pushed by the winds. With the combination of extreme heat and dry conditions, sagebrush flared quickly. Yellow flames flashed and jumped from one bush to the next, leapfrogging, pushing onward.

"Shut up, Wadlow."

Robby Wadlow groused that we could have driven to the edge of the fire, instead of hiking more than a mile and a half under the blistering sun. Although Robby had a reputation for being a complainer, his argument did have merit.

After a week in the shade of timber country, unbearable desert heat pressed the skin of my face and covered the body like a woolen horse blanket. Soon we caught up to the Supe. Kneeling on one leg, he huddled with Stew and the Killer, drawing directions in the sand. I took a breath and sipped a quick drink of water. They decided Four-A would attack the blaze along the northern flank while Four-B went after the southern end.

We'd been traveling for hours, sitting around, playing music and cards, passing time and joking. After lazy hours of boredom and waiting, without hesitation, we were smack in the middle of an honest to goodness wildfire in the hottest part of the day. No one made fun of the desert anymore. With the combination of scorching air temperature, dry flashy grass and light brush, flames flared with a violent burst and moved forward, throwing off intense radiant heat that hit in waves.

We punched line near the fire's edge, throwing dirt onto its base, trying to knock down the flames so we could get in close and uproot the sagebrush. Fire is alive and requires three components to survive: heat, fuel and oxygen. To stop a fire, you must eliminate one of those three parts of the triangle. The straightforward, most direct way to stop a wildland brush fire is encircle with a fireline and separate the fire from unburned fuel it needs to consume to continue. So we went to work. Ten guys moved in tandem, physically pushing at max effort while simultaneously getting cooked by the sun's rays and heat from flames.

"Heh heh, come on you slacker, throw that dirt." Vintage Supe led the way, everywhere at once, all over the place, pressing guys, encouraging everyone. "Have a drink. There you go, sport. Damn now, move your ass."

Pillsbury looked like he'd run twenty miles. His face flushed red and shiny like a waxed apple. The Supe was on him like white on rice. "Hot shovel that Drew. Come on. Keep going now."

I swung the Pulaski with purpose, breaking apart hard packed dirt and sod for the shovels to throw onto the flames. Adrenaline pumped through me from the excitement of going direct, but the heat took a toll. Whenever the winds shifted, hot smoke blew right in your face. The carbon gray, acrid gas choked when breathed in. Pillsbury looked ready to pass out. He still shoveled but weakly. His legs had the wobbly look of a boxer who caught one square, still upright and on his feet but doubtful to last a standing eight count.

"Pillsbury, trade tools with Lightning. Lightnin' let's see that hot shovel." Now I was in the thick of it.

I started in the groove too, body flowing, hands, arms and shoulders in fluid motion, digging into loose dirt, lifting the shovel full and throwing each load onto flames. The movements repeated over, over and over again for I don't know how long.

Lead hot shovel is no joke. You are the individual closest to the direct heat of the flames. The main fire spits embers ahead ten feet and more to new bushes, which smolder, ignite, and flare up. Fresh waves of radiant heat blast right when you move in close attempting to knock down the flames.

Grass and brush are much lighter fuels than the heavy woods of timber country and easier to set ablaze. Once started, light fuels flare quickly with flashy, intense heat. Combustion rapidly comes to completion, and the flames quickly burn out. Unless the fire grows and spreads new flames to unburned fuels, it will soon extinguish and die. We were trying to contain this fire by going direct, knocking down the head before it could catch new fuels. Although a straightforward plan, without water from engines, the onus to stop the blaze rested squarely on our shoulders. And I felt it. Reverberations of my heart beating pounded in my head. Hair in both nostrils burned from breathing super heated air.

My forearms were like rubber. I could not throw the dirt with as much power but was hanging in there. Salt from sweat stung both eyes. Dust and dry chalk lined mouth and throat. My breathing had a ragged rhythm, one breath to jam the shovel into sand and lift up, a burst exhale to throw the load onto the flames, then a deep, catch up breath as I moved to reload and start the process again. The intensity of being lead changed time perception. Minutes blurred into hours and seemed like forever. Like sand falling in an hourglass, steadily I grew weaker.

My heart thumped, ready to explode. Blood rushed behind my eyes, bathing everything in a hue of red and orange. The lungs screamed at me, each breath a desperate gasp.

Deep into anaerobic debt, I held on and blocked away the pain, pushing through to keep going. Shovel loads of dirt. Waves of radiant heat. Flash bursts of flame. Ragged gulps of breath.

"There you go, Lightning, have a drink now. Heh heh, just enough. Not too much."

The canteen water stung like drinking from a hot faucet. I needed the liquid. The Supe nodded. "All right, son. You got this now."

"You swing that tool like a chick." Lumpy's voice carried across the distance.

I looked to the sound and realized we were not far from tying in with Four-B. They were maybe two hundred feet away. With renewed energy, knowing how close we were and bolstered by the Supe's words, I started throwing the shovel as hard as ever. As the squad realized we were near the finish line, their intensity increased as well.

"For a dollar an hour. What is up with dat?" Kingman relished talking smack.

Another ten feet and I tied into the guys of 4-B. We now had one ragged line around the fire, containment of that JT blaze complete.

I stepped back. Super-P's and combie tools finished clearing the fireline. Resting one hand on the shovel handle, I drank freely from a quart canteen. Ridiculously hot, the water tasted like plastic. Not caring, I gulped with abandon. My body absorbed the fluid. The coarse, gritty sensation of sand and dirt lined my tongue and teeth. Water helped rinse the rough texture from my mouth.

Taking off sunglasses to wipe the lenses clean, I looked around at how far we had come. There were not many defining landmarks to judge from, except a steep outcrop of rocks a quarter mile to the west. When we started at one-thirty I did not remember that bank of rocks. Now a quarter to five, I placed the cleaned sunglasses back on. The world looked amazingly better minus the layer of dust and dirt. The rose tint of the lenses eased the sharpness of the stark landscape. The flat sweep of sand and rocks looked bleached the color of bone with speckles of subtle shades of yellows, browns, and orange. Distant in the east through the harsh sunlight, the moon's faint outline rose visible plain and white against the pale, faded cloudless sky.

The winds died down and with them our conflagration. The Supe directed us to widen the narrow, bare bones line around the eastern smoking but charred remnants of the fire's head in case the winds picked up later. After a brief respite, we restarted our work, making the barrier stronger. Punching line in next to the dying yet still smoldering embers went easier than the full on intensity of going direct against the head of the fire's flames, but significantly less dramatic. Not that anyone complained. The heat from the day took a toll on everyone. Blood pulsed in both forearms. The weight of fatigue blanketed my body. I forced myself to be mechanical in movement, conserving energy while punching out the line.

My name is Curtis Browning. The guys on the crew call me Lightning, or sometimes Molasses, a completely inane and undeserved nickname if you ask me. Back on my first season the crew cleared brush in a local campground with weed-whackers. We had partied hard the night before and were up late. Okay yes, I will admit to having some cobwebs that morning and being fairly well hungover. That said, although by no means a champion weed-whacker, I definitely cleared as much ground as anyone that day. The mistake was to so strenuously object when Stew said I worked like old people have sex. He used a different word. In retrospect, my vehement response to his criticism ensured the worst possible outcome. The surefire way for a nickname to stick is when you don't like it. Getting a nickname resembled stepping in quicksand. The more you fight, the more you get stuck.

I work for the U.S. Forest Service fighting wildland brush and timber fires on an elite twenty man hot shot crew- the Los Prietos Hotshots, based in the Santa Ynez Valley, northeast of Santa Barbara, California. As a kid my dad worked as a smokejumper in McCall, Idaho. I grew up idolizing firefighters. I remember looking up from my little boy's vantage point at the rough men in their heavy lug-soled boots, knowing they were something special. Whenever a fire broke out, the tower bell would sound across the neighborhood, one blast for every smokejumper needed. Each kid knew where their dad stood on the jump list. This was back before women smokejumpers. When a real large fire or a summer lightning storm set off a slew of smaller fires, the bell would sound loudly, repeating over and over. Everyone stopped in place to count the blasts, trying to figure out if their dad would be going away. Overwhelming excitement ran rampant because the jumpers were being called away to some unknown place of adventure. No one knew when they'd be back.

The summer of my sixth year was a particularly brutal fire season. The jumpers were gone for weeks and weeks on end, at that age what seemed like forever. The married couples and families lived in a trailer park on the other side of the hill from the jumper base and barracks for the single firefighters. A narrow path covered thick with fallen pine needles from surrounding trees connected the trailer park with the base. I spent that summer repeatedly pushing my single speed, banana seat bicycle to the top of the hill, checking out the jumper base from a distance and then riding back down the steep trail as fast as possible. Navigating the uneven surface of pine needles down the curving path at breakneck speeds proved tricky. I repeated that exhilarating, crazy ride over and over again. I remember the afternoon my dad came home after he'd been gone for over a month. He walked down the trail, a pack of gear slung over one shoulder, his tall frame blocking out the sun behind him. He had paused to pick a handful of ripe huckleberries from one of the many bushes lining the hill. In my mind he looked larger than life, strong and heroic. I can still see him walking that path, and remember dropping the bicycle and running to him, feeling a rush of happiness that my Pops came home. He dropped the bag of gear and lifted me high in the air. Giving me a big hug, his rough beard scratched the skin on my face.

He died a couple years later in an auto accident. Mom's eyes were red as she told me how his buddy swerved on an icy road to avoid a deer, flipping the pickup truck. Not wearing a seat belt, Pops died on impact. I stared without saying anything or even crying, her words not really registering, the enormity of loss more than I could comprehend. We moved from Idaho shortly after to be closer to my mom's folks and never went back. I will always remember the way my heart sang seeing him walk down that hill and home to us. Down the road, I may look into smoke jumping. Right now, I am happy to be on this crew, working with these guys.

The LP Hotshots are one of the most respected firefighting outfits in the United States. Our boss, the Superintendent of

Hotshots, the Supe, is singularly responsible for the high standard of the crew. He is like a real life character from a Louis L'Amour novel, tough as nails and salty as hell. He walks with a rolling cowboy gait that can eat through the miles, although less fluid now, due to five separate knee operations he's endured to keep going. After years of ground pounding, hiking up, over and down steep, rugged country while carrying a heavy pack, the wheels tried to give him some trouble. He had zero intention of slowing down though.

The Supe turned his back on a desk job years ago. He loved the outdoors, the fires, and the road too much. Instead of climbing the ladder, and no doubt he would have risen to Deputy Chief or Regional Forester or some other big time muckity-muck position, he fought forest fires. A ton of them. Over the years the Supe led the shots through fires across the US in every kind of situation. My mom always said the Devil wasn't necessarily that smart. He's just been around so long, he learned all the tricks. Well, the Supe has seen more wildfire behavior than most anyone. That firsthand experience made him a widely respected, fire fighting expert. Fireline- Summer Battles of the West is an outstanding and well researched work of nonfiction. Not by coincidence, the author Michael Thoele interviewed and quotes the Supe at length.

He has ruddy cheeks and a tan face, weathered from long years in the sun. With his mustache more gray than brown, he still cuts a dashing figure. Last month in Arizona, the local newspaper ran a photo of the Supe on the front page.

We were off the line for the first time in a week. Shaving and using the rear view mirror of the Supe rig to see his reflection, he looked right out of central casting for the Marlboro Man.

Over the years, the Supe built a remarkable hotshot crew, founded on a strong tradition of character. Personnel turn over every year, but the core leaders stay on, ensuring the highest standards are maintained. Chief among this group is Stewart, the foreman on Four- B. He has metallic grey eyes, a grip and forearms like Popeye and can hike the steepest mountains at an unyielding death march pace as if his legs were made from coils of heavy duty steel springs. Stew is capable and as tough a fireman as there is.

I associate Stew with Kirk Gibson hitting that game winning home run for the Dodgers in the World Series three years ago. Beat-up and physically falling apart, Gibson prevailed because of his mental toughness. Mark McGwire and Jose Conseco were juiced up and bashing bombs. The A's were great all season long. Their pitching staff and especially the closer Eckersley shut opposing teams down. Gibson's improbable pinch-hit, walk-off blast epitomized the word clutch and reversed the momentum of the Series leading to the huge underdog Dodgers' victory. We listened to the game on the radio driving home from a fire in the Angeles N.F. The drama of the moment made a huge impression on me. Whenever they replay the homer on television with Gibson limping round the bases, doing his fist pump, I always think of Stew.

When lead sawyer for the shots, Stew could run a chainsaw for hours, relentlessly. Guys joke, imitating him through clenched teeth, "Grrrr....Thirty-six hour shift, a tin of Copenhagen and one quart of water. That's all you need, you pussies."

Kingman is our lead Sawyer and does the best Stew impression. He has a collection of voices that get everyone rolling. I'm no rookie, but Stew still intimidates the hell out of me. A fearless crackup, Mike enjoys giving him a hard time. Kingman can also saw like a banshee.

On a hand crew each tool has a specific function. The chain saws lead the way, cutting trees and brush. The sawyers set the pace for the rest of the crew. Cutting brush through heavy thickets takes endurance and strength as well as excellent technique to be efficient. In a brutal rat's nest of chaparral you cannot simply muscle through, the bar will get stuck or throw the chain. With each passing season, Kingman learned more and grew better. Having such a skilled sawyer, we were that much faster and could punch in fireline like nobody's business.

Pullers are paired with a sawyer and physically grab cut limbs, branches, and stumps throwing them out of the way, preferably away from the main fire. The Super Pulaskis follow next, smashing the soil asunder and chopping roots that cross the line. A Pulaski is an axe with a grub hoe on the backend. The axe cuts tree limbs and branches, while the hoe breaks apart dirt, clearing the path of anything combustible. The Supe invented the Super- P years ago welding together two regular Pulaski grub hoes to create more tool surface.

We each carry backpacks loaded with enough gear to be self sufficient for several days: a head lamp with spare batteries, poly-propylene underwear, a space blanket for cold nights, food for several days and as much water as you can lug around. I haul a gallon dispersed between web belt and backpack and am referred to as a water buffalo. Staying hydrated is worth the heavy load to me.

C-Rations or MREs, army issue "meals ready to eat" serve for food. They are dreadful and must be Korean War leftovers. I carry two for emergencies and a small jar of Tabasco sauce to drown out the awful flavor. For real meals I pack cans of tuna, sardines, ranch style beans, spicy beef chili, individual packets of apple and cinnamon instant oatmeal, and both powdered hot chocolate and instant coffee. Usually an apple, a couple oranges and several peanut butter granola bars are stashed in a side pocket too.

Guys with gas packs also carry two quarts of gasoline and a quart of oil for the chain saws. Besides the extra weight, oil and gas leak everywhere inside the pack. The stench of petrol permeates clothes, food and even plastic canteens. Getting rid of that smell or sticky oil from your gear is next to impossible. Hence, rookies or FNG's were relegated gas packs.

The scrapers make sure the fireline is void of combustible material like leaves, pine needles, or roots. If a tiny bit of fire crosses the line by creeping through the duff, flames will take off and burn with renewed vigor on the unburned side. The squad boss inspects the line quality to ensure it holds. The width of line required depends on the height and type of fuel, as well as the rate flames spread, which is related to wind speed. That timber country fire charged like a freight train across the crowns of trees. We witnessed fire jump line five bulldozer blade-lengths wide. Sparks and burning embers float above in the updraft and carry forward distances across, starting spot fires anew. Spots quickly expand, grow and merge with the main fire to roll onward.

The winds were dying with the evening. Because of the light fuels, we made the Joshua Tree line four feet wide.

As the sun began to set, I began to understand why some folks might appreciate the desert. For the first time the air seemed actually pleasant enough to breathe. Random local wildlife started to come out and about. A hundred feet away a desert owl swooped down from high in the sky at breakneck speed and snatched a field mouse in one fell swoop. The owl flapped its wings effortlessly, rising smoothly into the air with prey firmly in grasp. The tiny mouse, visible in the distance, flopped about, tail swishing futilely.

High clouds formed in the west, mile long streaks of pink cotton candy stretching across the deepening azure of evening sky. The moon from earlier shined brighter now and glowed as if from its own phosphorus light. Shadows from caverns and craters spread across the surface, like scars marking a face. The first scattered evening stars appeared to have definition, each individual prick of light shimmering and dancing above.

"You don't understand, that tree was over a thousand years old. This is a protected wilderness." The Park Ranger's voice quavered as he complained to Killer. They stood feet apart, facing each other, the Ranger visibly upset.

"I am sorry sir, but you don't understand." Calm and low, the Killer's voice carried through the still air. Both hands were at his sides, waist high with palms up in a show of peace. Being reasonable did not mean backing down.

"That tree continued burning at the crown, spitting embers and sparks across the line. If we didn't cut it down now, for certain there'd be a spot fire tomorrow morning, as soon as the winds and heat ratchet up again. This fire would have roared off and more precious acreage and trees would have burned. Neither of us wanted that."

The Ranger did not give in easily, however. They went in circles about the proper course of action we should have taken.

In the distance a white Park Service truck slowly approached, a low trail of dust hovering like a tail behind it. The truck stopped near the Supe's rig. The Supe walked over and spoke with the driver.

"Bring 'em in boys," his voice crackled over the walkie-talkie. "Grubs here."

We lined up, single file and hiked down, threading between large rocks, yucca spikes, and lonely Joshua Trees, thousands of years old, one of the oldest living things on the planet. Nature showed a peculiar sense of humor creating such a homely, yet striking looking plant that could survive here. And not just survive, those plants truly flourished in this brutal climate, living long, fruitful lives. How fitting and proper they were named after the Israelite who led his people past Moses' grave, out of the desert and into the Promised Land. "Professor Bowers, dropping some Old Testament on you," I thought to myself. How poignant and sad to put down a thousand year old living being, even if only a tree. Looking at the downed Joshua Tree, bucked into pieces and lying on the earth, filled me with a shadow of regret.

A tall woman who resembled Big Bird from Sesame Street wearing a Smokey the Bear hat spread food across the tailgate of the white Park Service vehicle. There were buckets and buckets of the Colonel's fried chicken, containers of mashed potatoes, green salad with thousand isle dressing, cornbread with butter, and biscuits with gravy. She even busted out several gallons of ice cream. I grabbed a can of Dr. Pepper from the ice chest, loaded a plate and took a seat on a boulder next to Lumpy.

We ate plenty of chicken growing up but never the Colonel's, probably for some unknown ideological reason. Who knows. That crunchy and greasy chicken tasted incredible. After the day's mouthful of dirt, the spices and saltiness of fried chicken coated my tongue. Chewing the meat released pure joy. I caught myself inhaling ravenously like an animal. Big Bird must have brought enough food for fifty. The twenty of us tore through the buckets without hesitation.

When I finally came up for breath, the rest of the crew were joking and rehashing the day. The thrill of initial attack, going head to head with fast moving flames prevailed as the feeling in the air, increased by the tired satisfaction knowing we did a good job.

"That Ranger almost bust a fuse when Mike cut down that J tree." Metlox had a way of overstating the obvious and apparently found this humorous.

"Yep, the Killer sure gave him a crash course on fire behavior 101."

"How about Doughboy. I thought he was gonna go tits up on us there."

Guys were brutal. Always present, the pressure to pull your weight did not dissipate. Wadlow never hesitated to point out anyone else's possible weakness, perhaps hoping to bolster his own resolution. Although 6' 4", strong and in peak physical condition, an unstated question lingered about his mental toughness. In our business that tended to be a critical failing. A flicker of self doubt hid in the deepest recesses of his mind. Wadlow wondered whether or not he was a quitter. Everyone faces questions about themselves. How we choose to answer the tough questions defines us. Named after the giant in the Guinness Book of World Records, Wadlow was strikingly handsome with blond hair, piercing blue eyes and the physique of an Olympic water polo player. Instead of working this misery, slogging through caustic smoke and dirt, he should have been modeling, making a fortune and drinking champagne, gracing magazine covers and runways in Paris or NYC.

I dumped the empty plate of chicken bones in the trash bag and grabbed my sleeping bag from the crew truck. After the brutal heat of day, the night felt refreshing in contrast. We would forgo our single man tents and sleep under the gorgeous heavens wide open with stars. Hopefully, I wouldn't be bitten by a rare, poisonous spider or Gila monster, or some other desert nonsense. Without the warmth of the sun, the high desert air temps dropped dramatically. I bundled myself in the sleeping bag, head resting softly on a makeshift pillow of my dark green LP hooded sweatshirt stuffed with two leather Whites boots for cushioning.

Lying under an incredible array of stars, mapping out the galaxies in my mind and placing the Milky Way within the immense universe above, I felt peacefully in alliance with the cosmos. The clear sky appeared vibrant with stars grouped together closely in clusters that looked like bright neighborhoods. I imagined the possibilities of traveling through space, seeking other worlds and civilizations. Watching for falling stars, a faint light tracked far above the horizon. I lost the blip for a second but then focusing both eyes, found it again and watched the object sweeping methodically through the sky. It must have been a satellite, encircling the planet, tracking foreign troop movements, or perhaps monitoring the weather, or maybe sending television signals to remote rural homes. Imagination kept me company and awake for an hour. For my spent body, the desert dirt bed felt soft and comfortable. Life was good. Contemplating space travel I fell asleep.

CHAPTER

2

I awoke right before the Supe could lift the south end of the sleeping bag. Sitting upright, I murmured good morning. He clucked at me then shuffled amongst the sleeping crew, lifting guy's feet in the air, quietly rousting everyone from their dreams. A faint glimmer of dawn crept like a line across the dark edge of the horizon. The crispness of the high desert air surprised after the scorcher of yesterday.

Pulling each boot over somewhat-clean socks, I soaked in the morning stillness and quiet. Even the murmur of twenty hotshots could not disturb the peace. A pair of fold out tables were set with breakfast. The black sky turned pink and orange, then faded and washed into a translucent blue. Given the choice, I'd probably choose sleeping in. But the sunrise and optimistic promise of a new day proved hard to beat. Sunsets are romantic. Of course I love them. But sunrises are special. Whether up early on a road trip or adventure, or even when pulling an all nighter either partying or studying, sunrises can be magic. They're probably not so cool if you work on a farm and must get up every day with the chickens.

"Lightning, you look like a raccoon."

I looked at Lumpy confused.

"Yeah dude, check it out. You've raccoon eyes as if you were skiing."

Pulling my sunglasses from the sweatshirt pocket, the reflected face in the lens showed a dramatic tan line around my eyes. After months of sun in the midst of fire season, sunburn didn't seem likely.

"That's weird, right?'

"Must have been while throwing hot shovel. The fire seared your face. You notice your skin getting hot?"

"Well, yeah. Yesterday got a little warm. Haha. That's wild."

Wild hardly described how we spent this day. Mop-up consists of going through a blackened, burnt area and extinguishing any remaining hot embers or coals still present. Desert fuels are light. Except for a few random yucca heads smoldering, there were not many hot spots to worry about. We would break apart still glowing embers and smother them with dirt. In timber fires thick stumps and roots will smolder for days and even weeks or months. Mop-up prevents wind from fanning still glowing embers with fresh oxygen and reigniting the fire. In timber and heavy brush the threat of re-burn can be dangerous. After fire burns through, the remaining scorched fuels are dried out like kindling. If flames restart in a recently burnt area with wood essentially pre-heated and dry, the second fire or re-burn can rip through with potentially dire consequences.

Contrasted with yesterday's excitement going direct against active flames of a real conflagration, mop-up qualified as down right boring. Hotshots tend to think of mop-up as good duty for others. Without water from fire engines, the work exemplified dull and tedious.

We fanned across a wide coppery canyon, the drudgery calling. Although not as scorching hot as yesterday, the heat still felt suffocating. After a few monotonous hours, guys peeled off, looking for shade and bivouacs to hide out. The central concept being, if you're not visible while not working, no one will know the difference.

Either slow witted or maybe dedicated, I grubbed at a smoldering yucca stump, working to extinguish every last ember. After dislodging burnt black brands, I methodically mixed and buried them in the dull gray sand. The desert granules were not unlike beach sand, except coarser.

A flicker of movement distracted to the left. My vision took a moment to focus and finally make out a lizard, now stock-still, frozen in place on a grey rock a dozen yards away.

Perfectly camouflaged, I would never have noticed if she hadn't moved. I tossed a flat white stone with a flick of the wrist that barely missed by less than a foot. That fool lizard stayed in place too. After moving and gaining my attention, she now stayed put. A second rock fell short by inches. The shot landed close enough dust sprayed and covered her with a thin mist. A moment before I tossed a third stone, the lizard wizened up, scurrying away herky-jerky, long tail dragging behind.

The herky-jerking motion of the lizard reminded me of a fire in Oregon last year. Spider and I were away from the squad and nailed full on by an air tanker load of fire retardant. The pilot flew low, aiming to knock down the head of the fire but missed his target by fifty yards. We realized too late to avoid the approaching wave, the pink cargo masking the sky, crashing directly towards us. With no time to amscray out of the way, we dropped to the ground, hugging dirt with helmets facing in the direction of the DC-10. The velocity and weight of three thousand gallons of sticky, orange goop demolished us. The volume and force hit in a mini-tsunami that lifted and slammed us down the hill, tumbling and rolling for fifty feet. Worse than Waimea shore pound, we bounced down the hillside, stumps and rocks banging the way. With ears ringing and knees wobbly, drenched with pink orange slurry, I stood painfully from the tumble but in one piece.

Face down to my right and awash in the sticky stuff, Spider's torso lay still except both legs jerked with a spastic motion not human but more like a disjointed headless chicken. I rushed over and helped him to his feet. A gash crossed his forehead and across the right cheekbone. The skin of the face hung loose as if someone tried to peel it away. The Dermis layer appeared visible and pink with blood vessels and papilla like a medical textbook or grotesque slasher movie in bright light of day. Above his head when the slurry load hit, Spider's combie tool flew about and struck him when he rolled down the hillside, practically tearing his face off. I radioed for help, my voice stammering over the airwaves. We medivac-ed him off the mountain and to a hospital in Medford. Those trauma surgeons earned their money because when he came back to work and healed, barely a scar remained. I don't know what scared me more, the gruesome face or the way his body jerked like that fool lizard. The memory gave me the chills.

Looking around the Joshua Tree canyon with not another person in sight, I scanned the hillsides but could not make out anyone hiding. They were to the west, last I noticed. I started in that direction and almost walked past the squad and probably would have if not for a flash of orange from Pete Johnson's hard hat.

"Lightnin' you look like an idiot standing there throwing rocks at your own shadow."

"Whatever, Pete."

Six of them were spread underneath two woeful looking creosote bushes. With dusty green pants and faded yellow nomex shirts blackened from soot, they blended into the whisper of shadows on the hillside quite nicely. I ducked under a hanging branch, scooting in on hands and knees, positioning myself for a share of the shade. That morning I stashed a paperback in the backpack. Pleased for a break, I pulled it from the pocket and lying against the pack for support, began to read.

The book was a soft cover collection of poems from a romantic era literature class last quarter. Although I sometimes got lost in the assigned reading, the ethos and appreciation for the natural world of the pastoral romantic poets resonated with me. The idea of being a shepherd sounded appealing. To pull off the romantic ideal in today's modern world was a goal. I envisioned hiking mountains with a .30- 06 slung over one shoulder, keeping an eye for mountain lions or predators with a trusty German Shepherd dog as companion. Shearing sheep could be physical work. Casually hiking the hills, enjoying sunshine filled days sounded like pretty good duty. The poets tended go overboard, manically obsessing about the love of their life. That is where they usually lost me. Being that consumed about some gal did not sound too believable. Admiring the beauty of the physical world was a program to get behind.

Pete explained to everyone about his newest money making scheme. Because of Santa Barbara's poor water quality this was a can't lose proposition.

"Each filtration unit is two hundred dollars, with a lifetime guarantee. Instead of buying bottled water and corporate water companies clearing fat profits, we cut out the middleman. I'm telling you, direct product marketing is the wave of the future. You guys should really check it out."

"Wall Street, you're a freaking idiot. This is a pyramid scheme, no question about it."

"Lupe, listen. We have one of the first franchises and earn a percentage from everybody we sign up's sales. You just need to sign up four people. You'll be thanking me."

"No fucking way, or thanks. Real super proposition. Screw your friends over, then recruit them to screw over their friends. Swell system. This house of cards will topple over sure enough. When the money disappears, then come bragging about it."

Suddenly two fighter jets blew past, flying low to the ground, hugging the terrain. Deep in thought about a poem, I did not get a good look at the first plane. The second looked military, perhaps an F-14. They raced by in a mock dogfight, the booming roar of engines startling against the vast stillness of desert. Then as quickly, they disappeared, echoing booms reverberating and slowly dissipating, the only sign of their passing.

"Wow, can you believe that! I could see the expression on the pilot's face in that first jet."

"Holy crow, they were barely thirty feet off the ground."

"What a blast, can you imagine?"

There we were, biding time, holed up under sparse shade in the middle of one dusty, godforsaken purgatory while those pilots flew around sparkling fifty million dollar aircraft, playing fighter games at high-risk speeds. The contrast made our situation seem pathetic. Instead of feeling luxurious in the idleness, I suddenly wanted to be anywhere but there, and wished to be deployed to another fire or sent home. The feeling of hopelessness passed after a moment, however. I returned to reading. We hid out the rest of the day.

We slept in Joshua Tree again that night. The following morning the fire gods granted my wish, releasing us to return home. While filling the vehicles at a gas station near Yucca Valley, in the attached mini-mart, I found a dusty, two dollar cassette tape of theme songs from old television westerns. We played the vintage cowboy music on the boom box during the desolate drive home. Tumbleweeds blew across the road as the original theme to Rawhide played and the Supe rig sped along, leading the two lumbering crew buggies.

We'd only been on the road for a little more than two weeks, but I looked forward to getting home. After neglecting to pay a couple bills before we left, worries about credit history blemishes nagged the back of my mind the whole trip. Echoes of my mom admonished how financial missteps lasted on the "permanent record." Always full of wisdom, she would convey her knowledge while lying on the couch in the afternoon, smoking cigarettes and listening to her favorite sad songs. I used to refill the thick Scotch glass from a heavy, half gallon bottle, topped with crushed ice. Her drinks had to be icy cold. We usually played cards until after the third one. Then ready for her nap, she would tell me to go outside and play. Still really beautiful, a number of men showed interest, but no one ever lasted. She could not love anyone after my pops, and was pretty much broken after he passed. I tried to focus on the barren landscape and stupid cowboy songs as we drove down the bleak highway. Ignoring the voices of ghosts from the past wasn't easy.

After a long day, we finally pulled over the San Marcos Pass and into Paradise Canyon. Corndog fast forwarded the mix tape to "The Boys are Back in Town" by Thin Lizzy, the southern blues influenced rock staple always a crew favorite. Everybody especially loved the part that went something like, guess who just got back today, them wild eyed boys that had been away. They were clearly singing about us.

CHAPTER

3

We pulled into the hotshot compound at five-thirty. Quickly the rigs were gassed, dull tools unloaded and fresh ones restocked into the truck compartments. The next workday would be spent cleaning gear, sharpening used tools, prepping and getting ready for the next fire. Tonight, however, the comforts of civilization beckoned. After handling the immediate necessary chores, everyone gathered around the flagpole near the office until six o'clock, joking and recapping the trip. When the clock hit the top of the hour, the Supe said to get out of there. He would be buying the first round. Like a wave rolling outward the crowd headed for the parking lot.

My motorcycle rested where I'd left her parked under a tree near the edge of the gravel lot. The used Kawasaki GPZ 750 cost nine hundred dollars two summers ago and still ran great. Although not as quick nor nimble as other rice burners, the GPZ suited me fine. I did not care about being the only person on the crew who did not drive a pickup truck. Packed with an assortment of Fords, Chevys, Toyotas, and one old Dodge, the parking lot could fill in as a photo shoot location for Peterson's truck and four- wheel drive magazine. One day soon I'd save enough money to purchase a Toyota 4x of my own.

The GPZ started without hesitation. I sat and let her idle for a short while, listening to the steady dull clicking purr of the engine. Strapping on a silver Shoei helmet and slinging over one shoulder a large black duffel loaded with dirty clothes, I followed the line of trucks peeling from the parking lot onto the road towards the Paradise Canyon Store. The Store is several miles from the ranger station near the junction with Highway 154 on the eastern side and below the San Marcos Pass. The road is a narrow winding two-lane shaded by Piñon Pine, Scrub Oak, Manzanita, and interspersed near the creek with Poison Oak.

Although the valley gets warm in summer, shade from covering trees cooled the temperature. After that hellacious desert, our version of warm weather seemed downright pleasant in comparison. Riding a leisurely pace, I sat comfortably in the saddle and allowed the vehicles ahead to pull away. Wind blew through the open helmet visor. Smells of dried grass filled the air. I enjoyed being mobile again, content to breathe. Riding over loose gravel from a pothole, the rear tire spit a small stone like a slingshot.

Hugging the engine with both legs, I cranked my right wrist sharply, opening wide the throttle. The GPZ rocketed forward instantaneously. Applying pressure forward to the left hand grip, I pulled the motorcycle down to a forty degree angle, heading into a group of S- curves. Pushing the right hand forward, I swung smoothly across to a hundred and thirty degree angle, leaning through the turn, then back again to less than forty degrees through the next several banks in the road. I could feel the g-force as we hugged pavement and accelerated through each bend. After a final set of curves, the road straightened with clear asphalt ahead. Opening the throttle full tilt, I rocketed the final mile to the store.

I pulled in with a rush, weaving through the parking lot full of vehicles and stopped next to the Killer parking his '71 faded red FJ Land Cruiser. He stepped down, slamming the metal door shut. A backcountry veteran of countless fishing trips to Baja, the Land Cruiser sported an ancient winch on the front bumper, aggressive Cooper tires and a utilitarian lift. Still running like a beast, the Cruiser looked ready for an off road, cross continent rally. The Killer gave me a rye look, raising both eyebrows, but not saying anything. With the full black mustache curling at the ends and his expression, he had the jaunty look of a pirate captain. Pulling off the helmet and duffel bag, I left them stacked next to the cycle and walked to the store entrance past the crew already spread along the concrete wall, talking and passing beers.

The Store split duty as a combination hamburger stand and narrow corner market. The shelves were stacked high with various canned goods, non- food items, and one wall devoted to a walk in cold box, stocked full of sodas, juice, and most importantly, plenty of beer. I grabbed a quart of Coors Light and waited in line to order dinner. Set to one side of the front cash register, the kitchen took up as much space as a closet. Considering how constrained his work space, Rudy, the grillman, could deliver an assortment of tasty food in remarkable short order. He wore a white mesh ballcap, a blue t-shirt with a faded church group logo and a white apron, soiled with splattered grease from the deep fryer. Frantically flipping burgers and dousing them with seasoned salt and pepper, in a blur he dropped new batches of French fries into the fryer. The smell and sound of charbroiling burgers lined across the grill engulfed the Store.

"That sizzling of burgers sounds better than a symphony, Rudy."

I ordered a double hamburger with fries, and paid for the beer. The cashier was an attractive raven haired teenage girl with emerald green eyes and olive skin. She looked me boldly in the face and smiled while taking the money, handing over the receipt with claim number.

"Welcome back, Curt. I've been hoping you'd make it home soon." Her eyes were remarkable and inviting. They flashed in contrast with her brown eyebrows and dark features.

"Well thanks, Ally. How 're you doing?" I stammered, gathering the change and escaping outside, the screen door banging shut behind me.

J.C. made room for me on the wall. He was my best buddy on the crew and could always be relied upon for a good word. Lean and tall, J.C. loved beach volleyball and spent his free time playing on East Beach. A member of the Chumash tribe, he had a dark tan, like blackened leather, from hours spent in the sun. When guys started calling me Lightning, I did not take it well. J.C. calmed me down, explaining that as tough as they could be, everyone came from a positive place. The crew held each other accountable with a powerful expectation that everybody pull their weight.

"If you're hurtin' hungover, and dragging ass, whacking weeds in a campground, how are you gonna hold up when we're going full-bore initial attack on an intense brush fire?"

His steadying presence helped cool me down, and more than once saved me from making trouble for myself.

J.C. passed over a six ounce can of Snappy Tom tomato juice. I poured a dose into the open quart bottle and took a gulp. The spicy tomato added a tasty saltiness to the lager, and as an added bonus certainly made the beer healthier. That Coors Light was downright refreshing and good for you at the same time. Throw in a double greasy burger plus French fries with loads of salt and ketchup, and I was one content, happy camper.

Sitting on that wall with everybody, relaxing was the best. A murmur of stories and laughter percolated across the lot. By tone and body language crew 4 were clearly stoked to be home. The first quart went down fast. True to word, the Supe purchased a case for everyone to share. I grabbed a bottle of Bud Light from the cardboard box.

"Supe, when are you gonna get some good taste? Everyone knows they use too much rice in the blend. Budweiser just doesn't have that crisp refreshing quality of Coors."

"C'mon now, sport. How many times do I need to explain this? I'm starting to think you really are slow. Starkist doesn't care about good taste. We just care that it tastes good."

There are two camps for most everything, Coors vs Budweiser, Ford vs Chevy, and the debate over Stihl vs Husqvarna chainsaws. I am firmly in the Coors Light camp. For my money, there is no better thirst quencher. Coors is crisp, does not fill you up and even says "refreshing" four different times on each can. They could not state that on the label if not true. Alcohol is one commodity that actually enforces truth in packaging. From a frosty, ice cold bottle or mug nothing is better on a hot day. After finishing the Supe's Bud Light, I decided to head home. I have ridden the GPZ after a few too many and promised myself to never do that again. Riding is dangerous enough without mixing alcohol into the picture. City firefighters often refer to motorcyclists as "organ donors." I wanted no part of that. Life is good. I aim to enjoy it.

That said, I was light headed riding over the mountain pass and down the highway as the road snaked into Santa Barbara. The wide open helmet visor allowed in fresh air. The beauty of town spread below with red tiled Spanish style houses dotting the verdant and tawny foothills. If fog socked in the coast earlier, it had burned off and was no longer present. The sky was clear and turning a darkening blue with ribbons of whispery streaks slowly turning from white to pink with the coming sunset. I have not been there yet, but this beautiful view is how I imagine Spain looks. Juan Cabrillo must have believed he'd somehow magically returned home when first sailing into the harbor in 1542. Keeping myself company, I sang aloud an old ballad learned in language lab for Spanish class last quarter.

"Yo soy como la chile verde, picante pero sabroso.
La Llorona, la Llorona, Llorona. "

Surprisingly catchy with melodic guitar rhythms, the imagery and bravado of the old cancion's lyrics made me laugh. The singer compares himself to a green chile, spicy hot but more importantly, full of flavor.

In the distance the Channel Islands were visible in between the marine and leaden blue Pacific and the pale royal blue of the fading horizon. Random white splashes from wind swells rolled across the ocean surface. North of the islands a row of oil derricks perched across the water like mechanized beetles. I rode the GPZ ten miles over the speed limit the whole way home, singing to myself, taking it easy.

Pulling into the apartment, none of my roommates were home. I dropped the duffel in the bedroom, poured a pint glass of water from the kitchen dispenser, and crashed like a falling timber on the living room couch. We live in Isla Vista, the student ghetto adjacent to the University of California campus. Four dudes squeezed into a 900 square foot two bedroom, paying $275 apiece for the privilege. I don't know what rents are now, but that was a lot of money in 1991. The apartment was worn but relatively clean. Most importantly the location could not be beat, directly across from a grassy park on a cliff overlooking the ocean. Two blocks on the right lay the edge of town. A worn dirt path led through open space to Deveraux Point or officially, Coal Oil Point. In the quiet of night, you can hear waves crash against the wooden walkway leading down to the water. Lazy afternoons we'll hang on the old sofa in the front yard, watching people play volleyball across the street. A stream of college girls run by, working off the infamous freshman ten. This was my third year in the apartment.

I started fighting fires the summer after freshman year and now tried to balance the Southern California fire season, from May through November, with finishing the classes required to fulfill my degree. I inherited a little money from my grandmother. The money now long gone, paying for college rested on me. Although a five year college plan was

39

not uncommon, my quarters were missed   working and saving for tuition. I was midway through third year. Jesus spoke about watching the lilies grow and living in the moment. I try my best to follow that program and did not feel rushed to worry about what comes next.

My roommates Chris and Ben were taking summer classes. It was the three of us for summer. Our other roommate Marco went home back east for break. Sounds from the kitchen woke me.

"You can tell Curt is home when there's that smoky smell through the house."

"No doubt. First time I thought something was burning. That wood smoke is distinctive."

"Hey now, it's not nice talking about people who can hear you." I walked behind Chris, pinning his arms in a bear hug and lifting him off his feet. Over 6 feet and a solid 190 pounds, I needed leverage and both legs to pull him off the ground.

Chris and I met freshmen year and immediately hit it off. In a sea of pretty people, his punk exterior and spiked bleached hair stood out. Completely hardcore, Chris was also actually quite sensitive and one of the most positive guys you ever met. Bob Marley and Steel Pulse were his soundtrack as much as bands like the Misfits and Black Flag. Riding through town on a red, gold and green Vespa, with a goofy smile on his face and knitted rasta beanie cap covering bleached hair, anyone could have mistaken him for a Marin County deadhead. That notion would have been quickly dispelled with the violence and force he brought to the rugby field.

"Ugh ooh, Curt's been away in banjo country. Maybe looking for bro-mance." Ben chuckled. He had shoulder length, streaked brown hair, an open face framed by square features and a wide smile. Average in height, Ben was strikingly handsome. His eyes were different colors, one hazel brown and the other blue gray. That wasn't the only thing about him special. He possessed a magnetism hard to explain. Hearing his hearty and generous laugh across the room, you wanted to join in. We'd be at Pizza Bob's having slices and pitchers of beer. When Ben laughed at something, I swear nearby tables would start laughing along. His laugh was infectious.

"Romance? More like some buuttt!" I said through clenched teeth in my best Stew impression. The way I reeked, repellant was more applicable than butt magnet. I seriously needed a shower, having been over a week since the last.

Throwing crunchy, filthy clothes onto a pile in the bedroom corner, I jumped in the shower. An unpleasant sulfurous aroma not unlike rotten eggs permeated the hot water. I lathered with soap and shampoo and worked to get clean. A week's worth of accumulated dirt washed away in rivulets, pooling on the tub floor. I positioned the patch of poison oak on my forearm directly under the running water. Slowly turning off the cold, the water became scalding hot. This opened the pores of the skin and was better than itching. The patch was not large enough for a complete "oak-gasm" effect but still felt good. Using Ben's fancy fog resistant mirror, the disposable razor struggled to cut through the rough beard. I lathered again and shaved a second time.

"C'mon, Curt. Hurry up and get out here. We're going to a little get-together."

"Hold your horses. I'll be ready in three." Splashing Old Spice onto smooth cheeks, the alcohol stung, bracing the razor burn. I picked out a clean plaid collared shirt, khaki shorts and well worn huarache sandals. Admiring the reflection on the wall mirror, I smoothed my short hair with spread fingers. The catnap and hot shower were exactly what the doctor ordered. We'd been in the boondocks for weeks. I was ready for some civilization fun.

"I am ready to go off like a human time bomb."

"Well, don't point that thing at me." I swear orthodontists must dream of smiles like Ben's.

We poured from the apartment without locking the door, jumped onto bicycles and headed into the night. I have a beater, yellow Super Duty that although not pristine, still runs smooth. The town buzzed with energy in the air and people walking about. The three of us swerved in and through the foot and bike traffic down the street, zigging and zooming along like pelicans flying in formation. We'd been traveling long enough I forgot tonight was Saturday night, party night. Summer months in Isla Vista are far less crowded than when school is in session and the entire student population fills town. During school roughly 16,000 people pile on top of each other in an area six-tenths of a square mile, the most densely populated area in the country. Supposedly when built, the landlords needed a variance from building code standards to pack in so many students. I relish these months with fewer people. Everyone seems friendlier. Their normal crowd gone, people are open to meeting and making new friends.

Tonight we were invited to a girl's house that Ben chatted with that morning while having coffee in the quad. In summertime opening a conversation with someone you've never met before leads to snap, just like that, they've invited you over to their place. During the school year with five times the population, everything seems more structured and less free flowing.

Locking bikes at a rack outside, we entered a three story apartment complex with the correct address. A swimming pool was centered in the open courtyard. Lights shined from underwater, the clear water a perfect turquoise. The maintenance man went a little heavy with chlorine I thought. Rows of white plastic lounge chairs lined the deck. Ben's new friend, Kara, lived on the third floor. We bounded up the concrete stairway two at a time, using handrails to launch upwards. Ben knocked twice on the door marked #303 and we walked into the bright room.

CHAPTER

4

Stepping into the new and unknown, the countless different potential universes in the world fascinated me. Kara and her friends lived within their group of people and floated through life. My crew populated a separate bubble, going about our lives until BAM, the spheres met and worlds collide. We were now smack in their bright and fresh world. Definitely girls lived here. Freshly painted warm yellow, the kitchen was spotless. Lilies filled a vase on the kitchen counter. Colorful prints you'd find at Z Gallery decorated the walls. I had the impression the girls' families were well off. You could smell the money.

The front door opened into the kitchen and connected to a wide living room area. Four girls and two guys sat at a rectangular wooden table, playing a drinking game. Pop music added to the scene. Her friends were cute, but Kara was really attractive. She was part Japanese with smooth skin, long, dark hair and a sunny disposition. I sat in an open chair next to a curly haired brunette named Melanie who passed around Coronas, a perfect lime wedge floating in each clear bottle. The two dudes appeared mellow and turned out to be next door neighbors. After we passed their quick muster, postures relaxed, their protective brotherly responsibilities fulfilled.

Everyone was playing "Mexicali" which involves rolling two dice in a cup, slamming them on the table and without showing anyone, declaring your numbers or "hand." A lot of bluffing is involved. The next person needs to roll a higher number to beat the previous hand. If you don't beat the previous roll or someone calls the bluff, you have to drink. If someone claims you're bluffing but you actually did beat the previous hand, that person has to drink. It's a fairly easy game to play and suited our purposes nicely. I don't particularly need help drinking cold beer. However the game engaged everyone as a group and was good for a laugh. Three times in a row, I rolled 3-2 which is a "social" and everybody has to drink. When I called social the third time, everybody yelled that I was bluffing. They had to drink twice, once for the "social' and again for being wrong because I actually was telling the truth. I probably could have bluffed a fourth "social." No one would have challenged me.

Ben and Kara were hitting it off. Animated, he explained his plans to pursue a PhD in Bio Chemistry. Waxing poetic about chemicals and the impact science developments have on society and our lives, Ben made the history of benzene and its use in creating the first decaffeinated coffee sound fascinating.

"I never got the whole idea behind decaf coffee. What's the point?" I asked.

The two looked my way like I spoke in Swahili, and neither responded. While not completely ignoring the rest of us, they were engrossed in their own discussion, the energy between them plain to see.

"That's a beautiful poster of the Eiffel Tower."

"Thank you. I spotted it in the window of the Liberty Travel agency on De la Guerra downtown. They gave it away for free. Only had to buy the frame. Travel agencies constantly receive new posters from airlines and foreign travel bureaus. Don't you just love Paris?"

Melanie's dark eyes tried to capture mine in a look. She shared attention equally between both Chris and me, but I did not feel any particular attraction. My friend's interest, however, was apparent. The other roommates were clearly paired with the neighbors. Although pleasant to be in the company of people, I began to feel odd man out. Growing restless, when an opportune pause came in the game, I said how great to meet everyone and waved goodbye, thanking the girls for the hospitality and cervezas.

Stepping outside the bright apartment, I breathed in the cool night. The beers delivered a nice warm feeling, but my head was clear. A smattering of stars shimmered against the dark sky. Although not nearly as illuminated as in the desert, a rich purple quality lived within the blackness. My shadow followed as I traveled, bouncing down the stairs and across the side of the cream colored building, reminding me of a comic book hero. I paused and admired the dark figure, his features chiseled and sharp in contrast to the pale wall. An expansive bougainvillea draped across the arched entrance of stucco apartments, the bright flowers awash with a soft luminescence.

Past midnight but not yet ready to return home, I mounted the bicycle and rode towards downtown to check the scene. We were away long enough I could taste salt and the marine influence with each inhaled breath. Peddling rapidly, cool air washed across my face. The breeze teared up both eyes, making the street lights and reflections off the storefront windows appear festive and vibrant. Due to the proximity of the campus, local laws prohibited Isla Vista businesses from staying open past twelve. A few people milled about, but the town was shutting down for the night. Deciding to head home, I turned right on Sabado Tarde, rode past a community garden, veered left on a short side street then right again onto Del Playa.

Peddling lazily down D.P., a favorite Johnny Cash song played from an open window of a two story apartment building. I never heard this live concert version before.

Looping around, I stopped under the window and resting on the bicycle seat, listened to the sad, love song. Johnny's distinctive voice sounded plaintive, full of yearning and captured perfectly the heartache and regret of the lyrics.

When the song finished, I turned to peddle home but a girl stopped me asking for directions. Shoulder length hair, golden brown like honey, was pulled over both ears and away from her face. Full lips formed a shy smile. I could see them moving. When her eyes locked on mine, I may as well have been hit with a thunderbolt. My brain froze. Time skipped and paused before a jumble of sounds formed words and sentences. Finally I awoke from the trance and understood English again. Her name was Janine. She and a group of friends from Ventura came up for the weekend but were separated. Janine tried to retrace their steps and looked everywhere for them, but was now turned around and lost. She had no idea where they were staying. Please remember this was years ago before everyone carried smart phones and GPS apps can pinpoint your friends' locations.

Pulling myself together, I asked, "You know Bob Stout? He's from Ventura. I know where he lives."

"Yeah, I do. Bob's a couple years older than us, but we've partied with his sister Roxanne. She's our age."

"All right, now. That's good news. I can take you to Bob's place if you like. Maybe someone there will know your friends or who they're staying with. It's not far. You can ride on the handlebars."

She said okay, placed a palm on each handgrip, and jumped nimbly backward onto the bike. Bob lived on the other side of town. We talked as I peddled. Bob played on the soccer team with my roommate from freshman year. That's when I met him. He had a beautiful vintage blue Cadillac we'd pile into and drive to punk rock gigs down in L.A. For some reason, I usually drove. The whole trip we would talk politics. Bob was full of passion, persuasive and fiercely unapologetic about his progressive viewpoints.

"You ever eat at Corrales' taco stand?" I asked Janine. "It is the bomb. We get the four way chicken burrito with a chile relleno on the inside. I was raised on Mexican food and have never tasted anything close."

" Oh yeah. We love that place. I practically live on their carne asada tacos."

Janine sat lightly on the handlebars, leaning against me. Her soft hair touched my face and smelled fresh, like a tray of ripe strawberries. The warmth from her body rested on the inside of my forearms. I peddled a leisurely cadence to Bob's house. When we arrived, the dark apartment showed no sign of anyone being home. Opening the screen, I knocked several times on the front door and rang the bell. Nobody answered. I waited a minute before trying again, in case people were inside but asleep. No one answered. We looked at each other in silence and tried to think through what to do next. The town was shut down for the night, without a ton of options.

"You could stay at my place and figure out where your friends are in the morning," I offered.

"Can I, really? That would be awesome. You are sweet for helping me."

A slight breeze blew a strand of hair across her face. Absently she pulled the hair back over one ear, her expression forlorn and lost. In my imagination I had a flash of Daryl Hannah in the movie *Blade Runner* looking vulnerable and innocent, waiting to enlist the help of scientist J.F. Sebastian. Hopefully the badass Rutger Hauer character Roy didn't surprise us and squash my skull with his bare hands or maybe break me in half.

I swung back onto the bicycle. Janine hopped again onto the handlebars. We were silent as I peddled the distance to the house together. The Super Duty sure lived up to its name. The heavy frame and fat balloon tires absorbed every bump in the road. The ride was smooth and like magic. In the quiet, the spinning rubber tires softly hummed as we traveled over the pavement. When you consider I woke up that morning in a dusty, sleeping bag on hard desert dirt, the presence of this girl may have been a mirage. The apartment was dark when we arrived. Chris and Ben's bikes were missing from under the awning. The two were not yet home.

Opening the front door and turning on the lights, I showed Janine into the kitchen.

"Are you hungry? I make a pretty mean PB and J."

"That'd be awesome. Thank you. It feels like forever ago that we ate."

"Pizza is definitely numero uno in the food rankings. But peanut butter and jelly are right there in the upper echelon, top of the pyramid, as close to God as you can get in this here world."

Janine initially moved to sit at the kitchen table as I turned on the electric burner to heat the old school, black iron skillet. She turned and wandered to the front room, inspecting the assorted cut out magazine photos decorating the walls of the apartment. The record collection near the turntable caught her attention. She flipped through the stack of LP albums on the floor in the corner.

"Do you mind if I play something?" she called from across the room.

"Of course not. Sure. Go ahead."

The music collection was pretty diverse from our three varied tastes. Janine took some time before finally picking an album from the rear of the pile and placing it on the player. She returned to me in the kitchen and sat down at the little green Formica table and watched as I pulled the meal together.

The song she chose was "Wild is the Wind" from an old Nina Simone album that my mom loved and used to play repeatedly over and over when I was a little kid.

"Where'd you find this album? I love Nina Simone. Her voice is so beautiful and really expresses pain and emotion, enough to break your heart. The saddest songs are best."

"This was my mom's record and one of her favorites. She died almost eight years ago."

"Oh my gosh. I am sorry. " A crooked expression passed quickly across Janine's face. "I don't know what to say..."

"It's okay. How would you know? She had a rare blood disease and went fairly quickly once the symptoms came on, even after the doctors diagnosed it. I went to live with my grandmother after she passed. Mom used to say there was nothing like a really sad song to make her happy. That never made sense to me, but she sure loved a lot of depressing songs. I haven't heard this in a while. It is good."

Music filled the room and swirled around us like the wind and reminded me of being a child and confused. The song almost made you want to cry. But the lyrics were sweet and about being in love. I never understood and wondered why being in love did not make the singer happy. We were quiet and listened together, sharing the moment yet alone with our own thoughts.

On its last legs the ancient electric stove burner took forever to heat the heavy black skillet. Breaking the silence when the song ended, I said, "I inherited this skillet from my grandmother after she died my senior year in high school. T-bones, eggs and frying bacon, this pan has a strong tradition of down home cooking."

When finally hot enough I threw on a thick, burrito size flour tortilla and quickly browned both sides. "There is nothing like toasting tortilla on an iron skillet." With a flat butter knife I laid on a helping of Skippy from the jumbo size container then spread a dollop of natural blueberry jam. "Would you like a glass of chocolate milk?"

"Yes, please."

I poured two tall glasses of two percent milk and added three heaping teaspoons of Hersey's chocolate powder. I stirred the spoon in each glass with a ferocious velocity to really mix the powder. The exceedingly cold refrigerator made the milk full with slushy chunks of ice. The finished product was a frothy, chilled delight. I presented the food and drink to her and started preparing my own late night feast. Now quite hot the heavy iron pan toasted my tortilla ready in moments.

"That is super delicious." She said with difficulty, peanut butter sticking in her mouth.

I took a bite of my own, chased down with a slug of chocolate milk.

"Yep. The commercials sure have it right. Peanut butter and chocolate. They're really two great tastes that taste great together."

Janine beamed. "You are a smile, aren't you?"

After eating, we took turns combing through the album collection and played our favorite songs. Classic Motown, 70's top forty hits, some random funk, and especially punk rock loves songs, we enjoyed the gamut. Like a game with the ante raised each successive turn, we chose music to impress each another with its unique cool factor and specialness. Janine possessed an expansive knowledge and appreciation for a variety of genres from different eras. She insisted good music embody what could only be described as soul and the emotions be true. Her voice rose an octave expounding upon the song playing over the speakers.

"When Milo sings, the lyrics are from the heart and pure. Honesty plus real passion are why this so called 'punk' music is more relevant and important, with boatloads more insight about life, real life, than the manufactured crap on the radio these days."

In between songs and talking about where we were then or memories associated with the tunes, she told me about her family.

"My dad can be a complete jerk. He has his own law practice and is a workaholic. When around, which isn't that much, he takes his stress out picking on my mom, and sometimes me too. He's not physically abusive, but verbal abuse can be just as bad. It's pathetic the way he gets worked up about stuff that doesn't really matter. To be so bitingly critical and even cruel. My mom is over it. She hasn't said anything, but I know is just biding time until my younger sister Kelly is out of high school. Then she'll divorce him. I can see this clear as day. For the next couple years, she's simply going through the motions, waiting to be happy."

"That's horrible. I'm a real carpe diem kind of guy. You should never postpone happiness. Sure, that's a cliche, but it's a truth."

"I agree one hundred percent. I feel like her real life is in hibernation. My mom believes she's doing what's best for us. She justifies herself that he isn't that, that horrible. Happiness, whatever, is on pause for now. I don't ever want to live that way. But I understand her motives."

"Would it be better if they divorced right now?"

"Absolutely. Plus they would be happier too. They were good at one point, but stopped trying a long time ago. A line was crossed. There's no going back, undoing the awful words spoken. You can't be horrible to people you love and think everything's okay because you quote 'love' them. Love is delicate like thread. Once broken, you can't just tie it back together."

"My mom said you always hurt the ones you love the most."

"Your mom was right. My sister sees it too. My mom waiting isn't protecting or saving her from anything. It's selfish really. The worst part is Kelly only sees the dysfunction. That's her role model. At least they were better together when I was younger. Kelly was too little and doesn't even remember those days."

Janine's eyes sparked. She spoke with emotion, a combination of anger and sadness, feeling protective of family and overwhelmed.

"I think I know what you mean. My mom stopped trying. That's what killed her. At least my grandma never quit. With the emphysema and worn from life, she hung on long enough to make sure I'd be okay. At the end her body was barely a bag of bones. Although heartbroken to lose her, I understood when it came, death was a relief. She could never catch her breath and struggled, describing it like drowning. My grandmother kept on as long as she could, for me. Driving from the hospital in her old Ford the morning she died, I was overwhelmed with an awful pit of emptiness inside and loneliness. Just nothingness. My bones hurt. There was nowhere to go or anything to do. I remember feeling adrift like a lost ship with a broken mast and no anchor. Can you imagine being alone at sea, nothing to drink, surrounded by salt water. Or like a horseman after the apocalypse riding a desolate plain under black skies with nothing but dried out, burned prairie. No attachments held me in place. Not one thing to do, no clock to watch or anything, just emptiness. The vacuum of life, the world spinning along, minutes and hours clicking on, messed with my head. After that morning the concept of time and how we spend each second of the day has fascinated me. I don't know what made it click into place. Ever since I've tried to appreciate each moment. Life is precious. We should embrace everything about this life. Most importantly right now. Because that's all we ever really have."

A quiet look marked Janine's face. This was unchartered territory for me. I never talked about this stuff with my bros or anyone for that matter. For some reason I felt comfortable opening up to this girl. Something inside was awake. I wanted to share my feelings and experiences. Not just share, I wanted her to see and understand how I saw the world.

"My pops died when I was eight. Overwhelmed and clueless, I didn't really understand what was going on. Mom went into a downward spiral and like I said, she just gave up. It seemed like selfishness to me. After my grandmother passed, that rocked me. She loved me so much and was there when I needed her. Then she was gone. I blamed my mom because she didn't seem to appreciate the gift that is life. So precious and fragile. You have to treasure and protect it."

"Wow, I'm sorry you've had to deal with so much of death."

"I guess. That's why I try to be grateful for what we have. The world is so beautiful and special."

"That's an awesome outlook."

"It's true. Have you ever looked at the wings on a fly? First of all, I hate flies. They're freaking annoying, be driving you crazy and disgusting. But after you've swatted one, have you ever noticed, taken a moment to see how delicate and perfect their wings are?"

"No, I can honestly say I haven't."

"Flies are gross creatures. That's my point. But when you inspect their tiny wings, they're amazing. Bodies fine, like strands of thin black silk. The wings are beautiful, intricate and fragile, yet strong and functional. They fly. In the air. Flies are the lowest of the low on our planet. Yet they're incredible."

"I don't think I'll ever look at flies the same way again."

"Are you making fun?"

"Haha. No. Please don't think that. I'm serious. I've never paid attention like that before. You're very inspiring."

"Okay. Good. I could have said honey bees but everyone knows they're awesome. The point is even the worst creature on the planet is extraordinary. The world and universe are so phenomenal, you have to appreciate, embrace and live life to the fullest. To simply go through the motions, or worse give up, is wasteful and wrong and seems a sin."

Surprised we realized it was past four-thirty in the morning. Hours had passed on the living room couch. After one last soulful song, she followed me to the bathroom and we brushed our teeth. Janine used a new toothbrush I found stashed in the bottom drawer. I admired her reflection in the mirror the whole time while opening the cardboard package, applying fluoride paste and then handing over the toothbrush. Her eyes were the color of cold water with gold flakes splashed around the irises, framed by incredibly long eyelashes and dark sweeping eyebrows that arched and contrasted with the golden hair. She had incredible bone structure and could have stepped from the cover of a fashion magazine. We stood side by side in front of the mirror, brushing teeth in unison. At six feet three inches, I was a foot taller than her. She cocked her head slightly to the left, exposing the line of her throat. Brushing teeth together felt comfortable and seemed perfectly natural like a normal, regular occurrence. At the same time I was outside of myself as if an observer in the audience watching a scene of a play.

"You can sleep in Marco's bed. He's in New York for the summer. The sheets are clean."

Janine nodded silently as we walked to the bedroom together. I closed the door, sat on the edge of my bed and pulled the huarache sandals off one at a time, flipping them into the corner without looking. When each sandal hit the mirrored closet door, the heavy tire tread soles made a thick thump sound.

Janine stood near the doorway, checking out the room. Her eyes paused on the "Only You" Smokey the Bear poster on one wall. In super slow motion she glided over, bent down and kissed me gently on the lips. I held her face in both hands as we kissed. The lips were soft and kisses sweet. Her tongue darted into my mouth. Caught in a rush of air, I breathed everything in. She tasted cool and minty from toothpaste. Janine leaned forward, pushing my chest with surprising strength, causing me to lose balance and tumble backwards onto the bed. Then she landed on me.

We kissed for awhile, rolling around on top of the single bed. I embraced her, squeezing her body, which was petite but firm and solid in my arms. Slowly she started unbuttoning the buttons of my shirt and I reciprocated, helping to pull off her top. I undid the clasp on her bra with one hand and pulled it off, freeing her breasts. They were an alluring pale cream color that contrasted nicely with the brown tan of her body. I traced tan lines with the tips of my middle and index fingers and cupped a white breast in the palm of each hand. They were firm and full with skin unbelievably soft to the touch. Lean and fit like swimmer she had a flat stomach, fluid strong muscles and easy curves. I was awash in the warmth of her touch and presence, overwhelmed with wanting to envelop and soak in everything about her.

"This is enough, okay?" Her eyes were open inches from my own.

"Of course." Although I would have loved to keep going, it was enough.

We lay there sharing breath and kissing. Flooded with a wave of pleasant thoughts and feelings, a unique sense of tranquility washed over me.

Her head lay on my chest. One arm, half her body and one leg stretched across, resting on me. The pressure of her weight was not heavy but rather quite comfortable. She fit neatly on my frame, as though our bodies were two pieces of a puzzle, a natural match. I moved a strand of hair away from my mouth and listened to her relaxed, soft breathing, then fell asleep happy, holding her tight.

At 8:30 a.m. I awoke to sounds coming from the kitchen. I rose and paused, admiring Janine asleep in my bed. Golden honey hair splayed wildly across the pillow. With both eyes peacefully closed, her face was striking in its beauty. I stopped briefly in the bathroom then entered the kitchen.

The coffee maker gurgled, brewing a fresh pot. Chris was cooking turkey bologna and eggs. The smell of frying bologna filled the air. The kitchen was bright with morning sun from the open windows and alive with sounds of Chris humming, food cooking and the steady drip of coffee brewing.

"Buenos dias. How you doing, amigo?" he asked with a smile, grabbing a mug from the nearby cupboard and poured me a healthy cup as if running his own diner. "You get some needed rest last night?"

"Not so much. We barely slept for a couple hours tops," Janine said, following me into the room. "Hi, I'm Janine."

Her hair was pulled back in a loose ponytail. Dressed in last night's clothes, she did not have to be perfectly put together. Janine looked radiant and comfortable in her own skin and possessed a healthy beauty that would shame a Noxema advertisement. She positively glowed.

"Well, good morning, sunshine. I'm Chris. Like some coffee? I'm cooking breakfast." He smiled at Janine then looked at me with wide eyes, trying to maintain his cool.

"Thank you, I'd love some coffee. My friends planned on breakfast at the Omelet Shop downtown. I should meet them there. Do you think you could give me a ride, Curt?"

"Of course," I said, grabbing the pot from Chris and pouring her a cup. "Do you like milk and sugar?" The coffee was

63

steaming, full roasted and black like an abyss. Milk and two teaspoons of sugar turned it golden brown with a caramel note, rich and satisfying. I drank from my own cup and sat across the table, eyes locked on Janine.

"You leaving?" Chris asked.

"Well, I'm not Derf Scratch," she replied.

Chris clucked with appreciation at the obscure punk rock reference and hummed to himself, buttering two slices of wheat toast, making an egg and fried bologna sandwich. The lead singer for the punk band Fear was named Lee Ving. Their bassist was Derf Scratch. Chris nodded to us, grabbed an old surf magazine, walked through the front door to the yard and sat on the beater outdoor couch.

"Can I have your number? I'd like to see you.. come down and see you again."

"Before we go, you should know what an incredible time I had last night. I think you are really sweet. You are such a great guy."

That is a phrase you never want to hear. My stomach dropped and tightened. I immediately did not like the direction this conversation was taking.

"But I have a boyfriend, and don't think that would be a good idea. He is really jealous. It would not be good." Her eyes clouded. The expression on her face looked pained. She stared at the ground, then over my shoulder and everywhere but directly at me.

There it was. Not a sharp pain, more of an empty sick feeling. My stomach resembled a thick tire tube sliced by a knife. The air inside steadily escaped, flowing out, leaving the insides soft, formless and vacant. I sipped the coffee absently and stared at her a long moment.

"Really?" The kitchen that a moment ago bustled with happy sounds of food cooking, now seemed awful, still and quiet. "That sucks. Wow...Okay, I guess. I get it."

We drove downtown with Janine on the back of the GPZ, her arms wrapped tightly around my waist. I could feel the side of her face pressing against the center of my back the whole way before pulling over to the curb outside the Omelet Shop.

"You positive you'll be okay here?" I looked her in the face, trying to soak in everything, the gold and blue eyes, long eyelashes and sweep of eyebrows, the smooth skin and blushed cheeks. A poetry professor once lectured how nothing was as sad or poignant as a morning rose. For the first time I understood. That rose represented purity and the poet's love which would never again be as beautiful as right now, this very instant. Time and harsh rays of the sun would bear down to steadily fade and steal away the flower's luster, and burn the soft petals.

"We planned ahead to eat here this morning. I'll be fine." She gave me a strong hug and a soft kiss, gently touching lips. "Maybe I'll see you at Corrales sometime."

"Right, yeah maybe. Okay, be good." I kicked the cycle into gear and glided from the curb and onto the roadway.

When I got home, Chris sat reading on the outdoor couch, but came inside with me as I cooked breakfast for myself.

"Damn, Curt. That girl was pure gold." His voice crackled with hope, and a measure of disbelief. "She was bleeping hot. Beyond hot, dude, she was beautiful."

"She has a boyfriend, Chris." I tried to ignore my friend and focused on attempting to crack two eggs with one hand without breaking the yolks. I'd seen the trick on television and thought it looked smooth. I could not pull the move off however, and cracked both yolks, yellow goo dripping through and coating my fingers.

"Ouch." He looked at me with an expression that said it all. "That's messed up, bud. I'm sorry... What can you do?"

I picked at the pieces of shell mixed throughout the bowl of broken egg and bravely gave him a lopsided grin, shrugging. "It's all right. We'll always have Paris... Speaking of which, how was Melanie?"

CHAPTER

5

"**H**ey Lightnin', I hear you all are throwing a rager tonight."

"No, I don't think so, Lumpy."

We were hiking to the crew trucks after clearing brush that day along the San Ysidro Trail. I watched the back of Lump's boots as he picked and chose his steps over the steep incline, avoiding rocks and generally going the smoothest route possible. I liked following Lumpy because he kept a super methodical pace that ate through the miles without exerting much effort. Rounding a curve in the footpath, I could see his face in profile. He turned slightly at the response and grinned, crooked teeth smiling knowingly.

The trail work was decidedly basic duty: trimming overhanging mesquite branches and yuccas, building water berms, and filling in and redirecting the water drainage to stop erosion of the trail. The Supe always kept us busy in between fires, which was fine with me. After a couple days at the ranger station cleaning equipment, sharpening tools, and prepping for the next assignment, getting out and about was a welcome excursion. Plus, the San Ysidro Trail was one beautiful place to work. Starting at 3,000 feet on the Camino Cielo the trail runs downhill, snaking back and forth across the landscape to the town of Montecito at sea level. The view of the hills and south to the blue Pacific Ocean looked like a lush checkerboard of distinctive red Spanish tile roofs from mansions interspersed in a grid amongst layers of green Eucalyptus trees.

After the work was finished, the trail would be perfect for mountain biking. Starting at the Camino Cielo trailhead, you could ride downhill switching back and forth charging for almost five miles of continuous, uninterrupted fun. The question would be getting back to the Camino Cielo and your vehicle. The trail traversed the south-facing slope with non-stop sunshine the full day long. Riding or hiking that incline back uphill would require effort for the exhilarating but brief moments of rapid descent.

Lumpy and I were the farthest downhill, past the trail midway point, and the last to return to the crew trucks. Guys stood around talking as we walked up. I cut brush with a chainsaw the whole day. The Husky's weight pressed against my shoulder. With no shade to speak of and the sun bearing down, we hiked out at a fair clip. My breathing was strong and I felt good. That is what I meant about liking to walk behind Lumpy. He set a great pace.

"Come on Lightning, you're holding us up again."

Dempsey tried to get a rise from me. Everyone knew I did not go for that Lightning business, mostly because it was undeserved. The worst thing to do is let them know something bothered you.

"Blow me," I responded, always a solid comeback.

As we piled into the trucks, I put away the chock block from under the rear tire. J.C. asked if he could bring anything to the party.

"Cracker, I don't know nothing about any party."

"Well, Robby Wadlow said some rugby players told him there was gonna be a big blowout at your place," J.C. calmly explained.

"No, I don't think so. We haven't fixed the hole in the ceiling from that last one." The real estate management company was doing their yearly inspection next week, deciding how much of our security deposit to keep. A number of broken ceiling tiles still needed to be replaced where some numbskull decided to practice his head plants several months before. The cut on my forehead had bled more than you'd think.

Ideas start somewhere, who knows where, then take on a life of their own and gain momentum and converts until finally they become self-fulfilling. I was very much a swimmer caught in a riptide, trying to swim against the current, futilely paddling with all my might. The current was sucking me in on this party issue. Even the Killer asked what time he should stop by.

I was looking foreword to a nice quiet evening at home too. Maybe wake early tomorrow to find some surf. Santa Barbara does not normally have waves in the summer due to the cruel positioning of the Channel Islands, which shield the coast from the seasonal south swells. Talk was of a rare for summer north swell rolling through. I envisioned a Rincon dawn patrol. Tomorrow being Sunday, especially if there was surf, one would have to be in the water early to beat the crowds.

I did not mess around at the ranger station but left on the GPZ as soon as the clock hit six and was first to the Store. I grabbed a quart of Coors Light from the cold box and ordered a jalapeño burger with a side of fries. Taking the money, Alison the cashier flashed me that winning smile of hers.

"Hey Curt, I hear you're having a party tonight. Mind if I bring some friends?"

"Umm. Of course not. That'd be awesome."

"You're right across from Dogshit Park, right?"

"That's right, in the yellow house, one from the corner. You can't miss it. Bring your friends."

When caught in the current, there's no sense trying to fight it. The worst thing to do is paddle against the rip. You will get tired, exhausted and maybe wash out to sea. The best strategy is to paddle across the grain of the current, until free of the rip, then paddle to shore. What I could not figure out, as I was the first hotshot to the store, where had she heard about the party? Just what we needed too, a bunch of high school girls hanging at the apartment. You could spell that word trouble with a capital T.

I took a spot on the wall and watched as the rest of the crew and caravan of vehicles poured into the parking lot: four different Toyota 4x4s, a couple Ford F250's, both new and old school flare side Chevy pick ups, and one full size Blazer spitting gravel in a noisy, power slide stop.

The next two days were our weekend and everyone was in high spirits. Lumpy's latest misadventure from last night was the topic of the hour. Driving home to the hotshot barracks from the Cold Spring Tavern, he rolled his pickup. We worked side by side the whole day. The funny thing is I never thought about asking what happened.

"Aagh, sah what. Ma ma truuuck."

Lumpy didn't stutter but pronounced certain words with a unique inflection. He was supposedly a quarter Cherokee. The running gag was he gave Indians a bad reputation because he could not hold his liquor. Lumpy wasn't a bad driver but apparently had trouble with one stretch of the winding road home. Maybe the aggressive lift kits to jack up his rigs were contributorily responsible. This was either the third or fourth time he'd rolled a pickup. With a show for the dramatic, Daryl was recapping the different times.

"No, no. You forgot the Luv truck."

"How could you forget the Luuuuuvv truuuck?"

"Oh yeah, the LOVE truck!"

At that moment Lumpy pulled in and parked his white Ford Ranger, choosing an open spot in the farthest corner from the store as possible. Barely six months old, the 4x4 had a crumpled and dented passenger side. The cab was smashed, flattened on top and squashed down as if by a huge giant's fist.

As Lumpy came sauntering towards the group along the wall, everyone dressed in our uniform of green shirts and pants, he was greeted with a mix of catcalls and applause. He was average height but powerfully built and had an honest, open smile. Faced by twenty guys mocking and ripping him, Lump stopped, paused for a second, then raised both fists above his head in victory salute, smiling wide with the rest of us. Laughing, he pronounced to a chorus of cheers that he would buy a case of beer. You could not help but love the guy.

From what I heard, Lumpy's nickname came after rolling one of the earlier trucks. The joke was he resembled a character in a Bugs Bunny or Wile E. Coyote cartoon that gets clocked with a frying pan and a big exaggerated cartoon bump grows from his head. Lumpy rolled so many vehicles a permanent bump decorated his head.

Most folks getting ripped like that would get pissed and say something rude in return. Exactly how people got nicknames. A long and storied tradition dictated that sooner or later everyone was tagged with a nickname. Names never stuck unless the individual did not like it. Guys would often try to run with one they thought sounded cool. That never worked. If you liked a name, forget it. Unless the name got under your skin, where you lived and hit a nerve, that call sign was not meant to be.

The most recent addition to a long list of classics was for Pete Johnson. Pete's real name was Dave. Somewhere along the way everyone started calling him Pete. On a fire a month ago in the Lassen N. F. we were the road for maybe a week. Over the payphone, Pete's girlfriend broke the news his prized brand new pickup had been repossessed. With overtime and hazard pay everyone earned good money. Pete seemed to blow through paychecks faster than anyone, literally and figuratively. Within maybe five seconds Stew coined the name Wall Street Pete. Through clenched teeth, he mocked the visibly upset and frustrated man, stuck hundreds of miles from home unable to do anything about the situation. Stew was also the one who lent Pete five hundred dollars that spring when he was short on rent. Pete took a while to cool down, but even he admitted the Wall Street moniker was a good one.

On the way home I stopped by IV Market for some groceries. Especially during summer the market is the hub and social center to start the evening. People are buying chicken breast or hamburger to barbecue, chatting with friends or acquaintances, and in general socializing, finding out what's going on, where the parties are.

Sure enough, I ran into a friend from class, Joe O'Brien. Joe was a legend around campus and known as Guacho Joe. During basketball games he and a buddy from the swim team would run onto the court from the bleachers to lead cheers when the Gauchos were dragging and needed a boost. In front of three thousand they would pull their shirts off and pose, forming the letters U-C-S-B with their arms and bodies. The Thunderdome would go crazy. Handsome with short sandy hair and hardly a hint of that telltale swimmer's chlorine sheen, he had square chiseled features and an engaging honest smile. Whip smart and obviously confident enough to disrobe in front of thousands of people, at the same time Joe was super humble and neither vain nor affected. We chatted for a bit. As always I was impressed with how sincere, friendly and positive the guy could be. To me he epitomized the best Santa Barbara represents. He was genuinely stoked to hear about the firefighting. Shaking hands, we promised to surf together the next time a swell came through. Apparently the possibility of a north swell coming through this weekend was a myth. Realistically waves weren't happening until the fall.

In the produce aisle and lost in my head, I was admiring and trying to decide amongst the summer fruit. Something knocked me from the reverie of my Clash song. Glancing around, three girls in the express line were peering in my direction. One of them likely pointed me out to the others. I examined myself under the fluorescent lights of the market. Green nomex pants were shaded brown from a layer of sawdust. My green LP t-shirt was splattered by tiny wood chips and streaked with white salt residue from sweat. Both arms were dusty with remnants of blood caked on the right elbow, recently cut by some brush. Based on my overall dirty condition, the face was probably a mess too. Cute and dressed in thigh length cover-ups and bright tank tops over bathing suits, the girls were coming back from the beach. One said something and the three laughed together, white teeth gleaming against tan skin. My face flushed. Quickly turning in the opposite direction, I stared blindly at the colorful fruit in front of me and tried to ignore feeling embarrassed. Grabbing some nectarines, a handful of plums and then a gallon of milk I headed to the check out. The clerk smiled sweetly when I handed her the money, but I still felt self-conscious.

Carefully balancing the paper grocery bag on the motorcycle gas tank, I rode home and tried to shake it off. Pulling onto the grass front yard and parking under the sheltered porch of the apartment, my roommates and neighbors were in fact getting ready for a party. Chris' charcoal black FourRunner was parked in the street and not as usual on the lawn. Two huge Marshall guitar amplifiers sat in the driveway, wired to the stereo system in the front room. My protestations earlier were plainly wrong and wishful thinking. Yes, there would soon be a blowout at our place.

"Curt! Where you been?"

"We've been waiting for you, brother." Ben said, a bottle of silver tequila in one hand. A butcher knife was in the other hand, expertly slicing neat lime wedges.

I placed the fruit in a basket on the kitchen counter and milk in the fridge. Ben and Chris were with Rachel and Michele, our neighbors from the apartment to the left. Boisterous and partying already, they clearly did not wait for me. Raising fists overhead in championship boxer victory salute, I said yes, I am in for one but then need to jump in the shower. Bass lines opening a classic guitar anthem pulsed on the big amps in the driveway as I took back the shot. Everyone hooped up the moment. The tequila was smooth with no rough burn nor the typical brutal kick.

"That's nice, Ben. What's the brand?"

"Del Dueño, Curt. This stuff is the goods. 100% Blue Agave."

I accepted the bottle from his outstretched hand and admired the weight and unique, round shape. Tiny air bubble variations sprinkled throughout the opaque, hand-blown glass. A portrait of a Mexican landowner from a hundred years ago adorned the rustic label.

"Del Dueño? This is more like El Bueno!".

Murmuring agreement, Ben poured another round into mismatched colored juice glasses that function as our shot glasses.

"Here's to Luck," he toasted.

Everyone clinked glasses and repeated "Luck!" in unison, throwing down the shots.

You have to drink to Luck. Hesitating would surely be ill-advised and send a wrong message to the Fates. The second shot Ben poured me was even healthier than the first, a solid three fingers deep. He intended for me to catch up quickly. Both eyes watered. My face flushed from the rush of alcohol. Music from outside gained decibels in volume, like earplugs muffling the sound were now taken out. My four friends' faces smiled gayly with new definition as if in sharper focus.

I excused myself and jumped into the shower to finally clean off. All day we cut chaparral and overgrown brush under the hot sun. No one said anything, but no doubt I was more than ripe. The shower's strong pressure water hit with force. Quiet fatigue coursed through forearms and shoulders from carrying and lifting the weight of the Husky. Scrubbing with a soapy wash cloth, the muscles appreciated the combination of hot water and pressure. Although tired, the muscles pleasantly thanked me for the exertion, making them stronger. Have another tequila, Curt, maybe they'll start talking aloud to you, I thought to myself.

After not that long in front of the mirror to pick the right shirt and get the hair perfectly spiky on top, I finally came out from the bedroom. The party was on like donkey kong. Chris' bros from the rugby team were outside on the porch, tapping a keg of beer. People milled about throughout the apartment compound. Following the crowd, I sauntered to Rachel and Michele's to check on their scene. The kitchen was full but I did not recognize anyone. Dance music throbbed, drowning out the rocking music from the driveway amps. Michele saw me across the room, danced through the crowd and handed over a full plastic pint glass with a slushy cold concoction of 151 rum, orange and pineapple juices and Hawaiian Punch. I was thirsty and drank the punch down in steady methodical gulps. Michele gave a look of mock surprise then purposefully poured a refill from a clear acrylic pitcher with painted yellow flowers on the sides. If she were wearing a kitchen apron, Michele could have portrayed the quintessential smiling mom, serving kids a refreshing beverage on a hot day.

Part Samoan with long wavy dark hair and big brown eyes, Michele possessed an exotic sexiness tempered by her low key, friendly demeanor and casual appearance. She played soccer and was fit and athletic in a solid, but not exactly thick way. Smart, with a great sense of humor, I always thought if I had a sister, she would be a lot like Michele. Her roommate Rachel had shoulder length tawny hair and an attractive if unremarkable face. She was skinny with soft muscles that hung loosely onto her bones. Something hard to quantify about Rachel projected sex. She drew far more attention than Michele, with guys always sniffing around. I even hooked up with Rachel several months back, which could have ended up one of those drunken mistakes you regret. Thankfully, neither of us took our tryst seriously and we stayed friends. Although pretty sloppy, if my fuzzy memory served right, we both had fun.

I sipped the second curious rum punch. A sweet, chemical finish masked the heavy alcohol dose that would surely deliver a kick like a mule if you didn't watch out. The fruit sugars ensured the alcohol entered the bloodstream rapidly. In the living room a group of girls danced in a circle to the beating music. I chatted with Michele, watching them move. We stood close together to hear each other speak. Her eyes shined brightly. She was animated and engaging even if I only caught every third word. The punch went down too smoothly. I drained the second pint, chomping on a chunk of ice between strong teeth and excused myself for the bathroom. Someone inside had locked the door. I waited for them to exit. People slid by, entering the bedrooms, occasionally bumping me. Quite a crowd now filled the house.

Standing in the hallway, I noticed a poem cut from a magazine and displayed on the wall in a simple wooden frame.

> *But one day burst through the bricks of a dream,*
> *And realized there are green arrows,*
> *In places other than traffic intersections,*
> *They are everywhere.*

I stood a moment, thinking about that, then squeezed through the crowd and waved at Michele, now dancing with the group of girls. Cupping one hand over her ear, I asked if she knew who wrote the poem in the hallway.

"I'm sorry, Curt. No, I don't know. I cut it from an old LA Weekly, but never saw who wrote it. Isn't the positivity of the message terrific?" She smiled sweetly.

I nodded.

"Come dance with me, Guapo." Michele said, taking both my hands in hers. She leaned close, pressing against my body.

"Ahh, that's probably, um wouldn't be the smartest." I smiled weakly, shaking my head, sliding backward. "I don't think we're ready for that."

"You don't know what you're missing." Her hips twisted side to side like a hula dance. Glassy eyes stared at me boldly. She squeezed both palms and stepped in again, grinding close. Her warm hands in mine were small but strong.

"Ah, baby, don't say that. That's the punch talking." Sheepishly I extracted both hands from hers and backed away towards the kitchen. People milling about jammed the room. Hidden by their cover, I ducked out the side door, exit stage left, onto the driveway between apartments.

In the brief time at Rachel and Michele's, the party grew dramatically. Throngs packed the front yard and driveway, mingling with assorted drinks and plastic party cups of keg beer. Music boomed over the amps. A crowd of skate punks gathered near the curb, sitting on or holding skateboards in hand when not doing tricks in the street. Rugby players held court near the keg under the awning, and tons of girls milled about. I didn't see Alison from the Store, but wouldn't be surprised if she and her high school friends were around somewhere.

That's when I recognized that Janine girl standing amongst the crowd of skate punks. My heart literally leaped in the throat. She was everything I remembered and stunning. I reminded myself to breathe.

Everyone else may as well have disappeared with a spotlight focussed on her exclusively. Dressed in a sleeveless, moss green vintage dress with an A-line skirt and a pretty white floral pattern, she looked casually elegant and sophisticated and perfectly at ease standing in the midst of a group marked by spiked and dyed hair, ripped clothes and rebellious t-shirts and tattoos. Thrift shop dress or brand new, Janine looked amazing.

Smiling broadly, I started towards her. Then like a punch to the stomach, she leaned in casually close to and said something to a stout looking guy with short cropped dark hair. Dressed in jeans and a black Aggression t-shirt, he had a lean, fierce but handsome face. Smiling at whatever Janine said, I could see the square outline of his jaw as they looked at each other. One arm wrapped around her waist, holding tight, the veins on his forearm visible from across the yard. I stopped in my tracks thirty feet away and stood in place, confused and flustered. My mind went blank. Realizing she had not noticed me, I turned a one-eighty and headed in the opposite direction to the rear apartment where our other neighbors James and Dave lived.

Dave was behind their homemade wooden bar in the living room, mixing drinks in a penguin shaped, stainless steel cocktail shaker. I squeezed into a spot directly in front. He nodded at me enthusiastically.

"Hey, Curt. How are ya? Impeccable timing, my man. It's kamikaze time!"

Six people were lined up next to me. 60's surf music played loudly over the speakers. Everyone spoke loudly amongst themselves. Built from spare lumber and decorated with bamboo and leafy fronds, Dave was justifiably proud of his handiwork. Stained dark brown and a shade above waist high, the bar added a fun tiki theme to the apartment. *The Get-Down Lounge* was painted in swirling purple letters on the wall behind.

Dave wore a vintage red aloha shirt with large, colorful flowers. A bucket of ice, a plastic 1.75 liter of store brand vodka, one smaller bottle of triple sec and Roses lime juice were arranged neatly across the bar top. Deliberately he mixed the proper ratio of ingredients in the steel shaker and violently shook the concoction together. Removing the penguin head, leaving only the strainer, he smoothly poured eight shots into a row of assorted shot glasses in one sweeping motion. He distributed the drinks, lifted one for himself and toasted me.

"Cheers, neighbor. Slainte!"

Icy cold and bursting with the taste of limes, the shot went down easy. I sat at the bar silently freaking and tried to calm my thoughts.

A huge Lakers fan, Dave and I talked basketball while he continued making batches of drinks. I kept shooting them down, one after another. Dave was the model of efficiency mixing drinks, with measured movements and none that were unnecessary. He smiled, nodding and lightly dancing in place behind the bar, grooving to the music. I complimented his bartending skills, but he scoffed.

"You should see Frankie, the bartender downtown at Joe's. That guy is good. The bar will be packed and he just powers through the drinks, working the crowd. And you know who is truly great? There's an old school dude at the Tiki Ti on Sunset in Hollywood. I think he owns the place. Making Scorpions and those crazy rum drinks like Zombie's and Navy Grog, super complicated with a bunch of liquors and ingredients, moving smooth like a snake, all precision and grace. Fast but never looking hurried."

Plenty of shots were downed. I'm not exactly clear how many. But something still ached. The influx of booze brought a fuzzy, warm feeling and helped deaden whatever that pain was and hopefully send it back to sleep, buried away where it belonged. Sitting on the high back chair, my elbows rested on the bar top. I listened to the surf guitar instrumental jams and grew roots at the bar. Staying here for the night seemed an excellent plan.

"Hey Lightnin', what is up?!!" I looked around to find Dempsey and a group of hotshots squeezing through the door frame from outside.

"Come on in, fellas." I yelled too loudly. "Dave, please pour these gents a round. On my tab. Let me introduce you to some of them world famous, elite firefighters I've been telling you about. Toughest hombres in the West. The incendi proeliatores."

Dempsey, Corndog, Rob Wadlow, Boon and J.C. squeezed into the room and bellied up as near as possible to the bar. Smooth as silk, Dave mixed a new batch of drinks in the steel pitcher and poured one for each guy. Showered and dressed in freshly laundered clothes, they looked ready to tear it up. Wadlow grew up in nearby Goleta and sported a silk screen Primo beer t-shirt, shorts and flip flops. Corndog and Dempsey were in long sleeved, colorful striped western shirts, Wrangler jeans and cowboy boots more appropriate for a Santa Ynez ranch party than the college casual beach crowd. J.C. wore shorts, a collared polo shirt and a white visor that he loved even at night. He gave a wild look with raised eyebrows and a toothy wide grin that contrasted against his copper skin.

"Hey brother, where all the white women at?"

We tossed down two rounds of kamikazes then headed outside into the volume of people. While camped in my safety zone, belly to Dave's bar, a full-fledged rager was going off in our complex. So many people crowded the driveway Janine could have been ten feet away. I'd probably have missed her.

We navigated to the rear of the complex to escape the crowd. Some dudes were shooting around on the basketball hoop by the covered parking area. Corndog always bragged how he starred at Slama Jama High. Of course, he had to show that he could still dunk. Someone suggested playing half court, five on five, which we did for a while. I'm a good passer and have a decent post game, but am inconsistent. I'll sink a tough outside shot one moment and then brick a relatively easy one. No touch.

Boon offered some Copenhagen, which was fresh and compacted nicely between fingers, smelled strong and rich. On fires I occasionally chew Red Man tobacco, but rarely dip Cope. The fine cut chew plays havoc with your gums. Forget cancer risks, my mom hammered for years about flossing and gum disease. I knew well enough to avoid the periodontist at all costs. Copenhagen is stronger than Red Man. Nicotine rushed to my head and raced throughout the system. Faking left and quickly stepping right to get open, I caught the ball and drove hard for a layup. I jumped and launched a bank shot but the ball clanked off the backboard. The others scrambled to grab the rebound. We played half court, hack ball. I soon grew distracted by the tobacco which made me want to constantly spit. The head rush grew stronger. With a hot face, I began to feel dizzy. Checking from the game, I ejected the remaining wad into a bush near the corner of the house. Definitely hammered, I decided to grab another beer to help sober up.

I wondered through the crowd to the front porch and studiously surveyed the area where Janine was earlier but did not see her or the guy. A crowd surrounded the keg. I quickly figured the best spot to stand and maneuvered through and took position near the nozzle. This was our house after all. A refill was soon forthcoming. The keg enjoyed good pressure and poured a quality beer with minimal foam. I found that happy, woozy frame of mind where you believe everyone likes you and is smiling. Positive energy populated this party and especially around the keg. Beer flowed and good vibes filled the wave lengths. I manned the nozzle and poured beer for people and myself too. Three kegs stacked under the awning next to the GPZ would undoubtably be empty before the night was over.

A Youth Brigade song about California played over the big guitar amps. The rugby players knew the words about how we'll all sink with California, as she falls into the sea. They joined in, singing together. A dozen of them, arms around each other's shoulders, waving side by side, sang the refrain. Powerful and fit with the distinctive look of rugby players, they were barrel-chested like trees and solid.

I happened to be pouring a beer for Robbie Wadlow, when a cute girl with a blond bob hairdo cut in front and asked, "You find some nice ripe peaches at the market tonight?"

She was with other girls that I did not recognize.

"Why, you girls taking a survey?" Wadlow asked. "I'm partial to melons myself."

Even with my impaired judgment, I thought what a cheesy line. When you're as damn good looking and charming as

Wadlow, he could pull it off. Because he was such a butt magnet, hanging with him and going for his residuals was not a bad strategy. I have a healthy ego. Robby was so strikingly handsome and physically impressive, standing next to him could be a little intimidating. The guy looked like a Ralph Lauren model.

The self conscious wave returned from earlier realizing the perky blond could be one of the girls from the express lane at IV market. They were coming from the beach, but she was cleaned up now.

"You know, cantaloupes and honeydews. All kinds of melones." Wadlow would keep on to the bitter end.

"Nah, we just noticed this one at the store earlier today."

She smiled at him, but clearly addressed me. The awkward feeling flew away as quickly as it descended. Okay again and relieved, I realized the girls were not judging me harshly, but actually checking me out. Hey now. I should laugh at myself and the insecurities for being such a darn confused fool.

"Sure thing. I loves me some summer fruit. Steve Miller sang it best. How'd it go? Really love your peaches, wanna shake your tree."

Short, a shade under five feet, but built solid and curvy, the way her hair swirled made me think of a cupcake with buttercream frosting. Dressed in cutoff jean shorts, a light blue tank top, and open toe sandals, she looked good enough to eat. I felt like a hungry, famished cartoon character who envisions a face perched on the body of a roasting chicken, the legs, thighs and wings looking juicy and delectable.

I handed away the keg nozzle and wandered across the front yard with the buttercream girl. She said her name, and it sucks, but I immediately forgot it. We made none too subtle chit chat and tried to ignore how much my words were slurring. In the driveway some of Ben's friends set up a drum set with a snare, a Tom, a bass drum and cymbal. Two guys plugged electric guitars into the big guitar amps. The trio launched into a surprisingly decent, impromptu music set, playing a number of cover songs with a decided rocker sensibility. Into one microphone the two guitarists yelled their best with the crowd singing back up chorus. The bassist was lean and tall with a shaved head and a nice aggressive feel with the rhythm. The guitarist, a skinny eighteen year old lookalike of Robert Plant with shaggy dark hair and bangs was super talented. His fingers flew on the strings as he improvised and ripped through some complicated and difficult transitions. The guy could definitely play guitar.

I stood next to buttercream frosting girl and drank more beer, swaying along. Sound waves resonated, carrying the notes and chords on a physical level and hit me. I didn't just hear, but could actually feel the music. Playing live with help from the crowd singing along, these local kids sounded awesome.

In my addled state the lyrics to the pop song cover seemed particularly witty, with multiple puns and plays on words. Insightful about being young and in love, the song struck me as particularly meaningful and important. With a half cup of beer in hand, head bobbing and right knee rocking, I grooved along when someone bumped from behind, knocking me forward. The cup fell from clumsy fingers, spilling beer and foam across legs and sandaled feet, leaving me wet and sticky. "What a sad abuse of alcohol," was my first thought.

Remnants of dizziness crowded my head before making the command decision to go inside for a towel to dry off. Mumbling incoherently to the cupcake girl, "be right back" I made for the apartment. The masses in the yard were overwhelming. I forced through the crowd, bumped and wandered across the grass and into our place like a silver ball bouncing against the bumpers and levers of a loud and flashing pinball machine. If anyone did not appreciate getting jostled by me pushing through, oblivious me did not notice.

People dancing and milling about packed our place. On a mission, I maneuvered through and straight to the miraculously empty bathroom. Grabbing a beach towel draped over the shower curtain, I leaned over to wipe the sticky beer residue from my feet and legs. Bending towards the ground triggered the wave of dizziness to kick in, now more than ever. The bathroom began to spin in circles around and around. I parked on the toilet seat to wait it out.

That did not help. The room kept spinning more and more. Sitting in place, the situation did not improve and actually got worse. The room spun faster and faster like a crazy carnival ride. Standing and fumbling for the doorknob, I stumbled from the bathroom and to my bedroom mostly by sense of touch and muscle memory. Only steps down a hallway, the trip took a Herculean effort and every inner resource. I bounced off walls as if on a ship tossed about rough, stormy seas.

Finally reaching safety of my dark bedroom, I crumpled onto the bed and lay down, hugging a pillow in both arms. A couple may have been rolling around in Marco's bed, but I didn't care. Through thin apartment walls you could hear the band playing in the nearby yard and the din of partiers. With both eyes closed, I tried to breathe and regain control as the room spun like an insane record turntable. The entire room rotated around and around, forty-five revolutions per minute. I curled in classic fetal position and focused on the Bob Marley and the Wailers cover coming from outside. "Bob will get you through. Bob will get you through," I repeated to myself. The room spun on. Instead of closed eyes offering a refuge of darkness, an awful horror show arrived of brown, green and orange lights, assorted nightmare shapes, a patchwork of plaid colors and the doom of nausea.

The large black laundry duffel lay crumpled and empty on the carpeted floor next to the bed. Opening eyes, somehow I recognized it. Unsteady yet determined, I reached down, unzipped and opened the duffel while leaning off the wildly spinning bed and managed to vomit inside without falling over or soiling the floor or bed covers. Fortuitous positioning of the duffel preserved the room and the carpet.

I lay on one side, precariously leaning and puking, the violence hard to fathom. Wrathful, painful waves punished me without mercy. Stomach muscles clenched and wrenched like a self inflicted vise. The throat lining burned with bile and acid. I gasped for air when the spasms paused and appeared to be over, but was no way that fortunate. The sickness spewed forth again for an eternity. After nothing remained to emit, the contractions continued like deranged echoes, exacting their harsh penalty, heaving and constricting even though the system was drained empty.

Puddles of perspiration from my face and hair soaked the pillow sheet. Thankfully the spinning eased away. Spent and exhausted lungs gasped for air, trying to absorb oxygen. I closed both eyes and click, like a bolt locking a door into place, dropped from wretchedness into pitch black.

CHAPTER

6

If unconsciousness hit like a dark door shutting closed, waking up was getting run over by a truck. Too early morning sunlight glared through the open window waking me. An offensive shower of glass shards rained down on both eyeballs. I closed them in vain to escape the pain. Last night's internal torturer migrated north and was now in possession of my cranium. The vise clamped down with an inhuman force profound with intensity as if crushing the brain.

Low guttural noises murmured like a wounded animal. Summoning strength, I dragged to the kitchen for a tall water. Two Excedrin went down the raw throat like briar patch thistles. A fiesta bomb must have exploded littering shrapnel of red and blue party cups, empty cans, bottles, booze, and greasy pizza boxes. Loose record albums scattered across the floor around the turntable. Too spent to change the empty water bottle on the dispenser, I drank from the tap. Although horrible and like sulfur, the liquid helped ease the parched throat. I forced down a second glass, knowing hydration was crucial.

The headache was not the sharp stab of a knife but more like an unbelievable pressure, unremitting like an awful disease. I stumbled back to bed and tried to grab sleep. The only thing that could possibly ease the agony was to escape again into a sick unconsciousness.

Like a dead fish on the deck of a boat, I lay immobile. Hating it does not begin to describe the overwhelming loathing directed towards myself. An obnoxious telephone ringing penetrated the thick fog in my head, violating defenseless eardrums. A buzz saw of bell tones added a new layer of torture. I struggled for the nightstand and answered the phone.

"Harro." My larynx felt wrapped in sandpaper. Killer's voice was piercing.

"Curt. Gotta saddle up. The Supe set off pagers fifteen minutes ago."

"Where's the fire?" I croaked.

Fires in Oregon were in the reports. If we were flying I could at least grab some shut eye waiting for the chartered plane at the airport. Sleep was my only chance for solace.

"Look out your window. The West Camino Cielo's burning, below Bush Peak. Yata hey. Get up here."

Killer disconnected the line and did not hear my scream. You are freaking kidding me. This was the worst nightmare scenario imaginable.

I lay there as if shot by a tranquilizer gun, cursing myself. In a daze, more zombie than human being, I searched for clean clothes and methodically dressed in nomex pants and green LP t-shirt. Through the stupor I slowly pulled on clean cotton socks and two heavy woolen boot socks, then deliberately laced the worn brown leather Whites.

Once dressed I flopped backwards onto the bed for five more minutes, eyes closed, breathing laboriously. C'mon, Curt. You got this, kid. I bravely rolled over and staggered to the bathroom to brush teeth. The minty toothpaste hardly washed away the bitterness. Cold running water drenched my face. Reflected eyes from the mirror stared dully back at me, a lifeless road map of city streets marked by red ink. The wetness of faucet water helped minutely.

After a long minute I forced myself to move out and onto the GPZ, strapped on the helmet and fired the ignition. Kicking aside two empty kegs, I navigated the motorcycle from the porch, over the lawn covered with party cups and to the street. Yesterday's fruit was long gone, poached during the party. I stopped at the market and bought three oranges, two apples and two bottles of Gatorade. Empty at eight o'clock in the morning, a store clerk mopped the floor with bleach. The undiluted chemical smell hit in a wave, violating nostrils, almost causing me to retch again. I rested on the cycle's saddle at the curb outside and gulped down the first green sports drink. The thick peel from a hearty navel orange came away in one intact piece. Each juicy quarter section was devoured ravenously like a vampire eating sweet blood. Taking a bite from an apple, the crunching of fruit contrasted with the morning stillness. A bent over Cambodian woman pushed a shopping cart, searching for empty cans and bottles within trash containers lining the sidewalk. Her bounty inside the cart rattled noisily. The sticking of one metal wheel was audible as she made her way down the street. The round white sun bore through the faded, pale sky with nary a cloud in sight. No gray foggy marine layer would blanket us or cool today's temperature. At eight a.m. the air felt warm already. Today would be a hot one.

The fruit and Gatorade worked their medicine. Feeling practically human, I took my time on surface streets riding through town. At the 101 south onramp, I cranked open the throttle and rocketed to one hundred and ten miles an hour, hugging the GPZ's fuel tank to minimize the drag of resistance opposing our progress. The remaining Gatorade and orange tucked under the cotton LP t-shirt were cold and bracing against bare skin. Usually I stay within ten miles over the speed limit. Wildfire in local foothills must be as good a "get out of jail free" card as ever. Why actually, officer, the fire is right over there. How awesome to say that. Traffic was light. I did not see a single trooper the whole way.

A thin column of white smoke rose northwest of the San Marcos Pass, an unmistakable smudge in the clear sky and distinct from the dun and yellow faded green hills. Out of habit and clearly not thinking straight, I blazed a trail to the ranger station and hotshot barracks and should not have been surprised how deserted and eerily quiet the compound was when I pulled in. Everyone was long gone, responding to the fire. Did you think they were gonna wait for you, dummy? I looped the GPZ around and onto Paradise Road again, towards highway 154 and back over the Pass. Near the top I geared down, took the Camino Cielo exit and drove, speeding like a bullet down the undulating, crooked and narrow two lane road.

The GPZ handled the curves like a champion, better than I did. After almost spilling it once and a couple minutes riding the winding road, with repeated banking turns like a pendulum on overdrive, I felt sick again, pulled to the side and stopped. Barely throwing helmet off in time, I crouched in the long dried grass at the pavement's edge. Chewed mulch of fruit and fluorescent green liquid rushed from me without remorse, although thankfully not painful like last night. Obviously you don't want to be throwing up on the side of the road at 8:30 in the morning, or any time for that matter. I moved with clinical dispassion, callous to the routine, bent over with hands on knees, breathing and panting with mouth open like a dog. The motorcycle idled with a dull clicking next to me.

Pulling helmet back on, we continued down the Camino Cielo, searching for the crew. After several miles, I came upon the two green crew trucks parked in a narrow turnout. I positioned the GPZ between the rigs, rushed into the Four-A buggy, pulled on yellow long sleeved nomex shirt, threw on web gear, backpack and orange hardhat and grabbed a sharp Super-P from the tool compartment. After guzzling half the second Gatorade, I stuffed the remainder and the last orange into the pack then started hiking the trail that pealed from the road and appeared to head in the fire's direction.

The air was still. Heat from the sun's rays warmed my face. I hiked the dirt path at a lope for a half mile before rounding a curve and seeing fire ahead. Maybe five acres in size and mid slope of a moderately steep hillside, the blaze was building momentum, getting ready to run uphill through thick Manzanita and green chaparral. Shocking orange and illuminant yellow flames danced, breathed and were very much alive as the blaze enveloped and consumed new brush and fuel. We spend so much time training, thinking about, planning, and getting ready for fire. Finally seeing an actual one is always a surprise. Fire is similar to sex in the way we practically obsess and spend our days in anticipation, focussed on the potential. In the throws of action, both are new and unpredictable.

A white Bell helicopter dragging a red Bambi bucket zoomed in making a water drop at the fire's head. The clamoring cacophony of three buzzing chainsaws greeted me before actually seeing the crew. Rounding one last corner of the dusty trail, I came on Four- A standing in place, leaning on tools. The chainsaws were going full bore but having a difficult time in a thick wall of brush. Pullers could be heard yelling over the roar of saws trying to give direction. Manzanita is a hearty, drought resistant brush that can survive in climates with little precipitation. They grow exceedingly slow, resulting in the wood being incredibly hard, almost like rock. That dense, thick chaparral wood was chewing through the saws' chains, slowing the progress of the sawyers. The hand tools had nowhere to go and were backed up behind them.

"Nice of you to join us, Lightning," Dempsey cracked.

"Yeah, Bolt. What is up?"

Remaining silent, I stared dully at them from behind dark sunglasses. I breathed through nose and open mouth, catching my breath while resting against the Pulaski handle as if a cane. Pulling the navel orange from a pocket in the backpack, I quietly peeled and ate the juicy fruit. We stood in line, waiting and listening to the whine of chainsaws screaming full tilt.

"Where'd you disappear to last night, Curt? We looked for you." J.C. eyeballed me steadily, reading me like a book.

I did not answer him either but took a long pull and finished the last of the Gatorade, squashing the empty plastic bottle with one boot before stuffing it back into the pack. For the first time that day, I knew that I'd be okay and would make it.

The chainsaws soon broke through the troublesome thicket and began to progress through the brush. Hand tools started cutting line. I took my usual spot in the lineup and began swinging the tool with force, the grub end hitting the ground, breaking apart dirt, duff and short grass. I was at maybe fifty percent but the familiar movement swinging the tool helped my overall wellbeing. The movement of arms and shoulders helped the heart beat and do its job, pushing blood to circulate throughout the body. Pretty soon the chainsaws were stuck in another brutal rat's nest of ornery chaparral. We paused and caught our breath again. Although weak and easily winded, to my relief no one was the wiser. Holding my own was absolutely mandatory. While the chainsaws did not have much work in Joshua Tree, roles were reversed in today's heavy brush. The sawyers and pullers had their hands full. The scrapers' jobs would be much easier this time, which worked fine for me.

After years of drought, the Santa Barbara foothills were baked dry and extremely flammable. Manzanita leaves possess a unique oily component and burn with intense heat. Each time a new bush flared up, leaves crackled with an audible popping of oil. Moderate winds from the southwest steadily pushed the fire upslope. As the day grew warmer the flow of winds increased upslope and inland. Sundowners, or as they're known in other areas of California as Santa Ana winds, are the reverse and blast dry heat from the arid eastern deserts towards the west. Santanas will actually push fires downhill. When really gusting the only thing to do is try and protect as many homes as possible from the wall of fire marching to the Pacific. Sundowners usually hit in September and October or even as late as November and create especially dangerous conditions. Last year's awful "Paint Fire" started in the Painted Cave area near the San Marcos Pass and consumed almost five hundred houses and apartment complexes. Sundowners gusted forty miles an hour and pushed the fire downhill, burning five miles in a couple hours. The only reason the fire did not burn the whole way to the ocean was because the winds died. Thankfully, we did not have to worry about those conditions today.

Thirty-five feet away and not directly next to the fire, we were cutting "indirect" line parallel with the fire's edge. The line's path was straight uphill towards the ridge top. Once at the top of the ridge, the fire would lose forward momentum without the push from the wind and would spread downhill at a much slower rate.

Shaped like a V, with the bottom of the letter the initial point of origin, the fire burned and advanced upward, fanning out across the slope. We were on the southern flank of the newly named "Peak Fire". A helitac crew and firefighters from the district engines were working the northern flank.

Once we encircled the blaze with a line, the plan was to set backfires along the line's edge to burn towards the main fire. The backfire and main fire would meet and extinguish themselves without new fuel to consume. When setting backfires the line has to hold and no fire cross over or spot outside the perimeter. If flames do jump the line, the brushfire would be off and roaring again through the unburned fuel in its path. All our efforts would be for naught.

After three in the afternoon the Killer directed me to hoof to the vehicles, grab two drip torches and a five gallon jerry can from the Supe's rig, and carry them to the Supe, who was posted as lookout near the peak on the ridge above us.

"There's an old foot trail a half mile south of the buggies that leads to the ridge line. You'll find the Supe there at the top. He believes we'll tie into Division A early enough tonight we can backfire, and get this locked in with a solid black line."

In the middle of doing your job, a frame of reference or clear picture of where you fit into the situation is difficult to envision. Tramping down the finished line, I was impressed with the quality of our work. Thick and imposing chaparral lined each side like a solid wave of brush stacked high double overhead. The line cut through the green wall as if hacked with a giant god's sized cleaver. Where the anchor point started, blackened stumps of Manzanita smoldered and smoked. The sick, foul stench of burnt wood hung in the air. I love the smell of campfires and especially burning chaparral and mesquite which is unlike the distasteful odor of dead remains of fire. Something must change in the chemistry. Complete combustion converts sugars from the fuel into carbon or something. I need to remind myself to ask

102

someone that would know about this phenomena, because unless I'm crazy, there is a difference. Smoke from a burnt fire smells different than a burning one.

Arriving at the Supe's rig, the realization sank in this was not the greatest assignment ever. The five gallon jerry can contained a mixture of three parts diesel fuel and one part gasoline and weighed roughly fifty pounds. A drip torch is a metal cylinder with a handle, approximately one gallon of fuel mix, a burner arm and an igniter. The igniter acts as a wick that stays lit. When you tilt the cylinder's end to point the burner arm downwards, a broken stream of burning liquid fire drips from the igniter to the ground. The concept is to walk along, leaving burning drops of fuel on the earth as you go, lighting grass, duff and unburned material, spreading the new man-made fire to now act as your backfire.

I slipped the handles of two drip torches over the wooden Pulaski shaft and carried them together in one hand and the jerry can in the other and headed along the road, looking for the foot path to the Supe. The drip torches and jerry can were not too heavy although somewhat awkward to carry. Fuel sloshed inside the jerry can making the weight flow back and forth with a rocking movement. The foot path was not more than a faint deer crossing that would have been easy to miss had not the Supe flagged a bush with purple plastic marking tape. Hiking uphill was harder than the walk down and made more fun lugging the new weight. After good progress I paused, set the jerry can on the ground and drank water, catching a breath and stretching. The weight of the container bore across the shoulder muscles. A tweak chirped from my neck. Finishing the canteen brought the realization I was down to one quart left. I'd been sucking water like nobody's business.

Starting again I made steady, plodding gains pushing uphill. The old game trail meandered across the steep slope and terrain. Going straight upward would have been brutal. Hiking on, I squeezed through gaps in the brush, dry leaves and branches scratching my face and arms. After a ways I switched loads between hands, evening the weight and sharing the burden. The change helped temporarily. Soon the aching returned and I switched loads again. Back and forth I repeated this, stopping momentarily to catch a breath and shift the weight. More pack mule than firefighter, legs trudged on and both eyes locked on the stretch of dirt directly ahead. Without shade, unrelenting heavy air and heat covered me like a mantle. Trail dust coated the throat and roof of my mouth.

The smoke column to the left grew steadily thicker. Angry buzzing of chainsaws carried with the wind. The helicopter made regular drops and reloaded the water bucket from Lake Cachuma several miles away on the other side of the ridge. The steady slap slap slap of the Bell rotor blades reappeared after making the round trip. The hill took a steep turn forcing me to use the jerry can for leverage like a thick rectangular cane. The burden began to wear on me. Boots and legs kept shuffling like a slow bass drum.

For the first time I allowed myself to think about Janine. Since driving from the omelet shop that morning, I did an admirable job blanking her out and don't know why seeing her with that guy had such an effect. But geez, obviously it sure messed me up. I tried to drown her in a pool of Kami's and keep her away forgotten. Hangover and weakness combined to crush resistance and overwhelm the guard. A vision of Janine snuck into my thoughts like a thief in shadows. Once past my defenses, I did not want her to leave but focused and relished the memory of her face, the flash of blue and gold like rare jewelry when her eyes met mine and smiled. And the graceful line of her throat when she was sleeping and the smooth curve of hip.

The images kept me company as I marched in low gear with locked differential, body on empty and suffering. Like butterflies floating in, the sweet moments offered escape from the drudgery. Unfortunately the welcome illusions did not come alone. Burned into the memory, I kept seeing that guy and his arm wrapped around her waist. I could not erase the picture from my head and tried in vain to stop the scene from overwhelming me. Sifting through and focused on gold, I tried to ignore and quarantine off the bad stuff. I was not successful. In my imagination Ventura punker dude stood behind Janine and unzipped the pretty, thrift store green dress. She turned, staring him full in the face before the dress slipped from her shoulders and silently fell to the floor. Janine stepped from the crumpled dress, now naked. Mental pictures tormented and would not leave me alone. They were like poison and did me wrong.

The trail followed a draw in the hill, opened and wandered across one last knoll before hitting the ridge top. That is where I found the Supe. He squatted on one knee under the shade of some Chamizal and had a perfect vantage point to see the entire fire below to our left and the crews working on both flanks. Where earlier shaped like a capital letter V, the fire now looked like a ghost with wings raised. The northern line wavered with the topography. A swale in the slope gave the fire a chute to run. If not for the helicopter water drops, knocking down the flames to slow its progress, the fire would have blown clear across to the other side of the ridge. With plenty of daylight left, who knows where the blaze would have gone.

"Lightning Curt Browning. How's this fine day treating you? Heard you boys had quite a little shindig last night." Laugh lines crinkled behind the frames of his dark sunglasses.

In the home stretch but running on fumes, fingers of both hands ached numb from lugging the load. The final steps to a flat spot near his kneeling figure took a lifetime. Red jerry can and drip torches collapsed to the ground. I stood tall and paused for oxygen before responding.

"Supe...the sky is blue."

Relief at making the ridge was a gift. I never doubted the result, but the struggle definitely kicked my butt. Pulling out the last half empty quart canteen, I unscrewed the cap, stretched neck and shoulders to work out the kinks, and enjoyed a cool, heavenly pull of water.

The Supe looked from the orange fire below towards the thick white column of smoke in the east forming a cumulus looking cloud like a thunderhead mushroom in the afternoon sky.

"Why sport, I believe you've hit on something there. That powder blue looks exactly like the color a junior high school girl would want to paint her room."

I followed his line of vision. Where the white column faded, wisps of white broke off and floated across the horizon. The blue possessed a creamy, soft glow that reminded me of my eighth grade girlfriend. We would sit on her bed with the door closed when her parents were gone, practice kissing and listen to her favorite Top 40 dance radio station. Stuffed animals decorated the room with walls the same shade of baby, powder blue. The Supe's description brought me back to that time.

"You one of them cowboy poets I read about in the LA Times, Supe?"

The radio crackled. Supe barked into it, giving directions to the helicopter pilot for the next water drop. Then he switched to a different channel and asked Stew for an update on Four-B's progress. The two went back and forth. When done, he told me the drip torches and jerry can were good there and to head downhill and reconnect with Four- A.

"Yeah, I copy," I replied, turned and headed back down the path. Hiking away, the Supe chuckled to himself, "cowboy poet, ha."

Visions of Janine kept me company the hike back. Dressed in a sunny, yellow summer dress, she laughed. A rush of wind blew her hair, covering her face. Birds chirped and bugs buzzed in the brush. I plotted each step down the steep narrow path and imagined holding hands. My imagination helped her walk the trail, carrying a beach towel for a blanket, two brightly colored aluminum glasses and a bottle of chilled wine. The glass bottle was frosty and sweating from being pulled directly from a cooler of melting ice. Searching for a perfect spot to picnic, that open, flat space right there would be ideal to stretch out and spend a lazy day alone together watching the sun travel the afternoon sky. The ocean was a blur of deep marine in the distance. Quiet, warm sunshine would be our only company. We could make out and track the random specs of white sailboats on the blue surface.

Downhill without lugging seventy pounds of burn fuel was like a vacation. I remembered to refill water bottles from a canteen on the crew buggy. Hiking from there to the crew was no big deal. Thankfully, black t-shirt boyfriend did not bother us and left Janine and me alone in my imagination. The sweetness was like a bird's song, but faded away too quickly and disappeared altogether when I tied in again with the others. The blare of chainsaws and cursing crashed the pleasant solitude of the idyllic daydream.

CHAPTER

7

"**I** still miss him." After a couple drinks, the talk always returned to my dad. "You have his smile, you know. He was so handsome."

I heard the stories plenty of times, but loved hearing them again. Camping in Canada they awoke to snorting just feet away outside the tent, something large and wild rummaging through the food. Pops chased off the immense grizzly bear, arms raised and standing on tippy toes to make himself bigger, loudly bashing a tin pot with a metal mixing spoon. Or their big trip to Chicago and getting stuck with no money because mom left her purse in a yellow cab. Pops didn't stress but was cool as can be, like a cucumber and not upset about the bonehead move. He hugged and comforted my mom, ah baby, don't beat yourself up. That's an easy mistake and all part of the adventure. Of course, they rallied and figured how to deal until a friend wired some money. A favorite was their trip to see the bullfights in Mexico. Dad was the hero in every story and could handle any situation "no problemo" and always with a smile.

"He was wearing this ridiculous, embroidered black sombrero. We'd been partying and he was happy as can be shuffling through the dusty streets to the international border. Federales were on guard. Dark men with machine guns and very serious, no joke those hombres, not like the Tijuana police. There was a delay in the line. We stood waiting awhile, not sure what the issue was. Your dad kept singing the refrain to a mariachi song in his broken Spanish, and even got this big, scary looking one to crack a smile along with him. He had that way."

Those afternoons were the best, like she flipped a switch to find joy again and be carefree. We played cards and talked. Her eyes sparkled. The curtains were drawn open and the apartment filled with her laughter. During breaks in the game I'd refill her drink, grab a fresh pack of smokes and play her requests from the collection of LP records.

Nice times were rare and the thin period sandwiched between quiet melancholy and a sloppier depression. Three strong ones delivered the right dose for pleasant hazy moments. Unfortunately there was usually a fourth and sometimes more. When she decided to nap was better because that tall ship on the Cutty Sark half gallon did not guarantee smooth sailing. The calm often turned rough. The Sea of Tranquility is on the moon and was not meant for the world of my youth.

When she woke in the evening I'd cook canned soup and try my best to take care of her. The ragged mood tended to darken. Her schedule was backwards. She'd stay up late, sometimes the whole night long, watching television, muttering bitterly and steeping in her thoughts.

In the seventh grade I made the mistake of bringing a friend home after school thinking I could quickly grab my glove before baseball practice. The curtains were drawn and the apartment dark. He must have told someone because the next day at lunch an eighth grader Jay Burke made a rude comment in front of the main group at a long table in the cafeteria. At first the words didn't register. His lips curled in a cruel smirk as he stared at me. Jay was muscular and the first kid at our school with a beard. He flexed, arms crossed in front of his chest. I was skinny and waiting for my growth spurt. Jay was fortunate the vice principal was close by and pulled me off him before his windpipe suffered permanent damaged. Maybe he landed some punches. I don't remember. The memory is vivid of having his throat in both hands, skinny fingers trying with all my might to crush it. The school suspended me for five days. From then on I remembered my baseball glove and played with kids out and about in the neighborhood or at their house, never at mine.

When mom first complained she didn't feel right, I thought this a good thing and a chance for her to see someone for help to get better. When she came home from the doctor's office and told me about the disease, it was too much to comprehend and like a nightmare. What do you mean, there is no cure and we need to make plans?

Although the blood specialist explained the genetic predisposition had been hidden within my mom's system for years, I wondered if she brought it on herself, wanting to be done with this world. She was so unhappy. Wasn't this the escape she quietly prayed for all the time. Freshman year and being mad just happened. Anger was something tangible. Nothing else made any sense. First god took my dad away and was now hurting my mom. The world was not fair. People breeze through without a care, not knowing what a mess we were in. A part of me blamed mom for this happening, believing she secreted the sickness upon herself.

Her last months were a blur. The complete deterioration of her body happened within a rapid period of time. I was at the grocery store where I worked part time when my grandma called to say the ambulance had taken mom to the hospital. The store manager drove me there. When I entered the room, she was unconscious and stuck with a bunch of tubes from several machines.

My grandmother and I stayed at the hospital around the clock. Mom slid in and out of consciousness from the meds. The doctor advised we should say goodbyes. We tried our best, but she was really out of it. I don't know if she even realized who we were when the time came.

Late one afternoon when she was asleep, my grandma and I went to the cafeteria for a bite of food. Neither of us were hungry, but we needed a break and fresh air. Not that the air was fresh. The entire hospital smelled like chemical disinfectant and gave me the creeps. White enamel paint on the cafeteria walls looked yellow. Fluorescent lights hummed non-stop like static. We were there maybe a half hour. Back in the room, I immediately knew she passed. The shape on the bed didn't even look like her. Her skin was colorless and pale. That still empty shell was not my mom. There was no spirit inside. She was gone.

My grandmother hugged me, tears running down her face. The past months took a terrible toll, watching her own daughter shrivel away and then die. Thinking how cruel this was for her, I squeezed my grandma back. She was shrinking with age. Taking her thin frame in my arms, I gently held her tight. But I don't remember crying.

I lived with my grandma through high school. Although her health was poor, she was a fighter and never gave up. There was a spark, a fire, in her that I admired. She hung on long enough to know I'd been accepted to the University of California. It was her idea that I look at fighting fires.

"Your dad earned nice money doing that work. I think it would be good for you."

At first I started on the engines. After a month one of the hotshots got hurt and I got bumped up. Grandma was right. This job was a perfect combination for me.

After moving to Santa Barbara, I sold grandma's old Ford and bought the GPZ. A few clothes, a surfboard, some old records, and that cast iron skillet were the only things weighing me down. How liberating to feel free. Do you own possessions or do they own you? Maybe there's not a ton of money or stuff, but I think I got it pretty good.

CHAPTER

8

Tough walls of Manzanita kicked our asses the rest of the day until we tied in with the other crew after one-thirty in the morning, the line complete. After the pack mule hike to the Supe, I bumped in and helped pull for Kingman. Except for a short period of drama when Mike almost cut some fingers off testing the dullness of his still moving chainsaw, the shift was a slog of awkwardly wresting and throwing cut limbs away from the line and into the green. Fire made the ridge top and crept down the lee side in some spots but nothing substantial. Forty feet of green separated our line from burning fire. We started backfiring at the ridge top and headed down both flanks, spreading fire from the perimeter lines to meet the main fire in the middle. Two people carried drip torches and progressed downhill at roughly an equal pace. The rest of us spread along spaced fifteen feet apart, monitoring the fire's progress and stopping any burning material from rolling down the hillside and catching fire below.

The clean line in the dirt was five feet wide. The brush on each side was cut back twenty feet across. Dempsey carried one drip torch and lit grass, duff and brush from the line towards the main blaze. He doubled back, hiking downhill, zig- zagging the way, dragging and leaving a stream of flames steady as he went. Fire crept along the grass, fallen twigs, downed leaves and crawled up brush limbs and into elevated leaves. Once the leaves were going, chaparral would flare and quickly become engulfed. Twenty feet away we shielded our faces or turned in the other direction to avoid waves of radiant heat.

Dry chaparral turned brilliant yellow and red against the dark night, leaves popping loudly. Dancing flames gave the area a soft, vibrant glow in contrast with black and purple hills. Faces stared into the fire, illuminated and bathed in rich orange. The bright light now made our incandescent headlamp beams seem faint and barely noticeable. Tonight's job was to ensure no spot fires or "slop overs" jumped the line or crossed into the green. Nothing is more demoralizing than to work your ass off, then have the fire get away, escape containment and torch a whole new area. That was not going to happen tonight.

Dempsey was working hard, hiking and crawling through the bristly brush. The rest of us were content to watch the dry tormenting Manzanita, now burst into flames. My theory is firefighters have an tiny, inner touch of pyro. Of course, you hate the destruction and damage wrecked upon people's lives and property. Any loss of life is unconscionable. Even with the mortal danger, the dance of orange, red and golden flames was seductive and fascinating. I've heard of random firefighters in the sticks intentionally setting fires, mostly to drum up work. Violating the trust placed in us to safeguard the community is fundamentally immoral, unforgivable and repulsive. Tonight we were using fire to fight fire, clearly a good. With clear conscience I'll admit the flames were engrossing and beautiful. Campfires were the caveman's television after all. In the foothills above Santa Barbara we were entranced by a mammoth version of a backyard fire pit or chiminea meant for roasting marshmallows.

I leaned against the Super P handle for support, enjoying the show. For the first time in forever, I did not worry about losing it at any second. Tired, absolutely fried and run through a meat grinder, mostly I felt relief at surviving the day.

The night air filled with warm, spicy scent of mesquite smoke. If only Robby Wadlow packed in some tri-tip steaks, we could have done dinner right. Instead I opened a can of peaches with a Vietnam War era P- 38 can opener. The P-38 was my dad's and cut through the metal in short order, my thumb ratcheting down to open the lid in a dozen quick turns. I've looked for a back-up P- 38 in camping stores. The new ones feel lightweight, cheap and not nearly the same quality as old steel. There's probably an allegory there. I didn't have the energy to ruminate on it.

The peaches were thick, full of sugar and exactly what the doctor ordered. I drank from the can hungrily. Rich viscous syrup coated the throat and sweet, lush fruit practically melted in my mouth.

The backfiring operation went smoothly with no spots or breakdowns. We made excellent progress and burned until four in the morning. Killer passed word we could take a half hour to grab some shuteye. Parked on a slightly flat section, I unstrapped the backpack, sat straight down and curled onto one side. With hardhat functioning as a pillow against the dirt and hugging the backpack as blanket, I closed both eyes. Soft popping noises and crackling of the fire smoldered ten feet away. A half hour earlier I had downed a quart of instant coffee mixed with chocolate powder. The chocolate barely masked the thick, bitter "bonus cup" made with tablespoons of instant coffee and enough caffeine to light a city block. Electricity flashed behind closed eyelids. My heart rattled and I sensed the world around me, but fell asleep in less than forty seconds.

CHAPTER

9

The Killer shook one shoulder after what seemed a minute. Reading Casio time, thirty-five minutes passed.

"C'mon now Curt, let's finish this bad boy before the sun gets too high, and that heat kicks in."

"You got it, Killer," I mumbled, shaking away the slumber and standing upright. Throwing the pack on and adjusting the straps for comfort, I stretched head and neck in a circle. The false dawn made the night appear grey. Figures shuffled down the incline, quietly bumping down.

To the right of the line was green, thick overgrown brush. On the left, blackened and flattened earth with random Rorschach blotches of sick white ash that marked the dead fire. Smoke rose lazily from smoldering remains of burnt stumps and brush. Our line held perfectly and defined a textbook black line. I made the way downhill and joined half the crew stretched out near the anchor point from yesterday morning. J.C. was burning out the final corner. The green section filled with flames as the sun rose steadily in the east. We were awfully close to being done with this fire. Sure there would be mop-up, but major operations were complete. The "Peak Fire" was 100% contained. Engines crews with portable pumps and hoses from a progressive hoselay would help extinguish smoldering stumps and hot spots. That work would be straightforward and tedious.

Soon the pale yellow almost white sun asserted itself against the cloudless slate sky. Sunglasses were a comfort for bloodshot eyes. The half-hour nap was better than nothing but barely. For certain the lack of real sleep made me punchy and on a different plane. Though everyone spoke quietly and acted normal, a rattle of thoughts clattered in my head like echoes in an empty room. My brain needed a broom to sweep the cobwebs away.

The last brush flared and burned. Under the light of day, flames appeared thin, transparent yellow and lacked the rich orange that contrasted with the pitch black night. I mixed another "bonus" quart of coffee with my last packet of powdered hot chocolate. Cold water isn't the best for dissolving coffee granules. I screwed the plastic lid tight and shook the bottle violently, willing the instant crystals to melt and not leave a bitter brown sludge at the canteen bottom. The movement reminded of Dave and his steel shaker full of Kami's from the party a lifetime ago. It seemed longer than twenty-something hours ago. The high voltage coffee tasted like dirt mixed with chocolate. The extra dose was necessary to get to even.

We were on our own for breakfast, but hunkered down after ten for an early lunch. There were sack lunches with quality deli sandwiches on soft French rolls, a plastic single serving container of potato salad, one large dill pickle wrapped in waxed paper, a red delicious apple, a stick of Bazooka bubble gum and a can of either flavored iced tea or lemonade. Someone in charge outdid themselves by shipping in several heavy duty cardboard boxes of ripe watermelons, enough for each person to have a half of their own. What a treat. Broiling under the summer sun on a dusty, south slope with no shade for a second straight day, lazy smoke hung low like a bad cough. That mess of watermelons must have wiped out an entire supermarket's inventory. My belief is our benefactor pre-planned this years back when miserable on the fireline and promised themselves that when in charge, whenever that future day came, he or she was going to hook up the crew on the ground.

Sitting on the hill, quiet now with mouths full with food, everyone cut the melons with pocket knives and feasted on big chunks. We were one happy, content crew.

"Those fingers better not get infected, Mike, you dumb sucker. For sure I hope you don't lose one. And there's no sick leave here, son."

The Supe pretended to chastise Kingman for not seeing a doctor that night and sent Mike to town for real medical attention. The chewing out was just show. You'd have to be blind to miss the quiet pride the Supe had for Kingman while delivering the hard tone. When the fingers were cut and Mike screamed, I was right next to him. White bones were visible in two fingers like thin men in canoes. Dark blood gushed but to me that was not a big deal. I freaked seeing the shocking white of bone. My head hurt thinking how many nerve endings are in your fingers. That Kingman sucked it up and kept sawing the rest of the night with only some bandages and tape was something.

Even Stew, who had a famous quote, "I am the only man I know," acknowledged Kingman's toughness to work through the pain.

"Grrrr. No brain, no headache. Stupid, bastard. What were you doing testing the sharpness of a moving chain? Better lucky than good. Cause you're damn lucky that hand didn't get cut off."

He pulled his sunglasses off and looked coolly at Kingman, his gray eyes expressionless. The faintest hint of a smile curled on the side of his mouth. For Stew that was remarkably sympathetic. Maybe he was starting to get a little soft.

We sat for thirty minutes, enjoying the meal and view to the ocean. Pretty soon jokes started with people talking smack.

Daryl tried to push my buttons saying that I looked like crap yesterday morning.

"You were green like nomex pants, Lightning. Maybe you party too much the night before?" He had a gleeful expression, excited for ammo to give me a hard time.

Not taking any guff, I stared dully at him. "Remind me now, why do they call you Derelict, Daryl?"

"Hey Bolt, did you disappear with that sweet little blond? I lost track of you," Robbie Wadlow asked. "She was a cute one."

"You like her, Wadlow?" I looked in his direction. "Nah, we didn't hook up. You're right though. She was a cutie. Reminded me of a cupcake with buttercream frosting."

"Yeah, little chicken dumplings. Good enough to eat. And she was ready."

"Oh?" the Killer asked. "Was she ready?"

"Yep," Wadlow said smiling. "She was ready!"

J.C. piped in, "Cabron, she was ready."

The phrase got picked up and passed again like people hitting a beach ball in the stands at a ballgame and went for a couple minutes. "She was ready, Cabron. She was ready." Over and over again.

They could repeat the expression for hours. Who knew how long ago the phrase was first coined. It could have been from the seventies for what I know. The line had a life of its own. Each person placed a different accent on "cabron" and the word "ready", attempting to capture an ideal pronunciation. She, whoever this individual was, had become immortalized.

Another favorite guys could repeat for hours was from the movie <u>Full Metal Jacket</u>. "Me love you long time. Boom boom, long time." Over and over. We'd be hiking along and one thing about this job, we are always hiking, miles and miles across the country. Someone would start up, and the dialog would keep rolling. After awhile the unending repetition was enough to drive you crazy.

After six p.m. we were released from the fire and could go home. Engines from other districts rolled in throughout the day with more than enough personnel to finish mopping up. Fanned out across the blackened hillside, we reconvened into one line behind the Supe and Stew. Gravity guided the mellow hike down to the crew trucks, the Killer taking the rear. Tools were loaded into compartments on the buggies and smoky, blackened yellow nomex shirts stuffed into hardhats and placed in the netting above the seats. I rode the motorcycle back to the hotshot base, following the Supe along the Camino Cielo but in front of the crew buggies. I'd have loved to blaze ahead but no way would have gone in front of the Supe. Some things you just don't do. It was a short commute. We made the base in minutes.

The Supe cracked, "I hope everyone enjoyed your weekend. See you for PT tomorrow oh-nine-hundred."

I decided to forgo a stop at the Store and made home after seven. Pulling into the front yard only scattered remnants of the party were visible. My roommates had been busy because the apartment complex was in decent shape. Ben and Chris were parked on the front yard sofa when I pulled in. Coals glowed white on the Weber barbecue. They were about to grill swordfish, cut vegetables and corn on the cob wrapped in green husks.

In the refrigerator behind a half empty gallon of milk was an open twelve pack of Milwaukee's Best. Believe it or don't, that crappy beer looked heavenly right then. I cracked opened a can and sat on the couch, my friends sliding down to make room for me. Their beers were open. We clinked, "Luck", cheersing.

"You freaking owe me big time for throwing that duffel in the wash for you, Curt. Don't ever say I don't love you, dude, 'cause that was unmentionably horrible."

"I'm sorry, bro."

"Seriously. That was gnarly. We didn't notice for awhile until we thought something died in your room."

I leaned forward and nodded to Ben my appreciation and told them about the fire. Then we talked about the party and watched girls run by. The park was crowded with people playing volleyball and throwing Frisbee. Others gathered together in small groups, gearing up for the sunset. Waves softly splashed in the distance. You could not ask for a more peaceful evening. Ben worked the grill and said there was more than enough to share. The greatest splendor ever was kicking back without anything to do or anywhere to be.

I reclined with feet propped on a folding beach chair, rested my head on a battered spare cushion and closed both eyes. Tiredness draped me like a suit and settled in. When the food was ready they waited on me like I was a paying customer. Chef Ben's meals could rival the finest served in a Michelin star restaurant. Chris and I were the beneficiaries. Ben was a skinny kid with a burning metabolism. After his parents divorced his mom worked an outside job full time. He learned to feed himself in junior high with boxed Kraft macaroni and cheese and graduated from there. My idea of gastronomy is pouring beer over barbecue chicken breast when the skin catches fire and would probably starve if we ran out of peanut butter or canned soup. But Ben was into cooking and talented. Perfectly grilled fish and vegetables with a curry sauce plus buttered summer corn on the cob were tonight's deliciousness. I thanked him for the good grub.

"We didn't know you'd be home. You lucked out cause the swordfish was on special. I bought extra to make fish tacos tomorrow."

"I owe you."

"No doubt, you owe me. Pain in my ass."

"Hey Curt," Chris said. "I almost forgot. That gal stopped by yesterday. She did not leave a number but said that she wanted to say 'Hi'." He looked at me steady, waiting for a reaction.

Thinking he was referring to the buttercream frosting girl from the party, I said, "That cute blond cupcake? Nice."

Chris cocked an eyebrow. "Cupcake? Um, I don't know about that. If you say so."

I collected the dirty, empty plates and asked, "Who wants another of the Best?"

I tossed one to Ben, opened another and started washing the dishes by hand. Ben made a freaking mess. His ingredients literally exploded all over the kitchen. The food was too tasty to complain. No matter how exhausted and running on fumes, I would clean every night to feast like that. After finishing the dishes and wiping down the counter, I took a shower, dressed in clean shorts, brushed teeth, said goodnight and jumped into bed. The lumpy mattress felt like a bed of feathers. The sheets were soft and smooth against bare skin.

CHAPTER

10

The solid night of sleep did me right. I awoke the next morning refreshed and did not need coffee to feel awake. The sky was washed white and the sun bright. In my imagination today was like a movie musical. At any moment people might start dancing in the kitchen or in the street and burst into song. Of course, I was goofy thinking to be channeling Gene Kelly or a maybe Jet or Shark character from West Side Story. That's how the day was. My life's soundtrack was rolling sweet as any music video.

I rode to work singing the whole way. The Shoei helmet thankfully shielded the awful noise from passersby. We ran five miles on trails for morning PT. My breathing and legs were strong. I weigh two hundred five pounds and am no gazelle, especially running uphill. Today both feet were light. I loped the whole way with music bouncing in my head. At the station I did three sets of pull ups, sixteen the first set, powering through the reps without pause and then two sets of fourteen, the final tired reps slower but steady. After the last, I hung from the bar, my weight pulling and straightening the kinks, clicking and shifting vertebrae into place.

We did chores around the ranger station and I spent several hours sharpening chainsaw chains. The routine of the task let my mind wander and play games in quiet thoughts. I was not anti-social, but simply content and at peace within myself. Mindless routine tasks are the best to lose yourself in the moment. We would work the Santa Ynez trail later this week. Today was a chill day.

J.C. interrupted the reverie. He was clamping a tool to a vise on the work bench. We were alone in the work area.

"Hey Curt. I was worried about you this weekend." His tone was flat and somber.

"What do you mean?"

"Hell dude. You were a bleeping mess at the party. What happened? I don't think I've ever seen you like that before."

"What are you talking about? Yeah, I was rolling. So was everybody."

"You were demolished when we got there. The next morning when you finally showed to the fire, really. You were green like bad Sci-Fi aliens."

"Are you the party police now, Cracker?"

"You know it's not like that." His black eyes were steady and unreadable. "We don't talk about it much, but on the reservation I saw way too many good people hurt by booze. Everyone acts like it's a big laugh. Oh, the Indians are on the fire line, we'll pay 'em with heap 'um barrels of whiskey' and stuff like that. It's not really funny and no joke. Lots of good dudes have seriously messed up their lives. I'd hate to see that happen to you."

"I'm cool, bro. I appreciate what you're saying, but it's all good. I got a little carried away is all."

"What's the phrase, Denial ain't a river in Africa. Really, Curt. Think about it."

"Okay, okay. If you say so. But I'm good. I swear." Thankfully he let it go.

That was a downer. J.C. was a good bud. I tried to shake the lecture off and focused to bring the music soundtrack back. The channel changed in my head to a steady stream of reggae, the melodies grooving and mellow. Founded on oppressive poverty and laced with heartache, the songs strived to maintain positive vibrations about overcoming trouble. I hummed along.

Of course, we stopped at the Store after work. I relished in the quiet ease of the daily pattern. Guys told familiar stories and jokes. Though I knew the punchlines and heard the same lies many times before, the ritual was comfortable, sitting on the wall. Most important for me was to feel part of the group, to be joined with something greater than myself.

Pulling into the apartment, I still jammed to the internal music, smiling inside. I watched television with Chris and Ben. This was as peaceful a day you could ask for. Sure, J.C. was a touch dramatic, but he meant well. I even went to bed early again. Normally I tend to be a night owl. Going to bed early has never been a practice. Something about making the choice seemed luxurious. I felt rich lying in the comfort of bed again, cool sheets keeping me company. On the verge of falling asleep, something Chris said the day before tugged my memory that did not exactly make sense. Didn't he say that cute little blond, cupcake frosting girl stopped by to say hello? I don't remember Chris meeting her. How did he know her?

I rose and walked to the living room dressed in boxers. Standing in the doorway, I blinked to adjust eyes from darkness to the lit room.

"Hey, yesterday you said some girl came by asking for me. Who were you talking about?"

Ben and Chris were sprawled on the sofa and lazy-boy chair. Both looked at me with blank expressions. "That gal from a month ago, what was her name? Janine? That damn good looking one. I thought you knew who I was talking about."

"What did she say again?"

"That she wanted to say hi. She was in town. That's all."

"Okay. Thanks. If she comes back again, please do me a favor. Make sure to get her number."

And that whole at "peace with the world" crap left like a helium balloon after a child drops its string. You stand helpless looking up and watch the balloon sail away, growing smaller and smaller, until only a faint speck. Caught in the updrafts, it fades away and floats from view. There went the peace. Now lying in bed was not restful and luxurious but confused and fitful. Thoughts raced. Memories of the night with Janine crowded my brain. I lay for an hour unable to sleep, head spinning, replaying every moment in the jumble.

CHAPTER

11

Alone at the kitchen table with a cup of coffee the next morning, I came to more of an understanding than a conscious decision. After work I would jam to Ventura and grab a burrito at Corrales taco stand. Magically running into Janine on the street wasn't likely. Doing something, anything even if only heading closer to her possible location seemed better than waiting around on my ass for her to reappear. Plus, there was no guarantee she would show again.

Now with a purpose and something to do when work was over, the day dragged and tormented me with listless passing of minutes and hours. The pleasant mundane chores yesterday were now wearisome. I was antsy to get going.

At six I did not pause but jumped on the GPZ and hauled ass down Paradise Road, past the Store, over the Pass and onto the 101 Highway south to Ventura. Commuters clogged the road. I sped between stopped cars, zigzagging across and floating through the lanes. Sunlight reflected off the windows of houses stretched across the Riviera and glittered and sparkled in the early evening. I normally appreciate the view but mainly watched for obstacles on the way.

Traffic finally cleared south of Montecito. I pulled the throttle open wide and flew at a steady ninety plus per hour, vigilantly keeping an eye for hidden troopers waiting to write an expensive speeding ticket. The coast highway lives its name and runs feet from the Pacific Ocean. The water looked warm, soft and blue green with lonely little ankle slappers for waves. Dimples across the surface in the distance sparkled like gold encrusted jewels from sunlight shining through their prisms.

Zooming along I made Ventura in less than 40 minutes from the Ranger Station, decent time considering traffic.

I exited the highway, rolled past a Greyhound station, and found the taco stand. An open spot in the asphalt parking lot next to an old VW camper van welcomed me. Several people were waiting at the order counter. I went to the rear of the line. Of course, I did not expect her to be there. But yes, in the deepest recesses of my mind the hope was that she would be. I looked around expectantly. Janine was not there.

When they called my number I asked for extra salsa and sat at an open table. The special red sauce takes the four way burrito with a chile relleno inside to unbelievable heights. I paired the best food imaginable with a large fountain root beer served in a styrofoam cup with shaved ice. Sweet carbonation cooled the heat from the salsa. The chile relleno was not hot, but had incredible, spicy flavor and a rich texture.

I devoured the meal and watched other customers and new people queue up. A group of painters in splattered overalls and a young Hispanic couple holding hands waited to place orders. The guy wore a white wife-beater tank top and khaki shorts that hung past his calves. Dressed in jeans and a purple top, the girl looked a couple months pregnant, her belly bump just starting to show.

After one last delicious bite, I surveyed the neighborhood and cars passing on the street. I glanced at the Casio wristwatch, as if waiting for someone, maybe a date, running late. Without verbalizing the wish, I made a prayer for Janine to appear. Hope dies hard. I half expected her to show any moment. She did not.

The counter lady read aloud a new batch of numbers. The Hispanic couple collected their order, looking for a place to sit. I rose from the table, opening the spot and threw empty tin foil wrapper, paper napkins and empty styrofoam cup into the trash bin and jumped onto the GPZ. Pressing the ignition and kicking into gear, I eased onto the street and cruised the downtown area. People walked between assorted storefronts and restaurants. I did not recognize anyone and putted around, circling blocks aimlessly. Janine was nowhere to be seen. Except in my imagination she was everywhere, all over the place. Her image floated in and about as if a residue energy trail where I could see each place she had ever been. Traces of her essence populated downtown in a ghost dance shuffle.

Spying an open parking spot on the street, I pulled in and stopped at an old school throwback, hippie coffee shop. The strong, unpleasant smell of burnt beans permeated the air. The decor consisted of batik, stained wood, psychedelic music posters and a homage to the late sixties and early seventies. This was no yuppie hangout or wanna-be poseur Italian cafe. Behind the counter the server in her thirties wore a silver nose ring and a sleeveless brown t-shirt. An elaborate sleeve of red, purple and yellow flower tattoos interlaced with green ivy covered her left arm from shoulder blade down to her wrist. She eyed me listlessly and barely looked up from her book to take the order. I asked for an iced mocha with a double shot of espresso. When ready I walked outside to a rickety table on the sidewalk to escape the awful smell of burnt beans. From a small wooden chair I watched the foot traffic and cars slowly pass by.

Sweet with a large dollop of chocolate sauce pooled at the bottom of the glass, the mocha was like coffee ice cream compared with my fire line bonus cup. I sat alone with random thoughts and then went back inside and ordered a second drink. While paying, I asked the counter gal if she knew a Janine from around here. She looked at me blankly and shook her head. I tried to describe Janine but fell silent mid-sentence, frustrated, realizing the hopelessness. I felt like an idiot for even asking. Ventura is a small town, but not necessarily that small. Feeling judged a fool by some tattooed nose ring counter lady made the whole thing worse. Not bothering to sit, I drank the second mocha down in a couple long gulps and was rewarded with an evil ice cream headache. Cold icicles pierced the brain. I placed a palm around my throat which supposedly helps with a brain freeze, but that did not do anything. I breathed exaggerated breaths through my mouth. After a minute the pain subsided.

I left the cafe. The screen door self-closed behind me from a spring. A tinny bell rang, marking the exit. I fired the GPZ's engine and peeled down the street. Four shots of espresso coursed through the central nervous system. Pulling onto the highway heading north, I was speedy and not from the motorcycle. My skin crinkled like goose flesh and heart raced and jumped. The pulse bounced in the temples and behind the whites of my eyes. Leaving the town boundary I opened the throttle the whole way, the GPZ flying one hundred thirty miles an hour. The aquamarine ocean shimmered and glittered on my left, the last orange rays of sunlight dancing across the smooth surface. I did not pay that beauty any attention. My vision clouded with anger, the lion's share directed towards myself for wasting time with false hope and acting like a darn fool. I flew through scattered northbound traffic as if the cars were standing still. Hitting a rough patch of pavement, the rear tire wobbled sideways, giving a momentary scare. My heart skipped, but I straightened out and kept racing without easing or slowing down. We made Santa Barbara in nothing flat.

I slowed near the Milpitas exit and the bend where the highway rolls through downtown. Sometimes CHP idle near that section. After passing the Cabrillo exit to City College, I juiced the throttle again, not as fast as before but well above the limit. After one hundred and thirty, ninety-five felt sluggish. The espresso rush was strong. Not feeling like going home yet, I turned off the 101 and headed right on the 154 towards the Pass and Cold Spring Tavern. Wednesday night some hotshots would be around for sure. With skin coiling like a reptile, a drink or three would help smooth the edges.

Cold Springs was an old stagecoach stop from the 1800's nestled amongst tall forest on the Santa Ynez side of the San Marcos Pass and is divided into two sections, the romantic, hideaway restaurant and our stomping ground of a tavern. Dark floors pair with wide beams that crisscross the frame of the rustic original wooden buildings. The walls are decorated with an assortment of vintage black and white photos and mounted busts of deer and elk from long ago hunting parties. Known for quality wild game, fine cuts of local meats and fresh fish the restaurant is highly rated. The tavern is a dark, simple room with low ceiling, wooden bar and a side stage with enough room for a small band to play music. During the week a solo guitarist or duo usually plays to a smaller crowd. Sunday afternoons are the best when a roadhouse band gets the whole place rocking. Speakers are set outside and the parking lot will be packed to overflowing with Harleys and other motorcycles. Cars line both sides of the narrow road. The Sunday crowd is a cross-section of bikers in black leathers from across the central coast, authentic working cowboys from Santa Ynez horse ranches, locals, hunters, people from town. Of course whenever we're around sprinkled throughout the crowd in characteristic green t-shirts, the LP shots will be representing.

A smattering of cars and pickups were in the dirt parking lot. The night looked fairly tame. I parked next to Pete's Toyota 4x and sauntered in, ducking my head to avoid the low frame of the tavern door. A group of four hotshots watched a duo playing guitar and a mandolin. A half dozen other people milled about. I walked to the bar and ordered a Coors and a shot of tequila. The bartender Jimmy greeted me with a smile and handed back six single dollars as change from my ten spot. Jimmy had a pointed hawk-like face with bushy mutton chop sideburns low across lean cheeks. He gave me the workingman's deal of $4 for a shot and beer. Cold Spring charged two prices, a lower one for locals and a higher price for everyone else. When first receiving the local's price a couple years ago, I appreciated the milestone. Of course every dollar matters on a tight budget, but the symbolism meant something more. I nodded thanks, tossed two bucks for tip and pulled a chair next to Pete, Lumpy and Boon.

Three guys from town were in the corner talking with two good looking gals dressed in jeans and cowboy boots. The musicians were not half bad and played bluesy folk music.

The songs were melodic ballads with intricate stories and plot lines. Everyone chatted while the duo played their set.

Lumpy's truck was getting worked on at the shop. He was Pete's passenger tonight. Not having to drive was an occasion to let loose more than usual. Pete was in rare form too, complaining about some imagined injustice.

"We were on that fire from eight in the morning until six the next evening. It ain't right we only get paid eight hours of Sunday differential. Eight in the morning until midnight is sixteen hours."

Lumpy attempted to explain we earned hazard pay for the whole day and overtime for the other sixteen hours. Pete did not accept the logic.

"It was Sunday all day. We should get Sunday differential for the whole damn day."

"What, did you miss church? Give me a break. It works out in the end." His eyes rolled in frustration. Being reasonable wasn't working. They'd been going around and around for a while now. Pete would not let it go.

"I just want what's right. That's all."

Talk about Sunday reminded me Janine stopped by the apartment that afternoon, but I missed her.

"Lump, Pete has a point. It is B.S...Sunday was a full day long. Doesn't make sense we earn the Sunday rate for only eight hours of the twenty-four."

"What a pathetic, sorry bunch of complainers. Let me buy this round. I doubt you have any cash, what with you'se getting practically robbed and all."

So we had another round, those three with beers and another workingman's special for me. Though bottom tier well tequila that finished with a harsh sting, the special was a solid value. Espresso caffeine sharpness remained, but the drinks dulled the edges, at least a little. I ignored the bickering hotshots and surveyed the corner table with the three guys from town and two cowgirls. The gals looked familiar and had been around before. I did not recognize the men who looked in their late twenties. They were dressed in collared and preppy polo shirts with coiffed hair as if recently cut and blow dried at a salon. The three shared the same self-satisfied, arrogant look of rich dudes.

One stood from the table, walked to the bar near our seats and ordered two Dewars and three beers from Jimmy. Dressed in a red polo shirt with white stripes, he was large and thick like a former college offensive lineman. As he waited for the drinks, Pete asked, "Hey man, what's happening?"

The guy turned and answered, "Nada. How you?"

"Good thanks. How's it going. I'm Pete Johnson. You guys from town?"

"Yeah, that's right. You say you're Peter Johnson? That's kind of redundant, don't cha think. Is your middle name Richard?" He chuckled at his own joke. "Nice meeting you." Grabbing three beers in one beefy hand and the two scotch glasses in the other, he nodded and went back to their table.

Lumpy and Boon enjoyed a laugh at Pete's expense. I was quiet. The debate about overtime suddenly grated nerves, made me feel poor and pissed off. Where did this dude get off mocking my friend anyway? A moment later I stood silently in front of their table. They looked at me expectantly. Not knowing what to do, I asked the better looking of the two cowgirls to dance. She had clear skin and the angular bone structure of women that ride horses. Her long brown hair was in a thick single braid tied back by a green ribbon. The cowgirl laughed awkwardly, looked sideways at her friend and said thanks, not now. Awkwardly quiet, the rest stared blankly. Deliberately looking the three dudes over, I winked at the big one in striped red polo. Again addressing the brunette I said, "If'n you two get bored with these Barneys, come on over and sit with us. Promise to show you a good time. Always give the lady what she is after. That's my motto."

The women snickered into their hands. The dudes didn't say anything but looked like I pissed in their soup. Turning away, I made a circular motion to Jimmy signifying another round for our group and paid with a twenty from my wallet. Leaning elbows on the bar I watched as he grabbed four beers from the cold box. In the mirror's reflection above the backbar the three townies looked agitated, talking amongst themselves. I tossed back the tequila and carried new cold ones to my friends, smiling inside. We cheers-ed. After raising his can in salute, Boon stood to go outside to the restroom. I followed him out into the cool forest night. The tavern did not have the best ventilation and could get stuffy. The night breeze was refreshing in contrast. Boon told me a story as we walked. Carved into the paint of the windowsill above the long rectangular metal urinal was the outline of a lightning bolt. Although years old, I never noticed the graffiti before. The design was the classic lightning bolt graphic from the '70's surfboard company. The beauty of the symmetry struck me. This was a lucky sign. As much I hate the rap about being in slow motion and slow on the uptake, the name Lightning had a cool ring to it and was starting to grow on me. Maybe embracing the nickname was the answer because protestations and resistance were not helping it go away. The timeless simplicity of the logo would make a great tattoo across my tricep.

Boon decided to head out, said adios and walked to his truck. Pleased about my tattoo vision, I reentered the tavern. Their set over, the musicians were packing up gear. Without music playing, quiet filled the bar. The good looking cowgirls must have left. Three dudes were now alone at the corner table. As I grabbed a seat next to Pete and Lumpy, a presence crowded the space behind me. Striped red polo guy jabbered something about not appreciating how I spoke to their friend. Hollow eyes stared at me as I stood, looked at Pete and Lumpy as if to say, "Can you believe this bozo?" and without winding up, threw a hard left cross to the side of his head above the ear. I was flat footed and did not get my full weight into the punch but caught him square. His eyes rolled back and he stumbled to his knees. Dumbstruck his buddies could not believe what happened. After frozen moments of surprise they rallied and rushed me at the same time. The one in white on the right swung at me wildly. I ducked and the punch missed. The third dude with short curly hair was in a dark blue polo and did not try to throw a punch, but launched himself at me, wrapping both arms around my sides and arms. I was off-balance from dodging the other guy. He was able to tackle and drag me to the ground.

Everything happened supersonic, out of nowhere. In a blur we were wrestling on the floor, smashing against chairs and table legs. I tried to pull from his grasp, swinging short punches and elbows to ribs and torso, squirming to get away. His weight was heavy on me. Several of his sharp blows hurt, rocking my ribs and kidneys, the pain a flash and searing. The sweet, peaty odor of scotch whiskey came from his skin and breath as we rolled around, fighting for leverage and an advantage. Based on the ruckus echoing around the tavern walls, Pete and Lumpy were in a rumble with the other two. Ye Cold Spring was hosting an old fashioned barroom brawl.

My right fist landed a good one and hurt, the knuckles cut from sharp, hard molars. That was a solid punch. After the connection, his strength momentarily wavered. I was able to squeeze away, unwrapping from his clench, rolled over and stood on two feet. Scanning the room, my buds were each squared up with one of the other dudes and going pretty good. Overturned chairs and a table littered the room. The curly headed guy stood slowly, holding his jaw with one hand, eyeing me like a snake preparing to strike. He raised both fists and crouched low, measuring his best straight shot. Even with a couple inches and the reach advantage on him, I was wary. The painful shots to my torso when we were wrestling on the floor gave me pause.

He threw a massive right. Side stepping to avoid the blow, I got him with a crossing left, the same punch I leveled his buddy with. My fist landed directly above the ear and must have rocked him. This guy could definitely take a punch. He did not falter and actually came at me with combination of wild rights and lefts. I avoided the initial flurry, but he caught me on the forehead with a short right, the pain of the punch a rude shock. My vision clouded. Everything went red and hazy, blood and adrenalin rushing to my head. He then connected a left, this one on the neck. That blow hurt. The room spun and everything became a painful blur. Maybe I landed some decent shots, but he was much quicker than me. Taking repeated punches was not sustainable. My body couldn't keep trading blows and survive this punishment. Out of desperation I rushed forward and tackled him from above. Placing my full weight on him, I dragged his body down with all my strength, forcing him face first to the ground. Crashing to his knees with head and shoulders under the weight of my torso, he tried to crawl backwards and squirrel away, escaping my grasp. I now had his back and without thinking kneed him in the head, knocking the guy unconscious. The knee was a burst and powerful blow that caught him squarely on the temple of the forehead. He slumped like a rag doll, face down to the ground and out.

I staggered afoot. Pete and the guy in white stood across from each other. Pete's LP t-shirt was ripped. His opponent bled from the nose, the front of the white shirt stained brick red with blood. The original red striped polo dude sat on one side of the bar, holding his fist. Lumpy was across from him, already sporting a nice shiner. Red striped shirt guy must have broken his knuckles wide open on Lumpy's hard head. Both looked done for the night.

"What's your major malfunction, you fucking asshole?" The big guy screamed at me.

"Screw you. You guys attacked me."

Jimmy the bartender stood behind the bar, surveying the damage and strewn chairs and the slumped over guy on the floor in front of me.

"Lumpy, Curt. You boys better get the hell out of here. NOW!"

The townies kneeled over their buddy, shaking him awake. Thankfully, he came to and although groggy, was alive. He did not remember being knocked out.

Lumpy stood, grabbed me by the shoulder and dragged me out the door into the darkness away from the tavern and to the motorcycle parked next to Pete's Toyota. A breeze rustled softly through the trees lining the road and parking lot. The stillness of the night was shocking in contrast with the rush and excitement of the moments ago finished brawl.

"F me, Lightnin'. What the hell came over you?"

"That was nuts! Did you see that big dude's expression when you clocked him?"

"Seriously, when you dropped that other guy, I thought you killed him. The way he was lying there... What the hell, man?"

Adrenalin overloaded our systems. Giddy from the blitz of action, we stood next to the pickup, assessing the damage. Except for some assorted cuts, bruises and Lumpy's shiner, we were relatively unscathed. Instead of driving home to IV, I decided to crash with them at the hotshot barracks. We headed down the Stagecoach Road and passed under the suspension bridge I always forget about. When riding above on the highway, you don't realize it's a bridge. At the intersection we took Paradise Road to the east. Pete started in front and sped the way, drifting back and forth across the center of the two lane road, almost like he thought the Toyota could outrun me. I passed on the right and tore away in a blaze of speed. The GPZ's headlight lit a shallow arch in the dark road, which didn't really matter since I could drive this route by sense of touch.

Pulling into the barracks we met in the kitchen. A bag of frozen corn worked on the knuckles of my fist and Lumpy pressed frozen pees to his cheekbone to keep the swelling down. A bunch of the guys were deep into a movie rental but sat up when we came in. Hearing our story out, they soon focused again on the video action.

The thrill and excitement fading, my body suddenly felt drained empty. I said goodnight, found an old blanket in a closet and shuffled off alone to a vacant room on the side of the kitchen area with a mattress and box spring. Undressing into boxers, I settled on the bouncy mattress and smiled to myself.

CHAPTER

12

The empty room confused me in the morning until I remembered yesterday's events. I lay in bed staring at the plain white walls, listening to kitchen sounds of hotshots around. A nice perk of staying in the barracks was no commute to work. The flip side was dealing with hustle bustle first thing in the morning with the crew getting breakfast, mopping floors and cleaning.

I poached a bowl of cereal from Cornflake then headed out on a five mile PT run. The head hurt from last night's drinking and maybe from some punches. The run cleared the cobwebs. Back at the station I was about to jump in the shower when J.C. stuck his head in the locker room and said the Supe wanted to see me, pronto. His tone meant something was up. I pulled my shirt back on and hustled to the office in cotton gym shorts and shower flip flops.

The Supe was at his desk covered with topographical maps and notebooks. Stew sat in his chair at the adjacent desk. The Killer stood to their left, leaning against the window sill. The Supe was pissed.

"Curt, some of us live in this canyon year round. What the hell were you trying to pull last night at the Cold Spring? I got a call from Ms. Audrey at my house first thing this morning. Apparently you boys made a mess of the place she's put her life's work into making nice for folks to enjoy. Whatever possessed you, I don't appreciate it."

Stew and Killer were silent. I began to say there were others at the tavern, but swallowed the words, realizing that would be a mistake.

"When we break for lunch, you're gonna head to the office there, apologize and offer to pay for the damage. Depending how contrite, sincere and lucky, you might not get 86'd for the season. We had this problem before when some boneheads almost got the whole crew banned. I promised Audrey that would not happen again." He stared straight at me, eyes not blinking. Then his gaze wandered briefly in the Killer's direction.

A sick emptiness filled my stomach. I felt lower than an inch tall and stammered, "I'm sorry, Supe. I'll make it up to you."

"First priority is making it up to that nice lady. Then you can worry about me. Now get out of here."

"Yes, sir." I got out of there fast, the screen door slamming behind me as I bounded down the steps.

Instead of enjoying lunch, I rode to the Cold Spring, my bones full of cement and dread. A guilty feeling engulfed my being the whole short trip. I arrived in fast minutes, none too happy to be back at the scene of last night's action. Taking the blue LP baseball cap off and holding in hand, I sidled into the restaurant and asked for a Ms. Audrey. The lady at the reception area gave me a slow look up and down and said yes, she was expecting me. A half dozen couples ate quietly. Wine glasses and fine china adorning the white tablecloths. The genteel ambiance contrasted with the raucous tavern next door. The owner soon came out from the kitchen and greeted me, shaking my hand. She was an older woman, with wavy brown hair streaked with gray and pulled back. Bright eyes lit a weathered face lined with wrinkles. She had a quiet, serious presence. When Ms. Audrey said something, people paid attention.

"It is a pleasure to meet you, young man. I'm sorry this isn't under more pleasant circumstances. Why don't we step outside."

She gestured me to lead and we sat at the wooden picnic benches in front of the tavern. The cool shade from the trees made the warm summer day comfortable. Just like last night the wind whispered softly through rustling leaves. The scene was peaceful and serene. I sat and took my medicine. She was sweet and asked me about myself. Hearing I was a student at the University, she seemed genuinely interested in what I was studying, which made the whole thing worse. I was the biggest heel in the world. She explained how her mother fell in love with this place and originally bought the Cold Spring back in the forties. Their dream was to make a fine dining restaurant, while maintaining the charm and character of the old stagecoach stop for everyone to enjoy.

"Ma'am, I am so sorry to have disrespected your place here. I can't begin to apologize enough."

"That's fine, honey. I accept your apology. This is a special place. Of course, I abhor violence. But young men have been getting into tussles here for over a hundred years. It's surely part of the tradition and fabric here. I'm thankful no one was seriously injured and there was not significant damage to the property. Why, Mark knew that. I suspect he was teaching you a lesson making you come here."

I offered to help pay for the damage. She waved the words away and declined, saying there was not much to speak of. A chair was broken, but that would be easy for her workers to repair. When I asked a second time what I could do, she shook her head and even inquired if I had time for a bite of lunch. The rabbit special looked especially delicious today. I thanked her but had to get back to the ranger station. Apologizing again, I left feeling better than before, but still pretty low and not deserving of her kindness. The fact that she was so nice made me feel awful.

After work I bought two cases of beer at the Store as penance. Lumpy's shiner was now a full on black eye. He looked like the puppy from Our Gang. I was bummed that he got knocked around because of me. The Supe sat at his usual spot on the wall, talking quietly with J.C. He gave me a look like, "See what I mean, son. You don't mess with the good folks in this valley." They both nodded but did not say anything aloud. During the day Stew and Killer spread the word the whole crew would be banned from Cold Spring for the season if there were any repeats of last night's action. I drained one beer before deciding to head home to Isla Vista. Guys were rehashing the play by play action of the brawl, but I was not keen on the subject.

Pulling up to the apartment, a white Nissan two banger pickup was parked in the driveway. I shut off the ignition, coasted silently to the awning, parked the GPZ and walked through the front door into the kitchen. Chris and Ben sat at the green Formica table talking to a girl whose back was to me. Reggae music played on the stereo. Deep in conversation, they were laughing. I said hello and the three turned to the sound of my voice. Like the shock of an ice water shower, I stared directly into Janine's eyes again. Dressed in a t-shirt and shorts, her hair was tied back in a loose pony tail. Her eyes were that remarkable blue with the gold flakes that haunted me. There is no denying she had a giant hook in me. Seeing her again cranked the hook in hard and took my breath away.

"There he is. You see, J, I told you Curt would be here soon."

I heard Ben's words but could not take my eyes off of Janine. My head spun, trying to absorb her presence. I was tongue tied. J? What, they were best buddies already?

"Curt, we told Janine you'd kill us if we let her leave again without seeing you." Chris flashed a goofy, toothy grin, happy I was home.

"Hey, what's up. How are you?" I asked, cool as I could muster.

"I wanted to see you, to talk with you." Musical words were earnest and hopeful. Our eyes locked. The kitchen air pushed upon me with pressure.

"Yeah? That's cool. I saw you at the party."

"I wondered if..um, I thought maybe you might have. I didn't realize this was your apartment until recognizing your bike. I was all turned around that first night. Is it okay that I came here?" The halting words stumbled.

"Of course. No question. Let's go sit outside." She followed me to the couch in the front yard.

"What have you been up to?"

"My friend Elaine and I were looking at apartments. We're enrolled at SB City College for the fall and need to find a place to live."

"That's cool. Silly college. Did you see anything you liked?"

"Not around here. Everything is so expensive for what you get. Especially considering how run down they are."

"No kidding. This town is the dumps."

"Seriously. So many IV apartments are really sketchy. There was a cool spot in town near the Mesa we liked. We'd be roommates with two grad students. They were nice, kind of geeky but harmless. The house was clean and had a good vibe."

"That sounds awesome. You'd be closer to City College too. I like the Mesa."

I have a philosophy of not bringing up bad stuff. Especially when things are going well. Once when I was 14, near the end of summer, I was off work and surfing with some older kids. This was before mom died and all that. There was a gorgeous sunset. The sky was getting progressively darker and darker. The water had a magical golden tone and was warm and glassy. No one was getting out even though the sky was now black. It was night, but the waves were plenty and peeling. Everyone took turns catching good ones, hooting and having fun on this solid south swell. In between sets, I rested on my board, bobbing in the lineup, enjoying the moment. An older teenager named Mickey Sordo declared how killer this was. I commented we would not be able to do this much longer. School was starting in a couple weeks. The entire lineup grew quiet. Immediately I realized the mistake to remind everyone that summer was almost over. Reality crashed the party like a brick, breaking the good mood and vibe. Since that lesson, I try my best to not bring up bad subjects, particularly when everyone is happy.

Janine and I sat on the sofa and chatted oblivious to the neighborhood action around. Neither of us mentioned the subject we did not want to talk about, namely where was the boyfriend. What would he think about her being here with me?

"How long have you had the motorcycle? You copied the same one as the Motorcycle Boy. You think you're him, don't you? Or is it Rusty James?"

"Oh, was there a GPZ in that movie? It was in black and white, I didn't realize."

"C'mon, don't fib. Yeah, you did. I remember thinking that morning when you gave me the ride downtown." Chuckling she said, "I know my Matt Dillon." Something must have crossed across my face, because she laughed harder. "Ahh silly. Don't be jealous. You're sweet."

She kissed me on the forehead, then lightly on the cheek and finally on the lips. I closed both eyes, tried to soak everything in and still my brain. Her lips were warm and wet. Thoughts flew around like paper in a crazy wind. I let them go. She had the same smell of strawberries I remembered. Her face was smooth to the touch. The kisses were sweet and soft. Sitting on that beater old couch, my face inches from hers, the world could have crashed and the sky fall down around us. I would not have noticed.

Janine stayed until nine o'clock but promised to come back the next night. I stood in the driveway and watched as she reversed the Nissan pickup and drove away. Something about such a complete knockout driving a pickup truck cemented the deal for me. As if there was a fraction or sliver of shadow of doubt anyway. Being near her made my heart sing. Everything she did seemed perfect. After watching the little pickup's taillights round the corner and disappear out of my view, I returned to the living room and watched television with Ben and Chris.

Ben nodded approvingly. "Sweet."

Chris said, "Hey, good thing she came back, huh?"

I grinned in return but kept quiet. They were watching an old repeat of the original Star Trek. We enjoyed the cheesy dialogue and over the top drama of future worlds in jeopardy.

159

CHAPTER

13

The next morning was crisp and sharp, as if newly washed. I woke with a smile. In the kitchen since no one was looking, I skipped around doing my version of Snoopy's happy dance. My twenty-one year old bones may be a little stiff. I didn't care. At work the guys spent hours trying to goad me. Someone decided and everyone agreed today was "let's give Curt a ration of shit day." Nothing penetrated. Their flak bounced off like rain on an umbrella. Time crawled but I cruised with inner serenity, music in my head. Janine was coming over that night. I relished the anticipation and was bulletproof.

After work I shot home like an arrow. Sure enough, pulling into the apartment the little white Nissan was parked at the curb in front. Seeing that truck waiting was better than sunshine peaking from behind a cloud, the calm after a rough storm. My heart lifted. Janine sat in the front yard talking with Ben. I parked the cycle, walked over and greeted her with a kiss on the lips.

"Hey there. What's happening?"

"Nada. Just kicking it here with Benjamin. How was your day?"

"Agonizing. How about you?"

"It was great."

'You hungry? Want to grab a bite to eat?"

"Sure thing. What are you thinking?"

"I don't know. You feel like Mexican? We could go to Freebirds for a burrito."

"Mexican would be good. But a huge burrito sounds like too much."

"How about Mi Casita's? They have killer shrimp tacos."

"Now that sounds yummy."

I jumped on the old yellow Schwinn and directed the way. Janine borrowed Chris' black cruiser. We headed downtown, peddling easily along, side by side, weaving in and out of pedestrians walking the street. She wore sandals, white cotton shorts and a faded burgundy, sleeveless top. I was still in dusty, green nomex pants, green LP t-shirt, blue ball cap and brown leather Whites. She looked like any other student on a nice summer evening. I probably looked like a kook in long pants riding the bicycle, the heavy lugged sole boots big for the pedals.

A decent crowd filled the restaurant. We found an open booth in the corner and settled in. The seats were worn, faded red Naugahyde, wide and comfortable. A mix of old Mexican bullfighting posters decorated the walls. A large velvet canvas in the center of the room showed an Aztec warrior in a great feather headdress embracing a dark princess at the base of a volcano. A short Hispanic woman in her forties with a round, dark face brought over chips and salsa plus two menus. Janine asked about the turquoise ring on her hand.

"What a beautiful ring. Can I see? That is so pretty." The silver band was brackish with age and wrapped around a crooked heart shaped but striking blue stone in the center. The thin band was tight and cut into the lady's thick finger. Janine smiled generously. "I love the heart shape. How lovely."

"Oh, thank you. Gracias. It was a gift." The waitress beamed widely, pleased to appreciate the compliment. Her eyes lit up and chubby cheeks turned a shade rosier.

A tin sign on the wall announced they were proud to serve Cerveza Bohemia. I ordered a root beer and three carne asada tacos. Janine asked for two shrimp tacos and a horchata. We sat quietly and ate the salty chips, still warm from hot cooking oil, dipping each in the chunky, red salsa. When the drinks arrived, I gave Janine a quizzical look as she took a sip of the milky white beverage.

"I'm sure it's good. But the idea of that stuff gives me the heebie jeebies, like rice pudding."

"Oh, you're crazy. You have to try it."

"Nah. That's okay."

"Oh no, hombre. I insist. Yes, you have to try. This is so delicious. It has a unique cinnamon taste."

Steeling myself to take the smallest of sips, I must admit the beverage was tasty. The red salsa had complex flavors wrapped in heat. The sweetness of the horchata paired nicely with the spice. Reluctantly I shrugged acceptance. Janine smiled knowingly, cheerful to be proven correct.

I had to grin back. The thought struck me if someone offered a ticket to Paris, Barcelona, Fiji or you name the exotic locale and said I could go anywhere in the world, I would have said thanks, but no thanks. Right here, this exact moment, with this girl was the one place I wanted to be in the world. Now if we're talking two tickets, I would accept in a heartbeat and take her with me. Shadows covered the restaurant interior. A beam of sunlight shone through an open window, illuminating Janine from behind like an aura radiated around her.

The food came steaming hot on heavy, white ceramic plates. We ate and discussed the day. She and Elaine signed the lease to share the apartment with the grad students on the Mesa and would move in the end of the week. The carne asada tacos were on two soft corn tortillas with a generous portion of diced cubes of tender beef, chopped onions, cilantro and a dollop of hot sauce. A nice change from the daily Store burger, they hit the mark. Breaking my own avoid bad news rule, I raised the subject we had conveniently avoided.

"What's your boyfriend think about you being here with me? You know, that guy I saw you with."

"Oliver? Actually, we broke up."

"Really. When was that. You looked friendly at the party. What happened?"

"I found out he cheated on me. Again. We were rocky for a while. Everything went down the night of the party. He's cheated before and I told him I could not forgive that again." Her eyes looked away from mine and focused on the print of the Aztec couple on wall.

"You guys are finished?'

"Yes."

"Any reason you didn't want to say something?"

"I don't know. Embarrassed, I guess. What girl wants to admit her boyfriend is a serial cheater. It's not hot for your self esteem. If you know what I mean."

The blue behind both eyes shaded, the hurt visible. I wanted to give her a hug. Instead I leaned in close and kissed her on the cheek and then the lips. What a loser of a dude. Because this girl seemed the sweetest and coolest in the world. She was gorgeous, yet vulnerable and sensitive.

"I won't ever cheat on you, promise." I said steady and serious. This was what, our third date, and already declaring to be true blue. And happily. What the hell was happening with me?

"I hope not. You would be the first. I must put out a vibe or something. For some reason, every boy I've ever gone out with has thought it's okay to be unfaithful."

"You shouldn't be so hard on yourself. Lots of guys, when they get with a real knockout, grow super cocky and start believing they must be something special. It goes to their heads."

"That sounds familiar."

"And let's face it, when women see some random dude with a gorgeous gal they immediately think, hey, he must be a prize and get way competitive. To prove their own self worth, they'll often pursue an other girl's guy. Happens all the time."

"So it's the other woman's fault?"

"I didn't say that. But it does take two to tango. My point is, women notice men way more if they're with a good looking woman. The same dude by himself doesn't get nearly the play as when he's got a smoking hot babe on his arm. Of course, the boyfriend should resist temptation when women throw themselves at him. Because yes, girls go after each others' boyfriends."

"I'm not sure women are that hyper competitive with each other."

"What? Please. Sure they are. Buying new outfits or getting your hair done, who are you really dressing to impress? Other girls mostly. Unless they're gay, most guys don't have the first clue about any of that stuff."

"Well, maybe..." She looked at me, wheels turning. "You make a convincing argument. Generally speaking, there is some truth to what you say. I'll admit you could be correct."

"Of course I am." I smiled with satisfaction. For once my deep thinking had a real life application and hopefully brought her some solace.

After paying the bill we rode the bicycles together, peddling a lazy and mellow pace down D.P. The streets were now quiet and peaceful. Low ocean sounds carried with the breeze through gaps between the cliff top apartments. Thrashed and worn from lack of upkeep and years of abuse from thousands of parties, the rows of apartments housed students stacked upon each other. Cockroaches be damned, wide windows and decks possessed million dollar views of the Pacific. We stopped at the beach access stairway above a spot called Indicators. With the low tide, small and barely existent waves slapped and kicked at the sand. A thin line of foam from the shore wash hissed and softly popped. Barely audible squawks from shorebirds communicated with each other, circling in the darkening sky, searching for fish in shallow waters. Sandpipers scurried about, digging for buried sand crabs.

With feet touching ground, we rested lightly on the bicycles. A waxing crescent moon hung in the east. Glimmering lights rolled across the smooth surface of the ocean. A peaceful expression bathed Janine's face. Strands of seaweed floated in the shallows and stretched across to shore. The water looked like glass and shiny under the moonlight.

Back at the apartment, no one was home and we headed straight to my room. I sat on the edge of the bed. A smile tilted across her face before Janine sat next to me. Breathing steady, we absorbed each other. Finally Janine leaned in and kissed me with cool lips. In a dream we rolled around, kissing, breathing and slowly but surely undressing each other. Clothes peeled away easily. Then we were making love. Like a magnet and iron, my being was overwhelmed by her presence. I looked down and tried to absorb that this was really happening. Her body was right there and solid. In a dream long legs wrapped around me, connecting every strong muscle to calves and smooth thighs, the melody and curve of hips. Pressure and heat from her skin enveloped me. The line of her throat gave me pause. A knot formed in mine. With eyes closed, the profile of her face looked angelic.

Afterward, I put on a pair of shorts and went to the kitchen for a drink. I filled two tall glasses from the bottled water dispenser, one with ice cubes and a second without. Now dressed in underwear and t-shirt, Janine sat, leaning against two pillows on the bed. She smiled at my return like the sun shined for me personally, filling me with warmth and trumpets played. She chose the glass with ice which suited me fine. The water was already cool from the dispenser, plus ice water hurts the silver fillings in my teeth.

"I love how you smell, warm and rough. The scent of oil is really a turn on. What's that from?"

"Really. That's a new one." I looked at her sideways, unsure if she was mocking me. "Must be from the chainsaws today."

Janine placed her face close to my chest and took a deep breath. "Yes. I love that. Oil with a touch of petrol. Sure enough to drive me crazy. Your scent was different when we met. I couldn't get your smell out of my mind."

"Well I did shower that night. I've thought about you nonstop too."

"Where'd you get these bruises?"

Across my ribs, torso and back were several black and purple marks from the fight. I shrugged.

"I must have fallen into some branches or thick brush on that last fire."

Her eyes looked skeptical. "These look fresh. See how they're green and yellow on the edges. You were in the hills just outside of town, right? Chris told me you were there when I stopped by. The fire was all over the news. Made me think about you. I probably should've known you'd be there."

She traced fingers along the edges of the bruises and ribs, across my lats and to the shoulders. Light with pressure, her fingers were nice against the skin and gave me goosebumps.

"Yeah, we were initial attack on that fire." Maybe you didn't know, but you were there in spirit. "Hey. Cut it out!" I yelped and tried to squirm away as she tickled the vulnerable spot under one arm. Janine sat on my legs with her full weight and laughed a diabolical laugh as I twisted and turned, attempting to escape from torturing fingers.

"Oh, the big, tough fireman is ticklish. Ahh ha."

"Stop or you'll pay".

Rolling away, I managed to escape. Then revenge was mine. Pinning her down, I tickled torso and the soft skin under her arms. Finally I found a sensitive spot above one knee. She screamed, begging me to stop. After a suitably extracted moment to prove who was boss, I eased up and released her. Janine feinted as if counterattacking with a wrestling move, but it was for show. She hopped nimbly onto the pillow and rolled to one side, gazing at me.

We talked and listened to music, then made love again. The best was Janine did not leave after, but stayed and spent the night on the little twin bed.

Breakfast together in the kitchen consisted of cold cereal and bright morning sunshine through open windows, the sun's rays warm through the glass. I headed to work riding an idyllic cloud.

At six o'clock for maybe the third time that year, I didn't stop at the Store but flew past on the GPZ over the Pass and to IV. The motorcycle whined with throttle wide open. I sang like the protagonist in the novel Laughing Boy riding his pony, sitting easy in the saddle, thinking about heavy silver, turquoise jewelry and the gorgeous girl waiting for me at home. I even imagined the design for a wide bracelet with a chunk of turquoise in the center to mirror the beauty of the Santa Barbara harbor below framed by the landscape around. Not once in my entire life have I thought about jewelry. Suddenly I wanted to study and work as a silversmith to make this girl a bracelet. The ridiculousness made me mock myself.

That's how our time went. After work Janine and I would hang out and spend the night together either at my place or the Mesa apartment. Her friend Elaine was cute in a wholesome way and very funny. The grad student roommates Rick and Steve were mellow. For some reason deadheads usually kind of bugged me, but they were actually pretty cool. Janine's place was clean and cheery. However , we barely spent the night there. With Marco away for the summer, I had my own room. We'd have to figure out something when he returned, because I could definitely get used to this set-up. Not solely because of the great sex either, although it was incredible. Janine was phenomenal. Being together was uniformly intense and special. The earth did not have to move every single time. She left me spent, supremely at peace and content. We would fall asleep with me on my back and Janine on her side, her head resting on the nook inside my arm where the shoulder meets the chest, one leg on mine, curled in the most pleasant and natural position possible.

The fire season that started absolutely rocking, suddenly, as if now on pause, took a break. There was not a fire for weeks. I did not complain. Far from it. Each day after work I blazed past the Store. The hotshots lined along the wall passing beers would wave. My absence was noticed and remarked upon. I gestured in return with left thumb and pinkie in the "shock 'em, brah" hang loose salute. I did not pause nor slow but jammed home as fast as the GPZ could carry me, leaning low to avoid the wind resistance trying to hold me back.

Our first weekend together we slept in, then rode bikes along the packed dirt path to Sands beach. We spent the day laying on beach towels, reading paperbacks and chilling. Surrounded by rich, summer golden bodies, I sported a mean farmer tan from working outside in short sleeves. Janine looked so damn good in her bathing suit, only a fool's vanity would think anyone gave me a second glance. Except maybe someone might question who was the kook with that stone cold babe. I brought an old longboard and paddled around in the flat surf solely to get wet. There were no waves. Though summertime, the salt water was bracing and refreshingly cleansing. Globs of tar on the shore and the rainbow haze from an oil slick floating on the water's surface did not discourage me. I lay on the towel with eyes closed, knowing Janine was inches away. Everything appeared orange and red under closed lids. Warmth from the sun cooked my skin.

We barbecued dinner and enjoyed a luxurious quiet evening at home. The next day was the beach again and then into town to catch a movie. The show was a romantic comedy I'd never have chosen. Janine made the call and it turned out to be hilarious. Afterwards when the lights came on, the theater buzzed with smiling people standing, shuffling for the exit. I wrapped one arm around her shoulder and held close. We stopped at an ice cream shop around the corner and walked down the street holding hands, enjoying the warm evening, waffle cones, the lights of downtown, and life on a sweet cloud, effortless and floating.

CHAPTER

14

For my birthday Janine made a picnic.

"We have to do something special. I'll pick you up at 1 p.m. It'll be a surprise."

We never made a big deal out of birthdays, so this was new for me. Turning twenty-two had the potential for a let down in comparison to last year's twenty-first birthday. Janine was determined to not let that happen.

She dressed in a cream colored skater dress with red stripes and black Chuck Taylor high tops. Black framed reading glasses were just for show and gave her a combination nerd and hot for teacher look. The vintage dress and black Converse brought the look together in an goofball, punk rock way that Janine made look effortless.

Promptly at 1 p.m. she arrived and walked me to the little pickup. Before getting in, Janine made a big deal about tying a blue bandana over my eyes as part of the surprise.

When I objected she said, "You can't know where we're going, silly. That'd defeat the whole surprise."

Pulling from the curb, she made several loops in the middle of the four way intersection so I could not know where we were going. While driving she talked me through my horoscope sign.

"You're a Cancer, which explains a lot. Sensitive and nurturing are your two biggest traits. Under that tough guy, hard crab shell, you're soft and tender. I'm a Pieces. We're natural partners and go great together. Like peanut butter and chocolate."

"Oh yeah. What are Pieces like?"

"We're the best, of course. Dreamers and poets. That's why you like me so much. I'm like bottled poetry to you. You're a classic Cancer too with trust issues. Before fully committing to a relationship, you have to decide if it's worth the risk."

"I want to hear more about you."

"Well, Pieces are the most sensitive of the water signs. We absorb energy like a sponge and are very good at reading subconscious cues from people. The main thing is we are dreamers and have strong psychic inclinations."

"You have psychic powers?"

"Don't make fun. Everyone is born with certain abilities. You might understand them as intuition. Young children are open and receptive to the input the universe sends. As we grow older, society teaches us drown out the insights. That's one of the functions of schools, to tramp down individuality and get everyone to fall in line. Our society focusses on the rational. People are fearful of what they can't understand. Pieces are more in tune with these gifts."

"Okay then. What does your intuition tell you about what I want for my birthday."

"Relax, birthday boy. You don't need ESP to figure that one out."

I could tell we were on the 101 freeway. By the warmth of the sun direct on my face we were heading north. Janine pulled off and turned onto a frontage road. She made three right turns and slowed, navigating a curvy road. Under the tires something crunched softly. We were on a dirt path. The truck inched along and came to a stop.

"We're here. No sir buddy, don't you dare touch that blindfold yet. Let me help you."

I could hear her exit the vehicle and open my door. She took my arm and helped me from the truck. With one hand in mine and another on my shoulder, she directed me along a dirt path for a couple hundred yards. I walked hesitantly, unable to see and unsure, careful not to trip.

"Now just one more second..... Wa-la!".

Pulling the bandana off, we were standing on a bluff top, fifty feet above an isolated cove and our own private ocean. After a moment of calculation I realized we were several miles north of Isla Vista, near the Sandpiper golf course. Other than the creaky wood pilings of a dilapidated pier to the north, we were alone with nature. A row of eucalyptus trees lined the path back to the pickup and road.

Spread across a flat grassy area under a solitary Coastal Live Oak on a patchwork quilt blanket was a birthday feast fit for a king. An old school, woven picnic basket was loaded with avocado BLTs on wheat toast, a Tupperware container of sliced cantaloupe chunks, another container with green grapes and two packages of Reese's Peanut Butter Cups. In a separate plastic cooler a dozen Bartles & James wine coolers were packed in ice.

A terrific smile lit her face. The two of us stayed there the remainder of the afternoon. We laid on the blanket, cushioned by the long grass, ate the delicious food she packed and relished in the beautiful day. Jokingly she fed me grapes one at a time, like I was Marc Anthony or an Egyptian Pharaoh or something. Random birds chirped in the bushes. Others flew by and circled over the shallows in the ocean, searching for fish. There was not another person for miles. The hours passed lazily, the sun slowly tracking the afternoon sky. We drank through the wine coolers and enjoyed nature. Even being naked in daylight felt perfectly natural.

Before we left, she gave me one final, extra special present. Janine obviously spent some time on an artfully hand drawn map of Santa Barbara with her apartment on the Mesa marked with a bold X. Pirates would have appreciated the attention to detail.

"Promise to keep this with you, or in a secure location. That way you'll always know how to find me, and won't ever get lost."

It wasn't until a couple days later that I remembered the vision of Janine while on the Peak Fire with the picnic, the wine and love making in the outdoors under warm sunlight. I had felt close to death, hiking, hungover and absolutely hating life. The daydream of being with her saved me. This picnic surprise was even better than the scenario I imagined. Maybe she was onto something with this whole listening to your intuition thing. There's no other way to explain the similarities of how close my dream foretold this reality.

CHAPTER

15

Weeks later the crew was spread along the Romero Canyon Trail, north of Summerland, clearing brush and widening the hiking trail. The call came over the radio at 11:30 in the morning. I wasn't far from Killer and heard the crackle as the dispatcher rattled off a whole mess of apparatus, engines, air tankers and finally Crew Four. Guys whooped aloud. We had not been on a fire in what seemed forever. J.C. said that morning the Supe planned to donate at the blood center later in the week if we weren't called to a fire. Based on the dispatched resources, this looked to be decent sized. We were a half mile from the trucks and hiked the dirt trail in nothing flat, not exactly running but more of a fast lope, not messing around. Arriving at the rigs I grabbed and put away the chock block, then settled into the rear seat. Guys bounced in their seats, giddy with anticipation. Rolling through my head was how to get word to Janine. I wouldn't be home that night. Ambivalent for the first time, I had mixed feelings going to a fire. Everyone else was jacked. I was torn, not knowing how long we would be gone. The contrast of the squad's happiness with my own internal conflict was palpable. I sat in my spot and looked out the window sorting thoughts.

We turned north onto highway 101 after coming down the hill. I could see ahead through the vehicle and the front windshield to Four-B's crew buggy ahead. Robby Wadlow opened their rear door and hung his legs and feet out of the vehicle, resting them on the door strap. That was one perk to sitting in the rear seat. Following suit, I opened our backdoor and latched it in place. I laid back stretched across the seat, resting both boots on the canvas door strap. With legs supported and comfy as any lazy-boy recliner, I hung out the open back door, wind and concrete blowing past. With a bird's eye view into the cars behind us on the highway, we passed through Santa Barbara. When we drove past the Glen Annie Road Isla Vista exit, I watched the outline of the twin ten story FT dorm towers fade in the distance. Minutes later was the exit to the birthday picnic spot. We didn't exit though but continued on. The road headed inland and air temperature increased. Hours of dun colored hills sprinkled with dark oak trees blanketed the grassland on the drive north. The warm environment of yellow pastures again turned cooler after we veered towards the coast again and the proximity of ocean air. Deep blue and marine greens of the Pacific kept us company for the last section of the four hour drive. The majestic and rugged coast was marked by sheer cliffs and breathtaking views and rocky beaches. Muddled thoughts clouded the scenery passing along the winding Coast Highway to Big Sur.

Late in the afternoon we parked at a state beach called Pfeiffer Point. A ranger in a Forest Service green Ford Bronco stepped out and met with the Supe. We collected the gear and taped bunches of tools together into transportable packages to load aboard helicopters. Then everyone stood about and waited. The clearing was flat with matted down, long wild grasses and an unobstructed view of the deep blue ocean sweeping like a flat plate to the horizon. To the east green, jagged Santa Lucia Highlands rose sharply to the sky. From sea level the mountains rapidly jutted to 3,500 feet in barely a mile of distance. Faintly visible east of the North Coast Ridge a thick smoke column was building into a formidable gray and white mushroom bloom. The slap slap of helicopter rotors came towards our direction from the distance. The Supe yelled for everyone to get ready. We were going for a ride. "Buckle your chinstraps, boys."

On the front brim of everyone's orange hard hat, black block letters spelled out each person's last name and flight weight. We divided into three groups, each unit roughly equal in weight. Like a scene from a movie three Bell helicopters came zooming in over the horizon, blistering fast and low, barely feet above the tree line.

I yelled in the Killer's ear over the incoming roar of motors, "Those choppers swooping in are totally bitchen."

His brown eyes wide, he yelled back. "No doubt! They're the freaking best. But those are helicopters, Lightning. Geek writers and TV news folks call them choppers."

I nodded in response and filed that info away.

The helicopters hovered briefly, then touched down in the clearing, landing skids settling gently on grass. A flood of air and dust washed across our faces. Group one strode in, crouching, leaning forward and jumped aboard. The next group boarded the second helicopter. Then it was our turn. They teach you to approach the helicopter from lower ground and duck your head as you near to climb aboard. That big rotor violently whipping around with velocity makes that last directive seem self-evident. I automatically duck. Self preservation and instinct kick in big time when faced with the potential for my head to be chopped off like ripe fruit meeting the business end of a sharp machete.

We scrambled aboard and buckled in as the crew chief loaded tools and saws. Grins on everyone's faces shared the almost childlike excitement of riding in the helicopter. The Bell 204 is a civilian version of the UH-1 Iroquois single engine military helicopter or "Huey" common in the Vietnam War. We've ridden plenty of helicopters. The experience never gets old. Something about going for a ride was unbelievably cool, especially not having to worry about taking incoming fire from hostile forces. If you polled the crew's favorite movies scenes, the sequence from Apocalypse Now with the Hueys flying in formation, blasting Wagner's "Ride of the Valkyries," would undoubtedly place in the top ten.

The main rotor's velocity increased, the helicopter motor whining with effort. The slap, slap slap blurred together into a loud, steady hum as the Bell smoothly lifted from the ground. My stomach lurched opposite to the pitched acceleration upward. We hovered for a moment, banked and turned in the opposite direction. The 'copter flew rapidly over the trees, steadily gaining elevation, then crossed over the mountain ridge and above the green valley below.

The Killer spoke with the pilot through a headset with earphones and microphone as we buzzed along. Before he was foreman on the hotshots, Killer led a helitac crew out of Arroyo Grande. The thrill and love of flying was strong in him. A helitac crew is staffed with from eight to ten helishots. They deploy as Initial Attack via helicopter throughout the forest at newly started fires. A helicopter can quickly deliver and drop helishots into remote locations that would take hours to drive to. Their job is to knock the fires down while still in their infancy before they grow into big conflagrations. Helishots are frequently the only firefighters on scene and are expected to battle and contain the blaze on their own. They'll go full bore, balls to the wall for an intense but short period of time. An excellent analogy compared helitac crews to world class sprinters while hotshots are more like marathoners. The Killer was equally as proud of his time with Arroyo Grande as he was stoked to be foreman on our crew. I did not have earphones and could not hear their discussion over the engine roar. The trees below seemed close enough to touch. Soaring over the forest was not unlike surfing or skiing deep powder. We were riding on air, floating above the surface.

The terrain of the valley below made me think of an elaborate miniature model railroad set. The mountains and topography looked like hobby toy decorations.   In the distance to the north the fire was vivid, growing rapidly on a steep ravine, the orange and yellow flames like a prop painted for display. As we flew closer the scene grew bigger and life size. The rugged reality of steep mountains asserted itself. One hundred acres already, the fire burned with ferocity. The distant column of smoke originally viewed from the coast was now a thick mushroom cloud cap, gaining depth and layers of dimension as the blaze grew.   The northern Monterrey district mountains of the Los Padres National Forest were lush and a rich deep green in contrast to our dry Santa Barbara hills marked by browns, dun, and light shades of green. The dark greens were visible proof of the dramatically greater rainfall they enjoyed. In Santa Barbara we average ten to thirty-five inches of rain per year. Just a short drive north, the Monterrey district receives as many as eighty inches of rain along this coastal range. Instead of chaparral, impressive redwoods surrounded us. Scattered throughout picturesque meadows and swaths of mighty timber stands, an abundance of poison oak awaited. We needed to be mindful. Horror stories of firefighters breathing smoke from burning poison oak and suffering awful experiences were common. Throats swell shut and lungs bleed with major, critical respiratory complications.

Needless to say, I planned to avoid poison oak as much as possible.

The helicopters landed in an open meadow full of yellow, purple and orange wild flowers and knee high grass. We jumped down and scooted away, avoiding the whirling rotor. When clear, everyone geared up, cutting apart the packages of tools. I grabbed a super-P, grasping the familiar wooden handle in one hand and shielded my face from the blast of air wash as the helicopter rose again. The Huey hovered momentarily, then zoomed east, leaving us far from the vehicles and in the middle of nothing but miles and miles of forest and fire. Amidst the thrill of the helicopter ride and proximity to a now roaring blaze, the thought struck that we were miles from the nearest phone booth. Who knew when we'd be able to call home. Shaking the thought away, I marveled at the rare beauty of the wilderness scenery, the green lush meadow like something from a picture book. Sunlight fanned through the branches of a stand of enormous redwoods, giving everything a magical golden aura.

The Supe had a firm handle on the situation after the 'copter ride. Stew, the Killer and he pow-wowed briefly before we started hiking to our anchor point. Fire crept through the thick grass and brush thickets, working along the tree bases and climbed the smaller scrub, tanbark oak and California bay trees. Leaves would burst and then flame out. The gap to the next level of hanging branches on the much taller trees was too great. The flames could not make the leap upward as if too high of a step on a ladder. Thick massive redwoods showed blackened bark across their bases from fire creeping up, but they would not be crowning today. We've witnessed crown fires rumble through forests many times, an unlikely scenario for these redwoods at this juncture. At four in the afternoon the plan was to cut indirect line on the southern flank. Hopefully we'd make the next ridge before the fire turned the corner. This fire had potential to run for several days if not more. We weren't going anywhere for awhile.

We started our line at the edge of a shallow creek in the middle of a meadow, using the water as the anchor point. Sword fern and even California huckleberries lined the creek bed. Clear water gurgled across the bottom lined with tiny round, orange and brown rocks and past the edge lined with green mossy sticks. Random broken tree limbs dragged lazily down stream.

Originally in the Ventana wilderness, the powers that be allowed the fire to burn slowly and creep about for several days or maybe even a week. Now in the regular forest, the fire was building momentum and heading where no one wanted it to go. After watching and waiting, now they decided to suppress the wildfire. So here we were swinging tools and running chain saws, cutting line once again. I swung the Pulaski with purpose, breaking soil, taking solid chunks of grass with every swing of the tool, each swing deliberate and strong. I stretched out, extending arms, shoulders and wrists, using the full length of the handle to increase the velocity and power of the tool head to rip into the duff and ground. No one could accuse me of being gravity flow. Not today. The squad stretched out, spaced eight to ten feet apart, each cutting a share of line, settling into a steady workman-like pace neither hurried nor rushed. We would be going for hours. This was a campaign and not a sprint.

Hours later we stopped briefly in the dark to place head lamps on hard hats and stuffed down a quick bite. I found a soft flat section to sit and opened some sardines and then a can of ranch beans. The pungent fish packed in oil smelled strong like an old fishing pier. The salty protein hit the spot and were delectable. Ranch beans are better heated and reminded me of dog food at room temperature. They were nourishing though and fuel for the long night ahead.

We would work through the night, camp wherever we were, rise with the new day and keep cutting line. That is what we did. Once free of the meadow and heading uphill, the going slowed. Thick grasses led to copses of small oak and bay trees. Wide thickets of shrubs and brush entangled together like huge spider webs dominated the terrain. The shrubs were more whispery and not nearly as difficult to cut as the heavy manzanita and chaparral that gave us such a hard time in Santa Barbara. However the stalks were incredibly long, interlaced together and gave the pullers fits. The sawyers would cut a clump's base. The pullers would attempt to throw the bush to one side only to find the plant's stalks interlocked with others still needing to be cut. And those stalks connected with another group. Everything was entwined and unwieldily.

After ten o'clock Killer directed me to help Gus pull for Kingman. I rolled down long sleeves of the yellow nomex shirt, donned leather work gloves and a pair of orange earplugs. Enough hardcore gigs have probably already done long term damage to my hearing. But I don't want to be stone deaf. Now a muffled, dull roar, the steady growl of the chainsaw throttled next to me as Kingman cut through the thickets. I settled into the task, wrestling clumps of brush as best I could. When swinging a tool I don't wear gloves. Thick callouses layered on more callouses of both hands prove it. Grabbing and holding sharp sticks, thorns and thistles was another story. The gloves formed a welcome piece of personal protective equipment, PPE baby.

We developed a solid strategy to attack the thickets. Kingman cut into the main grove. I'd grab the brush in a big, bear hug, branches poking and jabbing my face and arms. Mike then cut the next connected group. I'd accordion this clump in, consolidating thin bunches onto each other. We repeated the tactic until the armful of brush was as maxed as I could handle. Then he severed the end with one last Husky cut. I then tossed the unwieldy package as far into the green side of the line as possible. Then we repeated the process.

My wingspan gave me an advantage grabbing bunches of branches and shrubs. Gus was six inches shorter with comparable arm length. Shorter arms were not as effective grabbing thick bunches. On the crew size was not always a benefit. Compared with someone one hundred seventy-five pounds, I carried an extra twenty-five pounds each hour of a thirty-six hour shift. That's like carrying an extra nine hundred pounds (twenty-five pounds times thirty-six) over the course of the shift. We go for days on end. Many of the best wildland firefighters were guys I'd describe as average height or even shorter but lean and strong- wiry, tough guys. A big Moke like me needed more water and food to keep the motor running. Fuel added extra weight, required more work and made the job harder. I'm not complaining, just making the observation.

Even with the cool night, I had a steady sweat going. Warm moisture ran from matted hair under the hardhat, down the sides of my face and trailed into the corners of both eyes. The salt stung. After throwing a load to one side, I wiped sweat from forehead and each eye with the shirt sleeve. Then I used the back of a glove and kept going. The clumps weren't heavy but unwieldy and a bear to handle and throw. We made outstanding progress though. From the increased activity of the scrapers behind, I could tell the pace was faster than before. Methodically Mike and I hammered through the wall of brush, only resting when the chainsaw needed petrol. We'd pause briefly to refill from the gas packs.

The crew kept on for unrelenting hours, chainsaws revving. Tall trees blocked the moon and cast black shadows that crowded the night. Even the stretch of sky you could see was a deep, dark purple of darkness. The narrow cone of headlamps illuminated our view. An orange and red glow of the fire peeked from the north behind the steep rise of the hill. We sliced through the pitch, brush and scrub until after two in the morning. Finally, the Supe appeared and said to sack out. He would have rallied us through the night if there were a chance to catch the fire. The blaze was too far ahead. With no shot, we would rest now and start again at first light.

Sweat lined the back of my t-shirt and long sleeve nomex shirt. I sat on a level stretch of soft grass to the side of the line and from a corner zippered pocket of the backpack unfolded a compact, space blanket to keep warm and bundled. Setting the hardhat on the ground next to me, I rested my head on the pack as a pillow, laid on one side and closed both eyes. The texture of the nylon backpack pressed against one cheek. The grass and dirt were firm but comfortable against my shoulder and side. I was cozy with the wrinkly space blanket pulled to my chin.

The Supe shook me awake with a firm hand to my shoulder. Still dark out, a wide band of gray hung low on the horizon to the east. A layer of dew covered the grass and beads of water spread across the space blanket. I sat and stretched, shaking the sleep away. I was in deep slumber too, smack in the middle of a dream. We were on a surf trip in Baja, Mexico camping on the beach. Cold moisture bathed me in a thick, ocean fog. In the gray the sounds of dogs could be heard scavenging through our trash. Janine wore a cowboy hat two sizes too large that kept blowing away in a gust of strong wind. We chased after the Stetson as it rolled, bounced and carried along the sandy shore. The wind howled. We bundled together in the tent, trying to escape from and shield ourselves from harsh sand biting against skin. Blowed out from the wind, the surf was one long foamy blur of whitewater barely visible through the fog. Disoriented, I could not discern anything in the haze. A waxed cardboard case of empty cerveza bottles clinked together noisily as I rummaged through them. There were no more beers. We needed to make a trip to the agency. Kneeling outside the tent, I searched the cardboard box. Surely I must have missed one. A full beer had to be here somewhere. The futility of the situation bothered me. Something was wrong and did not add up. We shouldn't be out of beer. But there were not any. No matter how I looked. A tension weighed and pressed on me like humidity.

Finally I said screw it and pulled open the zipper to the tent flap to go inside. Only Janine was with some guy. He lay on his back with knees bent, resting on both elbows. Janine faced him, sitting comfortably on his lap, her back against his thighs and legs. The brim of the cowboy hat was pulled low over the man's face. I could not make out who he was. Their laughter filled the tent. Janine turned to face me. "Oh," she said, "you're here."

That was when the Supe woke me. Wow, that sucked. I tried to shake the dream away and shrug the whole thing off. Stretching neck and shoulders, I twisted my head back and forth, getting the kinks out. My joints were locked stiff.

Where the hell did that come from?

In the half gray of dawn the crew spread along the hillside trailing below, rummaging through packs and preparing breakfast. Most were opening brown MRE packets. Beef stroganoff or some other vile leftover from the Vietnam War would not do it for me this early morning. I opened a can of peaches and mixed instant coffee and powdered Swiss Miss together in a canteen. Stew was right about the peaches. They were really all you needed. We sat on the ground eating cold meals. After a brief conference over a topo map setting the course for the day, we fired up the saws and went to work.

The fire laid down as if lulled asleep by the nighttime coastal influence. As the sun burned through gray fog and heated air temps, she would rip again. I pulled for Mike which was more of the same as yesterday. We went through huge thickets of brush across rugged, steep terrain, up and then downhill. Killer stayed close, keeping us on the right path. I worked hard with sweat flowing again with the increasing heat of the day. Exertion forced me to focus on the task at hand and not on that wacky dream and the image of Janine sitting on the cowboy's lap. Jealousy is an ugly companion, the whole thing unsettling and out of left field. Sweat ran down my face with salt stinging both eyes. I used the back of one hand to wipe it away, the leather glove soaking and redirecting the moisture. I drank water like a fish, sucking down quart canteen after canteen, working to stay hydrated. That afternoon I pointed out to Kingman the bank we were heading through was one solid wall of three leaf, green and red, Christmas tree looking shrub. The plant sure had the look of poison oak. Leaves of three, woe is me.

Mike took his hand off the throttle and rested the body of the Husky on one thigh. His hearty laughter carried above the sound of the idling chainsaw.

"No shit, Sherlock. We've been tearing through this stuff all damn day and last night too. Lightning, no joke. You are freaking slow on the uptake."

I looked at him bewildered. "You're kidding, right?"

"Ha ha ha. Dude, you kill me. It's everywhere, surrounding us. You are hilarious. We're good though. With gloves and long sleeves on, we should be fine."

Mike cranked open the throttle again, cutting through the thicket. I went back to piling brush in both arms, consolidating bundles into manageable bunches to throw to the side. We kept going until late that afternoon. Word came we'd be flying out and setting camp on the coast. After five we grouped up, formed a line and hiked two miles to a flat clearing marked as a helispot landing area. We divided into three groups again and waited until a Bell 204 helicopter came and picked up the first group. We were now down to one helicopter. The Bell made the round trip to the crew trucks parked on the coast and returned for the second group. With a cruising speed of one hundred and twenty-five miles per hour, the helicopter made the round trip over the coast range and back in under twenty minutes. The third group waited for our ride home, listening to stories and jokes.

"How does the rabbi make coffee?"

"I don't know."

"Hebrews it."

B.D. must have memorized a book of a dumb jokes. I stood in place, resting on the heels of both boots, chuckling at the puns.

"What time is the dentist appointment? Tooth hurty."
He could rattle them off for hours.

J.C. moved next to me.

"Haven't been hanging much lately. Didn't mean to come down like a load of bricks when we talked, if that's how you took it." Voice low, his dark eyes were searching.

I shook my head. "Ah, no worries, Cracker. I've been busy is all. There's a new girl I've been seeing."

"Oh yeah? Sweet. You had me worried. She cute?"

When I nodded, his expression brightened.

"Nice! Does she have any friends? C'mon now. Hook a brother up. Can't believe you've been holding out on me."

"Actually her roommate is cute. Cool too. Maybe we can arrange something."

"Now you're talking, brother. That's right." His smile opened in a wide grin, relief covering his face. "Hey, you better wash up real well when we get to camp. Looks like poison oak popping along your forehead in a line above the eyebrow."

I rubbed an index finger across the temple. Sure enough, a row of tiny bubbles or blisters were rising on the forehead. They did not itch yet, but most assuredly would soon.

"Great. I frickin' knew it. Thanks, J.C."

The sound of the returning Bell was audible before we could see it zooming in from the west, the rotor spinning full bore. The whoop, whoop, whoop sound carried and grew steadily louder. The helicopter hovered momentarily, then settled in the clearing. The rotor wash blew around us, raising leaves and dust, scattering them in every direction.

We scooted aboard, buckled in and lifted away. The view on our trip to the coast was something. Barely above the tree tops we headed over the steep, serrated mountain range, massive conifers only feet away. Branches, pine cones and even individual needles were sharply defined with amazing detail. You could practically touch them. Once we cleared the main peak of the ridge line and started descending again, the green mountains dropped like a sheer cliff to the wide expanse of the deep marine ocean below. The glorious landscape and dramatic fall off was impressive and more like a photograph from a coffee table book than anything I have ever seen before.

We touched down at Pfeifer Point, exited the 'copter and reconvened with the rest of the crew waiting at the vehicles. After the Bell flew away we piled into the crew buggies, pulled onto the highway and drove south along the winding coast until we came upon a hippie retreat called the Lucia Creek Landing. Individual bungalows were for rent nestled amongst a grove of redwoods and a little hamlet comprised of a restaurant, some random buildings that housed a church camp, a separate cluster of a detox center, and a general store selling packaged groceries and souvenirs. The settlement had a seventies zen and yoga vibe. We stopped to camp near the bungalows in a field on the side of the road. I changed out of the dirty, yellow nomex shirt and pulled on a hooded sweatshirt to protect from the chill. Fog banked along the coast would roll in any minute. From a side compartment I grabbed my sleeping bag, Thermarest and a sturdy one person tent. I set out next to J.C. as the rest of the crew lined tents in rows on a patch of flat lawn.

Soon after the Supe sauntered over. We would be dining in the main restaurant. He picked Lupe to lead us in. Lining into single file again, we marched to a faded yellow building marked by a large wooden sign with "The Lucia Squeeze" in bright, scrolling letters. A cartoon bear family eating from a picnic basket was painted on the wall. Two dozen people enjoyed dinner inside. In the rear of the restaurant through wide double doors a covered patio with several long community size picnic tables were waiting for us. We shuffled through in our uniform green nomex pants, LP logo-ed green t-shirts or long sleeve green hooded sweatshirts and blue ball caps, with twenty pairs of boots thumping on the redwood plank floors. The patrons hushed, conversations paused in mid-sentence, watching our entrance. After a couple days on the fireline, no doubt we were a pretty ragged looking group. A family of a mom, dad, two teenage daughters and a junior high school age son sat in one corner. The eldest daughter was gorgeous. A palpable shift rolled through the crew as guys noticed her. Wadlow walked directly in front of me. A new spring came to his step as we navigated between the tables. For good reason, the public loves their firefighters. But any prudent parent would likely pull their teenage daughter a little closer with us tramping in, unshaven and bleary-eyed. That dad was no dummy either. He seemed to physically make himself larger, like a blowfish puffing his spines, warning off predators, hoping to shield her from our gaze. Like most fathers of teenager daughters though, he was dust. Both girls definitely noticed Wadlow. They visibly reacted and elbowed each other when he walked by. The family vacation road trip just became a heck of a lot more interesting. If camped anywhere near here, those two would be back sniffing around first chance.

We actually received table service with a real life waitress in her mid-forties who looked like someone's hippy mom. She had long braided brown hair streaked with gray, well worn jeans that filled out nicely and a bright orange tie-died shirt. Fit and pretty in an earthy-crunchy way, with a commanding presence, she quickly took charge of the ordering process explaining to each table the shortened menu with choices of chicken, fish or a vegetarian rice and bean number. I looked at the main menu. Of the fifteen items listed, a dozen were vegetarian or even vegan dishes. Our server Pam worked her way table to table, explaining the three choices, taking orders. She skillfully maneuvered through the twenty of us, laughing and joking but not taking any guff. Several micro-brews were on tap at the bar in front where we walked through. A frosty cold beer sounded like heaven. Unfortunately alcohol was strictly prohibited. Pete and Lumpy noticed carrot and lemongrass juice at the bottom of the menu and ordered some in jest. If those two thought they could mess with Pam, they were sorely mistaken. Writing down the order, she explained how super healthy and yummy the juices were. The restaurant's custom designed juicer was amazing. With finality Pam informed the table those two had better finish their drinks. Everyone got a kick from that. After placing my I order for chicken and an iced tea, I stood and walked inside to the restroom.

Inspecting my reflection in the mirror above the sink, I washed my face, forcefully scrubbing with foamy, soapy hands. Visible above the right eyebrow clear to the left side of the forehead a line of bubbles were coming in strong, pink

198

and blistering. I took off the sweatshirt and washed both arms clear to the pits with soap and hot water. Then I rinsed with copious amounts of water and inspected both arms twisting and turning them. Neither arm displayed any signs resembling poison oak. My face was a different story. Oh well, goes with the territory. I've had plenty of poison oak. This wouldn't kill me.

Outside the restroom in the hallway was a pay phone. I stopped to call Janine's house. Without any change I dialed the operator and asked to make a collect call. I repeated the phone number to the operator from scribbled notes on a pocket size, folded up tide chart stashed in my wallet. Her phone rang and rang until the answering machine came on. The operator switched the connection off and said sorry, no one was home. Heading back to the tables, I sat with everyone and waited on dinner.

Spirits were high with jokes and stories flowing. The energy in the room bounced with levity. Pam clearly took a shine to the Supe and buzzed around, flirting. Kingman razzed him, suggesting his new name should be "Granola 4" or "Bran-pa." The Supe chuckled and hitched in his chair like a cowboy sitting taller in the saddle. His expression to Mike may as well have said, "C'mon now, sport. I've still got it."

After a wait the food came in waves. Pam, another server and a busser helper carried platters with entrees stacked high. The room went quiet except for the rattle of metal flatware on ceramic dishes and muffled murmur of chewing.

Everyone went to work demolishing the grub. The chicken needed salt and the rice bland for my taste. But I was famished and would have been satisfied with a hunk of cheese on a sourdough roll. After the initial rush, everyone caught a breath, slowed down and started talking again. Instead of enjoying the moment, which is supposed to be my philosophy, Janine was now on my mind. I could not wait to call again. Hopefully this time I would get a hold of her.

By dinner's end, the sun was down for the day. Loose groups walked to the camp area, breathing in oxygen rich air laced with the smell of pine forest. Dark woods contrasted with the bustle inside the well lit restaurant. I grabbed cash from my travel bag's stash pocket and high tailed to the general store to buy something. Scanning the selection of goods I bought a small yellow container of Carmex lip balm. I already had one, but Carmex is absolutely the best and like money in the bank. More accurately the purchase was an excuse to ask the clerk for a couple dollars of quarters. Pete beat me to the pay phone around the corner. I hovered a distance away to allow some privacy but close enough to hold the on deck spot. He was likely speaking with his girlfriend. His voice sounded agitated. I looked away and focused attention on the sky and stars above. Hopefully his pickup did not get repo-ed again.

When Pete finished his call, full with anticipation and a little nervous I plugged in a dollars worth of quarters. The phone pinged and an automated voice gave directions. I dialed the number. After two rings, roommate Steve answered. Janine was not in. He did not know when she'd be home. I asked

Steve to please give a message I called. We were in Big Sur. Who knew for how long. I would try to call tomorrow. He said no problem and that was that. I intended to call home but figured my turn was over with Daryl standing fifteen feet behind me waiting. I would check in with Ben and Chris tomorrow. Nothing major could not wait until then. I wandered back to camp. Guys were sitting around talking but I decided to get ready for bed. After brushing teeth, inside the one man tent I settled into the cozy sleeping bag. Cool ocean moisture was pervasive. The tent would protect against condensation though. I lay in the bag, head resting comfortably on my lumpy sweatshirt and two boot pillow. Trying to envision Janine, I wondered what she had been doing the past two days. Memories of last night's stupid dream reappeared randomly during the day like a bothersome shadow. I did my best to think about something else and not drive myself crazy. My forehead itched. I idly rubbed the skin with the side of my index and middle fingers. The line above the eyebrow oozed with liquid. I mopped the area with a sleeve from the sweatshirt pillow. Staring at the nylon ceiling of the tent above, I listened to low voices and sounds of the crew shuffling about. The murmuring eventually softened. The camp grew quiet and still. I tossed and turned before finally falling asleep.

CHAPTER

16

At six o'clock the next morning sounds of people starting the day woke me. Although light out, for some reason I could only see the profile of my nose through the left eye. Pressure weighed on the swollen shut right eye. The skin on my face felt tight, unnatural and puffy. The eyelids were crusted, stuck together and would not open. Gingerly I touched the forehead where the line of poison oak showed the night before. The surrounding area felt engorged and misshapen.

What the hell?

I crawled from the sleeping bag and walked barefoot to the Supe's rig parked in the driveway twenty feet from our sleep area. Squinting into the driver's side rearview mirror with my half shut left eye, I did not recognize the creature staring back at me. The right side of the reflected face bulged, swollen like a grotesque gargoyle. Formerly weepy but now dried out, a yellow, crusty buildup covered both eyes. I used the right forefinger and thumb to pinch the top eyelid and the other hand to hold down the bottom. Gently I was able to slowly break apart the scab-like buildup and open the two lids. I could now partially see. Still distended, the right eye would not open the whole way.

The Supe, Killer and Stew stood at the rear of the truck planning the day, reviewing a topographical map. When I walked over, the Supe looked at me and did a double-take.

"Oh no, Lightning. What'd you do now? That poison oak got you bad."

Everyone nearby heard his tone and turned. The exclamations were a mix of incredulity and repulsion.

"Dude!"

"Holy moly, Lightning. That doesn't look good."

"Whoa! You look like the Elephant Boy or something."

"Yeah, something awful. Awful, a lot."

Stew's gray eyes were flat. In a deadpan voice he said, "Somebody aught to pop you with a solid left cross. Help balance your face out."

I shook the misshapen head in disbelief. Everyone chuckled and enjoyed their yucks at my expense. The Supe decided I would head into town with him that morning after breakfast to receive a cortisone shot at the nearest doctor's office.

They opened the Lucia Squeeze early for us special. We ate scrambled eggs, fried potatoes and wheat toast. Sitting at the communal tables again under the covered patio, the sideways looks at me were a mixture of horror and fascination. I felt like a circus freak, the poison-oak face boy. After breakfast the crew piled into the buggies and headed to the helicopter landing zone for the lift to the fireline again. I jumped into the Supe's rig. We drove in the opposite direction south down the coast. Pete, Boon, Wadlow and Kingman each gave me cash for Copenhagen. We would be here awhile. They were running low. For those dudes, running out of Cope was not an option.

"So Lightning. How you doing, son?" The Supe drove the truck with one elbow casually resting out the open window, his right hand light on the steering wheel as easy as can be. This was no mellow Sunday drive though. He barreled down the winding road with a foot made of lead. "You've been keeping a low profile since that bar brawl business over at the Cold Spring."

The highway rose a thousand feet above sea level. Looking to our west and the ocean in the distance down below, I wondered if the metal guard rails were sturdy enough to prevent a vehicle from jettisoning off the cliff. I clenched the "oh shit" strap above me with my right hand and looked away from the edge. Turning to face him I said, "There's a new gal I've been seeing, Supe. We've been spending a lot of time together."

If by "a lot", you mean every single available waking moment, then that is a fairly accurate description, I thought.

"Oh yeah? That's good news. She's got a hook in you, huh?"

"Maybe a little," I said not very convincingly. He laughed. We both knew it was a lie.

"Hopefully she can be okay with you being away on these fires. A lot of good women have a hard time with this lifestyle. Some never get used to it. Takes a real special one to put up with us being on the road weeks on end." I murmured agreement but did not say anything. "What are you studying over there at the UC?"

"English literature."

"You want to be a teacher?"

"Everyone asks that. No. I figure if you can write, that shows you can think. Then you can get a job. Get a degree, dress in a sharp suit, get a job. Not to be too simplistic, but that's pretty much how it works, right? I don't know. Maybe I'll go to law school. I haven't really thought too much about the future, to be honest."

"Be a lawyer, gonna work in an office, get fat and rich? You could do worse I suppose. I read somewhere, I believe it was Vito Corleone who said lawyers steal more money with a briefcase than any mobster and all their guns ever did. If that's what you're after…" He was silent a moment.

"Hopefully you're learning how to think over there. That's the main thing. Learn how to think. There's way too many educated idiots in the world. You know what I'm talking about. We see these bucket heads all the time."

"Maybe I'll get on with one of the big city fire departments. San Fran or LA County."

"Those are fine departments. What about the Forest Service? I can see you as an engine captain here."

"Ah, I don't know. Seems like they're forever mopping up. How much fire do engine companies really see?"

"That depends where you're stationed. The urban wildland interface is getting problematic. As communities expand into the foothills, more and more houses are being built. Towns keep creeping, stretching into the wild. Engines are the name of the game for structure protection. Work hard and there are tons of opportunities. Get assigned with one of these inter-agency overhead management teams and travel the country. You can't be pounding the ground forever."

"You're doing all right."

"Heh. Trust me, you reach a certain age and sleeping at home in your own comfy bed starts to sound pretty darn good."

"I don't believe that for a second. I'm sure you'd go stir crazy if you were home too long. Maybe after college, I might try smokejumping. My dad was a jumper."

"That's right. I forgot you told me that before." His eyes lifted from the road towards me briefly. "He passed away several years ago, right?"

"That's right. When I was eight." I looked back over the edge.

"How much more school, how many units do you need for your degree?"

"A couple years give or take. I'm trying to decide if I should enroll for fall quarter or finish out the fire season and start up again in the winter. I have until the end of the month to submit the paperwork to take the quarter off. A lot depends if I can get certain classes I want and need for the major."

"Well, if you ask me, and I know you're not, but I say go to school. There will always be more fires. No worries, we'll have a spot for you next summer. That university and your education are a golden ticket. Never forget it. Just let me know what you decide. We'll make the arrangements."

"No problem. I will let you know, Supe. I have been leaning towards enrolling for the fall quarter. I've enough money saved for the whole year and really should knock out some of the required classes for the degree."

My lips were moving. I heard the words spilling. But this was news to me. The plan was always to take fall quarter off, work through November end of fire season then start school in January again with the winter quarter. This new development was all about Janine, missing her and nothing whatsoever about school credits. The fiction sounded plausible. The Supe bought it.

"Well, be sure to let me know when you need to be there for classes if we're on the road. Once the fires start popping, we'll be in the thick of it. I have a feeling this season will roll through Thanksgiving. We'll be eating turkey sandwiches on the fireline more than likely."

Quiet then I watched the scenery speed past with plenty to ponder and not simply school or how my love life seemed to be complicating everything. As we hurtled closer to our destination, the impending cortisone shot loomed ominously. I have a thing about needles. Not a big deal. I just don't like them. During an absurd lull in the middle of fire season two years ago, we did not see action for over a month. Saying enough is enough, the Supe volunteered everyone to donate at the local blood bank. The Supe believed donating blood was a patriotic duty, especially with the on-going blood shortage. Giving blood is noble, makes complete sense and is the right thing to do. That's all well and good. My theory is deep down, he was superstitious. In a messed up voodoo tribute we were giving a blood sacrifice to the fire gods.

When the buggies pulled into the blood center, the wide eyed staff looked like Christmas came early, they were so happy to see us. Vampires would have been more discreet, the way they eyeballed twenty fit, young firefighters rolling into the clinic, loaded with healthy, iron enriched plasma. At the entrance a middle aged woman handed out pens and clipboards with a form asking names, basic health information and one question if you engaged in homosexual sex. When completed, another woman escorted you into the main room with rows of comfortable stuffed chairs. Needles have been a thing with me since forever. I took my time filling out the paperwork. When I couldn't stall any longer, with air and walls pressing in, I followed the lady to a chair and sat while a nurse made small talk, fixing the needle. I ignored what the nurse was doing and focused on a television in the corner with a daytime game show playing. I never looked at the needle in her hands and did not even feel the prick when she poked me. Lying back on the stuffed chair my forehead and shirt were instantly sopping wet with cold sweat. My head grew light. The television white noise appeared muffled and distant. The nurse broke open a small packet in her hands. She ripped with steady fingers and held a small square under my nose, waving back and forth. After long seconds, a sharp wave of ammonia hit like a smack to the face and burned the nostrils. I jerked my head back and away from the smelling salts. Apparently I passed out. That part confused me though, because I was aware of the room and surroundings the whole time.

Long story short, sure enough twenty minutes after leaving the blood bank, a fire started near Dos Pueblos. The sacrifice worked like magic. We responded to a fast burning brush fire in the lower foothills and were worked over for about an hour. With help from two Forest Service engine crews and an engine from Santa Barbara County we knocked the blaze down. I remember watching Robbie Wadlow wobble like a tall tree in strong wind, about to pass out any second. He wasn't alone. Everyone was running a quart low. Our asses were kicked but good that day. No one would ever admit the fact, but it was true. I struggled big time especially with the residual shock and stress from passing out. Thankfully, no one realized what happened at the blood clinic. I would never have heard the end of it.

The Supe's face hiking back to the rigs that day enjoyed a supremely satisfied look. I swear he knew the blood donation would break the mini-slump, and we would soon see fire action again. I wondered if how quickly the sacrifice worked surprised even him. It was damn near instantaneous.

Driving together now, we pulled into a small coastal town, read the street signs and tracked down the medical clinic. I glanced sideways at the man behind the wheel. He wore the same happy contented expression. Flecked with salt and pepper, his mustache needed a trim. The Supe was at peace with, pleasantly ready and expectant for whatever the world would bring today. The guy had life down.

I was quite the opposite, thinking about needles and the imminent shot. The doctor's office walls were painted soft peach and echoed a low buzz of fluorescent lights. Two other patients sat in the waiting room, reading magazines. The receptionist handed over a clipboard of paperwork to fill out. The Supe told me the information needed for the Forest Service, or rather the fire itself to be billed for the doctor's visit. The minutes waiting were torturous. Finally a nurse opened an adjoining door and called my name.

I followed her to a large room divided into sections by plastic curtains and hopped onto a flat examination table covered with thin white tissue paper. The nurse took my pulse and blood pressure. The doctor would see me shortly. I sat on the paper covered table for more excruciating minutes breathing through both nostrils. The office smelled of disinfectant. Finally the doctor entered the room. In his late fifties, he looked thin and fit like a distance runner with tousled gray hair and an amiable personality. He blew in, inspected my face, especially the swollen eye, and clucked low.

"Yes sir. We'll treat this with a strong dose of cortisone. That will relieve the symptoms. The swelling should subside today. But you need to take care and avoid further contact with poison oak. That's very important. New outbreaks can be even more severe. We want to avoid prescribing more cortisone if possible. It's a powerful steroid and can accumulate in your system. Too much can be problematic. The nurse will take good care of you."

The nurse returned after a couple minutes. I closed both eyes as she took a swab of cotton and swiped the left triceps with alcohol. Without hesitation she gave the shot, the poke over before I knew it. So far so good. Then the cold sweat began in earnest. My head grew faint. A green checkered wool sweater may have been pulled over my head. The lights and room around cascaded bright and dark. The nurse said something, probably that we were set, I could now go. A river of sweat drenched the cotton shirt. A sensor hooked to me would have sounded an alarm, blood pressure dropping like a stone. I don't know where the blood went. Was I wounded from a gun shot with blood flowing out like a river? This is what dying must be like, I thought and did not move. Returning the nurse handed me a paper cup with orange juice. Sugars from the juice soon helped.

"How you doing, Curt?" The nurse must have called the Supe in.

"Hey, Supe. I'm all right." The shaky voice probably said otherwise. I jumped from the table anyway. "We're good. Let's yata hey."

"Good.. sure now? You look like a corpse. I don't think I've ever seen anyone so devoid of color."

"No question. I'm fine."

We walked together into the bright sunlight. He started the truck and we pulled away from the curb. A few blocks away I said, "That was pretty trippy, Supe. Like I was looking through plaid wool with lights flashing around."

His eyebrows raised. "You don't say."

We soon found an independent supermarket, parked next to a bread truck in the mostly empty asphalt parking lot and walked in. The Supe gave me a once over, double checking that I really was okay. Deciding I would live, he wandered down the non-foods aisle shopping for incidentals. I went to the refrigerated section at the rear of the store to grab a quart of chocolate milk. Next to the dairy was the Copenhagen. I collected the loose cans, then flagged down a clerk in a green apron rotating and stocking packages of eggs.

"Are there any rolls of Cope in the back?"

"I'll check. How many do you want?"

"I'll take everything you've got."

He came out with five rolls of ten tins apiece shrink-wrapped together. After checking the dates on the bottom tin to verify they were fresh, I bought the fifty plus cans. The checkout lady raised her eyebrows but did not say anything.

Somebody had a major chew problem. The Supe wandered around in no rush, a shopping basket in one hand. I went outside to the payphone in front of the store and called Janine. The phone rang five times before the answering machine clicked on with Steve's voice saying to leave a message. Because I already left a message with him last night, I simply hung up and did not leave another. Which meant a waste of coinage too. Because the call connected, I did not get my change back. Steve's a decent enough guy with a friendly voice. "We'll be real sure to get back to you just as soon as humanly possible." The recording bugged me.

I hate your answering machine, I thought, opening the chocolate milk and taking a pull.

A roadside burger stand beckoned on the way out of town. We stopped for cheeseburgers. It was a midweek. A group of construction workers were before us. We sat on a long bench under a red patio umbrella. Supe remarked the swelling was already way down. I could tell without looking in a mirror. The pressure on the skin definitely eased up. Waiting for the clerk to call our order the Supe chuckled.

"We're gonna have to call you 'Spike' from now on. That business with the cortisone shot was something else. You got a problem against needles? Your face was pasty white, pale as a ghost, almost green even. I thought for certain you were about to pass out."

I murmured something unintelligible and guffawed along as if this were pretty funny stuff and did not object. That was the last thing I needed. After finishing the burger, I wiped the messy sauce from my hands with paper napkins, crumpled greasy wrappers into a ball and threw them into an open trash bin. We jumped back into the truck slamming the doors shut.

After stopping for gas we headed up the coast. By the time we made the heli-spot and the parked crew trucks, it did not make sense for the helicopter to take us out to the fireline. The Supe spread a topo map over the truck's dashboard and steering wheel then spoke with Stew over the radio. He marked the progress the crew made on the map in relation to the fire. Past two ridge lines to the east an old logging road curved and meandered along a meadow. By his estimation we should be able to reach the road within two days. Once tied into the logging road, we would backfire along the road heading north. Steady winds were breezing from the west and not in our favor. The Supe believed the backside of the peak was steep enough the fuels would preheat enough from smoke rising. The backfire would burn uphill against the flow of wind and create a solid blackened space to protect against the advance of the main fire.

The key element of the plan utilizing the road would allow us to move rapidly to get in front of the fire's forward progress. The fire followed the topography of the ridges running north to south and was being channeled and burning both towards the east and northeast. A straight shot to the road was due south. We would initially go in the opposite direction of the fire's advance and write off a huge swath of forest. The road being two ridge lines away, a significant amount of land would burn. The Supe believed this strategy more effective than to go one ridge over, cut line by hand and hope to beat the progress of the fire.

"We can dick around and fool ourselves into punching line along this dry creek bed here or along this ridge, but that'll be beating our heads against a wall. More than likely this fire will move past us. Instead of holding the road two ridges over, if we over-think and are too aggressive we'll lose the first ridge. I hate to say it but we'll probably lose the second one too. Then we won't get a handle on the fire until this third or even fourth ridge here."

This made complete sense to me and was a rare opportunity to see strategy being developed. With a big picture vantage point I could visualize the fire's advance and our efforts in relation to containment. Usually I am swinging a tool, staring at dirt directly in front of me and never really understand where we fit in a dynamic and ever changing situation. The ranger in the Bronco was acting IC or Incident Commander, in charge of the fire, and unfortunately not on the same page. The ranger believed with enough air support to slow the front we should cut line along the first ridge line. We could catch the fire there if we went hard and sucked it up. The unstated but prime motivation was that he did not want the whole second valley to burn. Since a logging road was in place, I am sure he knew fairly accurately how many board feet of lumber would be lost if the second valley burned.

The Supe gave me a look and a slight nod. I stood and excused myself to check on something and left them to work it out. In Forest Service hierarchy the ranger was senior, the official IC in charge and ultimately responsible for the suppression of the fire. He was no dummy though. The Supe was The Supe and our version of Red Adair. When I returned ten minutes later they had decided to move forward with the Supe's plan and cut a beeline towards and make our stand on the logging road two ridges away. The Supe did not pressure nor bully the ranger into agreeing with his plan, far from it. He was simply persuasive in explaining why this strategy would be more effective, made sense and was ultimately the surer method to save as much forest as possible.

The crew flew in at the end of the day, and we drove back to the Lucia Creek hippie village. I did not like being separated from everyone even if only for a nine hour shift and was happy to see the guys. Immediately they started heckling me.

"Hey you look better already, Elephant Boy."

"I don't know. He's still pretty freaking ugly."

"You sure the doctor could not do anything to help with your face, huh?"

'"We need to start calling you Fugly Boy."

"Hopefully someone took a photo of him this morning looking like that. Damn, that would have been awesome."

"We should place an ad in the local newspapers asking for donations. 'Please don't let this kind of deformity happen to more kids. It can be prevented. Please give.' "

"Just think, Lightning. You'd make a valuable public service announcement."

"Too bad Halloween is a couple months away. You were set for a scary costume."

"Ha. Ha. Ha." I laughed along. The Supe chuckled too. Thankfully he did not mention the almost passing out business, probably believing I was getting good enough already. More would have been piling on.

At the hamlet we set out camp with tents and sleeping bags and marched over to the Lucia Squeeze. The scene was a replay of the night before with some minor changes. The menu had two new entrees to choose from. Pam wore a different t-shirt than yesterday, this one aqua green with a silk screen of a sea otter and the Monterrey aquarium logo. For her age she did fill out those faded Levi's nicely. Kingman immediately asked the Supe if he was able to find any patchouli oil in town. How about special scented candles or incense? The table rolled with laughter. It took cajones to poke fun of the Supe or Stew. Mountain Mike was universally respected and could pull it off. Whenever he started up, they joined in heartily and obviously got a kick from the teasing. No way would you catch me popping off like that. Nor would I poke a grizzly with a stick. Happily for everyone Mike relished the opportunity.

After dinner I returned to the pay phone outside the general store. Looking at the dark sky above, I took a breath and plugged four quarters into the coin slot. A buzzing came across the line and then the beep, beep repetition of a busy signal. Quarters clattered and dropped down the coin slot. I scooped them out with one finger. Someone's home, I thought, looking on the bright side. I wandered into the general store and looked around at nicknacks, dawdling.

Corn Flake was on the payphone when I stepped back outside. I waited five minutes for him to finish before trying again. The phone made it's mechanical beeping noises before the call went through. When Janine's voice answered after the second ring, my heart skipped.

"Hello! How are you?"

"Who is this?"

"Umm, it's Curt, silly."

"Oh, I was just messing with you. I'm glad you finally called. How, where, why? How are you? Where are you? Why didn't you call before? I was worried."

"I did call. Steve should've gave you a message."

"Yes, he said you were in Big Sur?"

"Yeah. That's right. We're southeast of Big Sur near the Ventana wilderness."

"I miss you. I waited at your apartment and couldn't stop thinking something happened to you or worse. I wish you had called. Chris and Ben said you must be on a fire. It was nerve racking not knowing what was going on."

"I'm sorry. When the word came, we had to go. We spiked out the first night with no way to call you."

"Really. None at all?"

"It's the middle of the forest. There aren't any phones out there. I'm not Gordon Gecko with a satellite phone. Come on. You know I wanted to speak with you."

"Okay. I was just worried and felt like a fool not hearing from you. I waited with no word two nights in a row."

"I'm sorry, babe. I've been thinking about you non-stop. Twenty-four- seven. Non-stop."

"I missed you too. This isn't fun with you gone. I kept thinking something awful happened."

"I'm fine. You don't have to worry about me."

"Of course not. You think you're invincible. Fires are really dangerous. What if something happened. How would I know?"

"Nothings gonna happen. You can forget about that."

"Well I won't. When do you think you'll be home?"

Who knows. I can't really say. We're going to be here several more days at least."

"Yeah. This sucks."

'It's okay. I'll be home soon. I promise."

"That's not a real promise. You just said you don't know when you'll be home."

"Yeah, you're right. I don't know how soon we'll get back. I'm sorry. What else is going on?" I asked, trying to change the subject. "Have you found a job yet?" Janine was looking for part time work she could continue during the school year.

"I applied at this cool boutique on State Street and feel pretty good about it. The manager said they would me call back later this week."

"That's great." The phone clicked. An automated voice said for more time to deposit fifty-five more cents. I fumbled in my pockets and dropped three more quarters into the slot.

"I knew you would find a job, no problemo."

"Well, I hope so. This boutique would be great too. I love their clothes. The shop has a super cool vibe and would be an awesome place to work. Plus, there's an employee discount on everything."

"Hey, no doubt about it. Whatever you go after, you'll nail, for sure."

"They're supposed to call later this week. It's not a done deal yet."

"They'd be crazy not to hire you." I tried to envision Janine holding the other end of the phone, lying on her bed, looking cute. For pajamas she had taken to wearing a green LP t-shirt that was too big on her. That look matched with bikini underwear, drove me crazy.

"The clerk made a point that I did not have any retail experience. I don't know. We'll see. I feel pretty good about it, but... sure wish you were here. It's not the same without you."

"Come on. I've been gone a couple days."

"You disappeared and never called. Plus, it's been three days. I didn't know what to think."

"I'm in the middle of nowhere. What could be going on?"

"Yeah, maybe it sounds silly. I can't help sometimes getting a little nuts. When I didn't hear from you.... I'm glad you called."

"You are silly. You're my silly girl, like the song. We knew I would be going on a fire again. We'll be home soon. Promise. I'll call you the same time tomorrow. We should be here again tomorrow night."

"Okay. Okie dokie, Smokey. Please stay safe."

The phone clicked again. The voice repeated to deposit more money for more time. Now out of change I told Janine I had to get going but would call again tomorrow. We said good night. I repeated the promise to call tomorrow around the same time. The hard plastic phone dropping down on the cradle sounded cold and final. I looked around if anyone could hear the conversation. I was alone and felt alone too.

CHAPTER

17

The next day followed the new same routine. After breakfast at our restaurant, the helicopter airlifted us to the fireline. They moved me back to swinging a Pulaski to minimize contact with poison oak. At the end of shift we flew out and ate dinner at the Lucia Squeeze again. Sitting around community tables on the back patio, telling stories and jokes, eating restaurant quality food, we practically owned the place.

As promised I called Janine after dinner at eight-thirty and spoke with her roommate Steve. He said she and Elaine left earlier for the movies. Okay, I would try back in an hour. Lounging in the one man tent, resting on pad and sleeping bag with clothes and boots still on, I used the headlamp to read a paperback thriller from a favorite author. I had trouble focusing and kept losing track of the story. With no idea what was happening in the plot or even the words recently read, every couple of minutes I needed to stop to reread a passage. We did say I would call tonight at the same time, right? C'mon now. You didn't expect her to sit by the phone and wait for your call. Well, did you?

I read off and on for an hour then wandered back to the payphone. Steve answered the phone and said the girls were not home yet. Hey, no big deal. I played cool and asked him to please let Janine know I called and thanked him. I tried to smile while talking. Supposedly people can tell from your voice when you're smiling.

This was uncharted territory. I've never been the jealous kind. But her not being home bugged a little. I wondered where the girls were and what they were up to. The mind can play mean tricks and be a tormentor which is not cool. It's because of that dumb dream I advised myself, but tossed and turned in the sleeping bag before finally falling to sleep.

Next day's work held an added intensity with the finish line within reach. We did not stop to be helicoptered home but charged on until well after sundown and finally tied into the logging road the Supe showed me before on the map. Built by bulldozer several years ago, the narrow dirt road was a barely fifteen foot wide chevron cut through the woods. Mostly void of shrubs, brush or other flammable material, the road would have to work.

With the sky a deep blackish purple we stopped for a quick bite of dinner. The Killer handed over a radio and directed me to lead a group of five guys to hike the road north for approximately three miles. Another crew was ahead waiting for us.

I jumped up and took the lead position. The others fell in behind, swallowing last bites as we ventured into darkness. My headlamp's narrow beam nominally lit the shadowy road and forest around. Leading the pack, especially at night in new country is way different than following along. Normally your eyes acclimate to the dark. This black pitch was disorienting and somewhat unsettling. I kept a steady pace, footsteps crunching on leaves and soft packed dirt. The familiar wooden handle of the Pulaski, clenched tight, gave comfort like a security blanket. The tool's metal head would prove a decent weapon if necessary. After a couple hundred yards, Boon asked me to hold on. He needed to switch headlamp batteries for new ones. We waited as he rummaged in his backpack.

"C'mon, Boon. You're supposed to double check the gear before we're alone out here in the anxious black."

"Blow me and your 'anxious black.' ...Anxious black...Who the hell even talks like that?"

Standing still without the accompanying noise of tramping footsteps accentuated the quiet. As a descriptor for this night, anxious worked as an adjective. With Boon finally ready, I started hiking again. An ominous feeling filled the air as if predatory eyes observed, tracking our movements, watching and waiting. I was not the only one who noticed because guys started joking. We better watch out. What was that spooky noise? A cough from a bear or maybe mountain lion? Hopefully the bluster would warn away any nocturnal critters ahead in the night. We're coming. Please don't mess with us. We don't taste good and are not food.

"Is it dark enough for you?"

"This will have to do until they figure out how to get inside a cow's belly."

"Hey J.C. Isn't there an ancient tribe of Indian zombies round here?"

"Nah, but supposedly there's werewolves and definitely vampires."

"That's right. Didn't they base the *Lost Boys* on a true story around here?"

"You know it. I heard about a whole village on the coast populated entirely with vampires."

Enormous black trees thick with wide branches blocked the night sky, hiding the light from stars. The jagged mountain range to our left covered the moon, further masking the night. And these creeps were trying to spook me with talk of vampires. Along with that whole needles thing, I'm not real keen on vampires either. It's not the blood part. I'm fine with blood. The idea of sharp fangs piercing skin and draining blood tweaks me a little bit. Complete wilderness surrounded us. Who knew what deadly hunter might be tracking us by our headlamps cutting through the darkness. We played with the scary thoughts like a game, trying to come to terms with the emotion. Everyone faces fear differently. The main thing is to not to let the feeling overwhelm you.

One night last summer we were in Oregon with Daryl leading the way. Somehow he got turned around. We hiked for over an hour before realizing we were not where we were supposed to be. Not nearly as black a night as this one, the terrain was also more wide open. Marking specific landmarks on the topographic map, we finally found the correct path. For a while though, it was sketchy. After going in the wrong direction we were definitely lost. A feeling of panic hit everyone. There's good reason to describe panic as a wave because the emotion smacks, washes over and can carry you away. The wave hit Pete hard.

"You damn derelict, Daryl. Golden compass we'll call you."

Completely stressed out, Daryl did not respond. He stared unblinking, studying the topo map, trying to place the visible peaks around us and differentiate what was what. Finally he decided we needed to hike in the opposite direction. After a while, recognizing we were on the right track, a giant sigh of relief went through everyone.

Sure enough, with me leading the way, we came to a fork in the road where I was not expecting one. I paused a moment and took the road that went left. The ridge we were following ran to the northwest. Going left seemed to make the most sense. No one said anything about a fork in the road. I was not going to radio for directions.

"Hey Lightning. You sure this is the right way?"

"Maybe you aught to radio the Supe and ask."

"F. you, Boon. I've got this." I said with some venom and kept hiking on. Though fairly certain we were on the correct path, the limited visibility added stress and confusion. A nagging tension of doubt made me second guess myself. The uncertainty would not ease until we tied in with the other crew. Boon tried popping off about vampires again. The joke was not funny anymore. The road was nothing more than a glorified dozer line, bumpy and strewn with rocks, roots and an occasional stump. I ground out a solid pace and focused intently where to place the next step on the uneven surface, working to avoid tripping or twisting an ankle.

We carried on for almost four miles before finally rounding a corner and seeing headlamps from other crews. The road veered right and rose upwards, following an embankment and hillside. After the isolation of pitch dark, other people's lights were welcome. I walked up and greeted the nearest ones. They responded with hellos. Bright yellow nomex pants distinguished the group as a California Department of

229

Forestry crew. Stretched along behind them, lining the road like a strand of Christmas lights, beams of numerous headlamps shined in the dark. More men than I could count were dressed in the telltale orange jumpsuits of Department of Corrections inmate crews. They reminded me of a scene from an old western. When the lone cavalry rider rounds a bend, the mesa is covered left to right with countless native warriors. They outnumber him a hundred to one and move forward in full battle dress with warpaint, lances and feathered headdresses. After hiking in the dark, the mass of people was a contrast.

I radioed to let the Supe know we tied in with the other crew. His response squawked loudly and crackled, breaking the quiet of the night.

"I copy, Curt. How far did you go? What's the status there?"

I turned the volume down and answered. "It was more than three miles, Supe. Probably three and a half minimum. There's a CDF crew and something like a thousand convicts here."

Behind me J.C. snorted softly. The proper terminology was inmate crew. Calling people "convicts" was not exactly PC, especially over the radio. Plus, there were more like a hundred.

"I copy you, Curt. Head back to our position here and have them follow and fan out along the road in this direction. We'll start backfiring when we meet in the middle."

"Yeah, I copy." I clicked the talk button on the radio twice for good measure.

I reviewed the Supe's directions with the CDF captain, then turned and started back the way we came. Hiking along the same road was easier now knowing what to expect. I marched with purpose, leading the train of people stretched behind me. We met Stew waiting two miles down the road, standing straight like a noble statue, alone in the dark. He emerged from the shadows like Batman making an entrance. Stew grunted a couple words to the CDF captain, flipped on his headlamp, and handed me a drip torch.

"J.C. you fellas bump down and space along the road until you meet with the others. Lightnin' you're with me. Let's get going. We ain't got all night."

Grabbing a fusee from the backpack, I snapped open and struck the tip. Using the sputtering fire as starter for the drip torch wick, I followed Stew into the foliage. Lifting one end of the torch and pointing the nozzle to the ground, I deposited droplets of burning fuel as we passed through the brush. Stew pointed to different shrubs, piles of dead material and specific areas he wanted to light. I followed his direction. Soon he grew quiet, and I lit whatever looked promising. The three to one, diesel gasoline mix flowed onto the ground as liquid fire. The fuel kept burning and slowly caught the surrounding grass, leaves and twigs. The flames grew and spread through nearby bushes and small trees. We hiked back and forth leaving a trail of fire behind us. I lifted the drip torch to the base of some smaller trees, catching lower branches on fire hoping to get them to crown out. The pine needles were dry enough they immediately crackled, flared and engulfed the whole tree. After a couple times of this, Stew said to not get the fire going too hot, too soon.

"We want a good base on the ground before the trees start crowning."

A golden reflection of flames danced across his face. I nodded that I understood. "Okay. Copy that."

The crew on the road had a perfect view of the backfire spreading through the forest. They waited and watched the red flames grow. Their job was to ensure fire did not carry across the logging road. When fire did creep close, if it looked possible to meander across, they would quickly scratch out some dirt, solidifying the break. Stew and I zig-zagged in and away from the road, down the line and did not pause until the drip torch ran low on fuel. We refilled from a jerry can the others bumped along, following our progress. After several hours we came to a rise in the road. Looking back, the fire behind us was something to see. Bright orange and yellow covered the sky with red demons coursing across the ridge in a steady pulsing wave. Heat and smoke rose uphill, pushing the flames onward and upward.

232

We kept hiking and setting more fire. Stew stood with the combie tool resting on the ground and directed me into a grove of trees. I searched for fallen branches, rotten logs or other dead brush that would light easily. I'd give an extra dose of burn fuel and pause a second to watch the material smolder and catch, then hiked through the brush and back to Stew's position. The going was easier now. Flames illuminated the area around and behind us. Being able to see and navigate the woods made a huge difference. Whereas earlier the night was pitch black like tar, we were now bathed in glowing red and orange light as if from a giant jack o' lantern.

I hiked across thick grass and uphill, down twisting ravines and around gnarly rat's nests of bushes, through open space brush and over fallen logs. Working hard, I dragged fire everywhere. The fire crept along, expanded and grew behind me as I made my way through.

We kept on through the night. I never gave away that drip torch. Stopping to refill the cylinder I'd stretch my neck back and forth pouring the diesel gasoline mix. Obnoxious fumes contrasted with the pure, oxygen rich forest air. A half quart of water and the moment of rest recharged me. Starting again, we hiked and hiked for hours, lighting miles and miles of fire, more than I've ever set. Over the ridge behind us, a wave of flames worked uphill like an awesome, dancing yellow and orange curtain whipping across the landscape. Most importantly the fire charged in the opposite direction from our line. Whenever we'd return near the logging road, I could feel eyes of con-crew members watching me, marking our progress. Each time a tree crowned or made an explosive run in the distance, they would hoot and holler like at a fireworks show on the Fourth of July.

With Stew leading the way, I continued, focused on the moment, each clump of fuel and where to place fire for maximum benefit. Perception of time evaporated like driving on a marathon road trip and losing oneself in the right side, spatial hemisphere of the brain. Suddenly you snap to, realizing you're home with no recollection how you got there. That was me noticing daylight the next morning. Completely cognizant of our surroundings, I knew where we were but felt as if coming out of a hypnotic trance. The digital Casio watch read six-forty-eight in the morning. We backfired almost nine hours straight. Red and yellow flames rumbled across the hillside for miles behind us. The drip torch and Jerry can now empty, Stew nodded we were good.

"Okay," he said, "Let's go" and started hiking up the road. I followed, my eyes locked on the back of his boots churning methodically forward, each step lifting from the ground like the advance of an army. Steep mountains to the east blocked the sun. The gray morning was slightly out of focus. Not much later we came on the crew trucks parked on the side of a paved road that intersected with the logging road. The familiar green crew buggies were a nice surprise. Someone must have gone for them yesterday to drive the long way around to meet us here. I was fuzzy on the mileage from the map when the Supe showed me the plan of attack a couple days ago. We must have burned over fifteen miles along that logging road to our present location. The milage actually hiked was a different story because we zig zagged, back and forth, up and back the whole way. I followed Stew to the Supe leaning against the front of his rig casual as could be. They spoke for a while. I barely grasped the words. Taking his glasses off, Stew blinked repeatedly, trying to lubricate both eyes. Probably dirt irritated them. He stood straight as ever, making a point to the Supe. His head nodded and almost imperceptibly, Stew wavered in place.

"Go inside and get some sleep, Curt. We'll grab a couple hours here."

The words were garbled as if speaking with leather lodged between his teeth. For the first time I realized he was tired. Too easily people throw the word stud around. That dude was as tough as any centurion who ever marched the Roman empire. If not worn to the bone myself, the realization Stew was human would have struck me.

"Thanks, Stew." I climbed into the 4A crew buggy and curled up on the rear seat, stretching both legs onto the seat across the aisle and dropped like a rock.

CHAPTER

18

They woke me after a couple hours. We spent the day posted along the logging road, monitoring the line, keeping an eye for spot fires. Mostly we tried to avoid hazy, white smoke drifting our way from the smoldering hot spots. The breeze shifted in and out towards our direction carrying the acrid fumes. Except for a couple minor sections where the fire slopped a little, the road held the night before. Supe's plan worked as mapped out perfectly. Backfire carried uphill and burned the ridge to the west. When meeting the main fire heading east, the two collapsed together and extinguished each other in an anticlimactic evanescence. Now that's a juicy word. Have you ever seen ocean waves during a heavy backwash bounce away from shore and slam into an incoming wave? They meet with a powerful clap. Surf pumps into the air with force because the water has to be displaced and go somewhere. Two fires connecting with each other are not nearly as dramatic. When two fronts collide, the power and velocity of both fires nullify each other. With no new fuel to feed upon, the forward momentum fades like the fizzling of a candle. Main fire and backfire meet, snuffing each other out.

I was fine standing around after last night's effort. Of course thoughts soon turned to Janine. Lazy, luxurious hours were spent in a sleep deprived, echo chamber of my head. Daydreams abounded about being at the beach. I imagined her lying on a towel next to me wearing a bathing suit. Her tan skin glistened, wet from swimming. I wanted to devour every graceful line of her body and especially the firm meat and splendor of her thighs. A ravenous, inner cannibal possessed me.

After five we grouped together, hiked to the vehicles and drove to a nearby campground and recently erected fire camp. Expansive canvas tents were arranged with cots for the CDC crews to sleep. Opposite the tents, an outdoor kitchen and dining area were set with folding tables and chairs. We positioned our camp in an open field off to one side away from the inmate crews and the turquoise portable toilets. Large fire camps tend to be dusty, dirty and noisy from diesel generators running non-stop through the night powering overhead electric lights. This camp was junior in comparison to the massive ones like little cities built from nowhere. Huge fire camps accommodate thousands of firefighters and support personnel battling the major fire complexes that last for weeks and longer.

Dinner consisted of thick, juicy t-bone steaks, mashed potatoes, green beans, corn on the cob and ice cream. The adult inmates serving the meal were the personification of big house convicts, yoked from lifting weights with enormous biceps and forearms. Rough green and black tattoos covered necks and thick, stout bodies. We passed through the chow line with brown plastic trays. Dressed in white pants, white aprons and t-shirts, the cons ladled food onto our plates from large stainless steel pots and containers. Serving t-bones was a huge man in his forties with long gray bushy sideburns, a goatee, and a hairnet over a thick gray ponytail. A couple teeth were missing from his wide goofy smile. Over six foot five inches tall, he easily weighed two hundred and sixty pounds of solid muscle. He joked with everyone while passing out their portion.

"Making conversation, jus' having an enjoyable time working kitchen duty here in the forest. Breathing fresh mountain air."

When the con caught sight of Robbie Wadlow, two spots in front of me in line, Cupid's arrow must have struck. He was in love.

"My my. Get a look at this one. Oh, aren't you a solid chunk of a man. Here, let me pick you a nice chop. Wow, the world I'd love to show you."

Wadlow tried to shrug the words away, "Take it easy, Pops."

"No offense, honey. You are a sight for sore eyes."

Definitely not comfortable with the attention, Wadlow kept quiet and moved down the line. Girls falling for his looks was a daily occurrence. I'm sure gay dudes occasionally hit on him, but you could understand Robbie feeling awkward. Ice cream would have melted from the heat of that dude's leer. The giant inmate kept clucking to himself and did not stop talking, going on and on while serving J.C. and then me. The big man was all in too, owning his attraction to Wadlow.

"Damn me. That is some good, good stuff. Chunky stuff. Now son, you gots to admit that is one fine looking man. You're not bad either, young 'un. But that blond one is really something."

"Thanks, boss," I said as he ladled a thick steak onto my plate, shuffling down the line, happy to not receive the same attention. Separated only by a fold-up table, the inmate was more than imposing, his large frame powerful and muscled from years of lifting weights. Overgrown eyebrows with random hairs twisting and curling, coupled with the two missing teeth presented a wild but goofy demeanor. An unmistakable craziness permeated the air around him like a scent seeping from pores. To be locked together in a cell if he were in the mood to get cozy was one scary proposition. If California ever wanted a poster boy deterrent to scare kids from crime and onto the right path, the prospect of that dude having his way with you absolutely qualified.

239

Inmate crews have always fascinated me. CDF and various county departments work with them way more than we do. If you pay attention, you'll start to notice the red crew trucks driving down the road. Lined up in orange jumpsuits, I pretend to ignore and act like I don't see them. But I quietly check out different individuals and wonder what they did to land in prison, what their story is. Since fire crews are staffed with non-violent offenders, the majority were incarcerated for drugs. A Daily Nexus editorial espoused a theory the whole war on drugs was really a big conspiracy to supply the state with cheap labor. Maybe that's true. A large percentage of CDC crews are inner city African Americans and Latinos who seem to enjoy the woods even if this is the first time they have done such hard, physical labor. Last year in Oregon we came across an inmate on the side of a trail by himself, sitting on a flat stump with his boots and socks pulled off. He complained non-stop to everyone walking by how hard they were working and for only a dollar an hour. That "dollar an hour" phrase became a popular refrain to bellyache. The choice between doing time behind bars or getting credit against time by working in the woods, even if only dirty, tedious mop-up, seems a no-brainer to me. Recidivism rates for inmate fire crews are significantly lower than the general population of prisons. Doing hard physical work to be proud of and contributing to society surely has a powerful positive benefit. Except for the fact Prohibition did not work the first time and the war on drugs is a huge, nothing burger waste of time and resources, the firefighting piece of the correctional system, seems a win-win each way around.

We ate dinner together at one long fold up table, invisible barriers separating us from the other crews nearby. Thick and juicy, the steaks were sprinkled with salt and cracked pepper, cooked medium rare and to perfection with a strip of pink in the middle. Most camp food is okay. This was a feast. Those convicts knew how to cook. The table grew quiet as we dug in, cutting bites with plastic knives and forks, enjoying the meal. In classic grrrr voice through clenched teeth Stew declared that Wadlow really was the "butt magnet."

Others piped in. "Don't worry, sweetie. I'll be tender."
Robbie's expression looked like he'd just swallowed a charcoal briquet. This subject did not sit well with him.

"What if we run into a "Rainbow" crew? Them gals surely won't be able to control themselves neither."

"Rainbow" crews are drawn entirely from female inmates. We've run into those crews before. Talk about some hard characters. Smoking cigarettes and oozing venom, the look of several female inmates put a scare in me. Maybe the attitude was all for show or self protection. "Contained Fury" described that crew and could be a title for one of those cheesy women behind bars, exploitation B movies that play on late, late night television.

We sacked out after dinner under the stars. Cozy again in my North Face mountain bed softened by pine needles and duff cushioning the ground, thoughts of Janine filled me with warmth. We rolled around in my imagination before I fell asleep.

The next day we tramped through the burn, falling hazardous dead snags, known as Widowmakers. White ash covered the ground where fire burned through, the flames meandered and curved across the countryside, clearing foliage and overgrowth through a vast swath of land. Contrary to how you'd imagine, the fire did not level virtually every tree and bush in its path. Countless Redwoods were blackened and singed across their wide trunks while the giant trees' upper branches remained intact. Utterly random, scattered pockets of brush were spared, leaving splotches and splashes across the hills like green islands or large camouflage patterns. Sporadic unburned green contrasted with gray and white ash of sections burned clear to the ground.

CHAPTER

19

The next day we mopped-up again until late afternoon then released. A strike team of engines arrived to finish the job. We loaded into crew trucks and headed for home. Early that evening we pulled into a gas station fast food complex along the highway and stopped en masse at Taco Bell. Three Taco Bell Supremes with extra hot sauce and a large fountain Dr. Pepper hit the spot. We were in, out, and back on the road quick. Between possible fast food joints, the variety of dishes available and ability to turn food around for twenty but pronto made Taco Bell the consistent choice. The Supe had this stuff down.

We rolled into the hotshot barracks well after nine, gassed up the rigs, loaded new tools on board and amscrammed out of there. Most headed to the Cold Spring for some cold ones. First out of the parking lot, I made a beeline over the Pass and into town. I thought to call ahead to Janine's but did not have change for the pay phone. Anyway I figured surprising her would be fun. Traffic was light into town and I flew, the motorcycle purring and running strong, carrying me fast to my girl. The yellow reflectors dividing the lanes formed a blur of a solid yellow parallel with and overlaying the painted on white lane lines. After dark woods, the lights of cars and town appeared bright and encouraging. Filled with excitement I rocketed down the highway.

The Mesa house porch lamp was lit. Though curtains were closed, lights were on inside. I parked next to Janine's white pickup on the street and did not hesitate to ring the bell. Standing still on the porch made me realize how my pulse raced while waiting for someone to answer. Steve opened the door, said howdy, let me in, then yelled down the hallway for Janine. He and Elaine were watching television. I stood in the foyer between the living room and kitchen suddenly feeling tall in the room and shy, not sure if I should walk to Janine's room or what. Thankfully she glided down the hall, dressed comfy in t- shirt and sweat pants.

"Hi there. Look who the cat dragged in. When did you get back?"

"We just rolled into town. I couldn't wait to see you."

"Well now you've seen me..."

I did not expect her to run to me like in a field of flowers with an orchestra playing, but this was frostier than how I envisioned our reunion.

"I'm just messing with you. Come here." The mischief in her grin lifted my heart. Finally we hugged, her body warm and firm in my arms. I squeezed tight.

"That's better. We arrived a half hour ago. I couldn't wait to see you. What's happening? How are you?"

"I'm good and started my new job. It's awesome. But I missed you. You're not supposed to go away from me like that. I don't like it."

"I know, I know. I didn't like it much either."

Sitting in her room on the edge of the bed, we talked about her new job, the fire, Big Sur and the back fire operation. Her eyes drifted and the spark of interest faded. I grew silent. She asked if I wanted to take a shower.

"You're a little stinky, buster."

Her nose crinkled. I had changed into a semi clean t-shirt and pants this morning. But layers of grime and a week's worth of sweat coated my body. Suddenly embarrassed to seem dirty to her, I nodded that would be a good idea. Undoing the laces, I pulled boots and both pairs of dirty socks off. Janine handed me a towel. With the shower started in the adjacent bathroom, I discarded t-shirt, pants and underwear into a pile on the floor. The reflection in the mirror looked ragged with a week's worth of beard and black soot smudges covering my face like a coal miner after a long shift. Thankfully the cortisone shot worked its magic. I no longer looked like a circus freak.

Janine found a baggy pair of blue cotton gym shorts for me to wear after I toweled dry. We kissed on her bed, but nothing more than that. She was shy about Elaine coming in and disturbing us. We laid together in the single bed with clean sheets and talked softly until Elaine slipped into her bed across the room and turned the overhead light off. The two girls talked briefly about people I did not know. After they grew silent, we kissed again. That was nice except a couple times when I scratched Janine's face with my rough beard. I had not yet shaved. We fell asleep holding each other which was sweet. Having her tight little body next to me was not easy though. I was ready to burst and could not get over the crummy roommate luck.

I slept hard on my back with Janine's head resting on my chest. There's a vague recollection of Janine shaking me, saying I was snoring. Early the next morning while still dark, I extricated myself from under Janine, rolled from the covers and padded into the kitchen for a tall glass of water. Roommate notes to each other were on the grease board. I idly glanced over assorted papers pinned on a cork board near the door.

"Kurt called. A couple times." was written messily on the left top corner of the grease board. Someone named Eric called too. That was written in a girl's handwriting. The soft click click of the second hand moved across the face on a wall clock above the kitchen sink. I could hear the sound of time passing. Yellow daffodils lived in a planter by the kitchen window. Beautiful white lilies in a vase decorated the table. Known as Casablanca's, the lilies have always been a favorite.

Work wouldn't start for a while. I went to the laundry area in the garage with the big duffel and threw dirty clothes into the washing machine. Setting the control to cold water, I poured an extra dose of detergent, clicked the knob for extended soak and did not care that socks and underwear were mixed together with colored shirts and pants. Everything was beyond filthy dirty. They didn't really qualify as whites any longer.

As the day grew steadily lighter, I sat at the kitchen table reading yesterday's newspaper, catching up on the world. Janine did not awake until after I switched the clothes over to the dryer. I smiled as she wiped sleep from her eyes.

'I didn't want to wake you but figured it would be okay to use your washing machine."

"Of course, that's fine.   Do you want some cereal for breakfast?"

"That'd be super."

She poured Cheerios and milk into two bowls. We sat together in the bright kitchen and ate in silence, metal spoons clinking against ceramic with each scoop. Finished, I walked to the sink and rinsed the bowl and spoon with dish soap and hot water. When Janine finished I took her bowl and washed it too, then hand dried the two bowls and spoons with a dish towel hanging from a hook.

"You're working today, right? What time do you get off? Do you want to come to my place tonight after?"

"I get off work at seven. That would be nice. Why don't you give me a call then? We'll confirm." Her eyes were clear but thoughtful.

"Okay. I guess." I did not understand why she would not just come by like before, but was not going to sweat it.

Walking to the garage, I took the laundry from the dryer and dressed for the day in now clean clothes. The heavy duty cotton t-shirt and nomex pants smelled clean. Holding heat from the dryer they were warm to the touch. Barely pausing to fold them I stuffed the rest into the duffel, threw the bag over one shoulder and walked back to the kitchen. Janine still sat at the table.

"Well, I have to vamanos for work. Hope you have an awesome day. I'll call you tonight."

"Okie dokie, smokey. That sounds good."

She smiled, walked with me to the door and standing on tiptoes, kissed me on the lips and said goodbye. I absorbed the soft kiss and lowered the duffel, passing it through the open door. Outside I slung the stuffed bag back over one shoulder and sat on the motorcycle. Facing the street, the sound of the door mechanism clicked into place when Janine closed it. Starting the engine, I settled on the cycle's seat, pulled on the Shoei helmet, tightened the chinstrap, turned and looked at the closed door.

Heavy morning commuter traffic filled the highway. I floated between the lanes and cars and did not pay too much attention.

We ran a leisurely paced five miles on paved road over gentle hills for PT. Harder runs were usually dirt trails or fire roads with exceedingly steep sections that would be a test to hike, let alone run. After showering I finally shaved, the disposable razor doing a passable job against the rough beard. I don't have the thickest of beards but two passes were necessary to get clean shaven. We broke into smaller groups by squad and worked on tools, sharpening edges and saw blades, prepping for the next fire. After a week on the road today would be nice and mellow back on home turf. I looked forward to closing time, getting back to Isla Vista and seeing Janine again. Last night's reunion was okay, but tonight would be better. We'd get back on track and in the groove. As they say, some things were not meant to be.

At eleven- thirty word came that we were heading to Montana. Instantly the casual vibe transformed into deliberate hustle. Everyone scrambled, loaded gear and jumped into the crew buggies.

"I hope all you Romeos kissed your girlfriends goodbye," the Supe said, chuckling. "We're gonna be gone for awhile. Ya-ta hey now."

"You have got to be shitting me," I thought looking at the pay phone on the wall outside the Supe's office. Calling now wouldn't work with no time to mess around.

Adjacent to the University campus and completely encircled by the town of Goleta, the Santa Barbara municipal airport is somehow officially considered Santa Barbara. We did not check in at the old school Spanish mission style main terminal but near a low slung airplane hangar a block to the east. All our tools, saws and gear from the buggies were unloaded, stacked, organized and ready to be loaded as soon as the charter airplane landed. With the gear set on the tarmac, the Killer said we had an hour before the plane would arrive. Go grab some food. Absolutely, positively everyone needed to be back in forty-five minutes, no ifs, ands, or buts.

Everyone vamanosed. J.C. and I walked through the open fence together and across the frontage road to a hamburger-sandwich stand that's been there forever but I never visited.

A dark brown, single story building covered with wooden shake shingles, The Shack already enjoyed a heavy lunch crowd added by the influx of twenty hotshots sharing the same agenda. We took a number and waited our turn.

"This is awesome, huh? Looking forward to some beautiful, big sky country. We'll earn some nice oats too." Oats was slang for overtime pay, when we were paid time and a half the usual scale. J.C. was a GS-5 and earned ninety cents an hour more than my GS-4 rate.

"Something, yeah I guess." In no mood to explain the thoughts swimming around my head, my heart was not into it. After we placed our order, clutching change, I found a pay phone in the hallway outside the unisex restroom. Janine would be at work. I rifled through the thick yellow phone book, found the shop's number in the woman's clothing section and called her there.

The phone rang twice before my favorite voice answered. "Azalea's. Can I help you?"

"Hey, it's Curt."

"Hey, you. How's it going? I didn't tell you, but I'm not really supposed to talk on the phone too much or have people call me. There are customers here. I'm working."

"It's just that we're at the airport and are flying to Montana. I wanted to speak with you."

"What? Seriously? Okay, but I'm sorry. I'm with a customer and can't talk right now."

"We're flying out in an hour. Who knows when I'll be able to call you again."

"That sucks. Oh well. Unfortunately, I can't talk right now. Thanks for calling."

"Hey. I'll miss you."

"Okay. Me too. Take care and be careful." The line clicked. A hangman graffiti scratched into the enamel black paint of the pay phone above the coin change slot mocked me. I felt empty as the stickman figure.

"Hey Curt, they called your number." I walked to the counter and grabbed the "to go" bag with tri-tip steak sandwich wrapped in tinfoil and an order of curly fries. I stood next to J.C. dully eating fries while waiting for his number to be called. We probably had enough time to eat at the stand, which a number of guys were doing, but returned to the airport anyway. The Killer said to be back in forty-five. I did not want to push it or feel like dealing with uncertainty. A coach in high school preached that if you're not ten minutes early, then you're really late. I never bought into that philosophy but did not need a hassle now.

"Bummed about leaving your gal again so soon?" J.C. could read me like a book.

"Yeah. Don't rub it in."

"Hey, it's natural. You're not the only one. Don't think for a second you are. Every guy here has dealt with that shit."

"Everything was incredible. Then Monterrey happened. Now we're leaving again. I don't know how to describe the feeling other than it sucks. Last night something seemed a little different. Nothing major but I could sense a shift, a barely perceptible distance."

"Ah, c'mon. You're probably being overly sensitive. You guys were going hot and heavy every night. Then we took off and she didn't hear from you for days, right, which probably made her trip a little. I'm sure it's all good. If this girl really likes you, she'll wait. If she can't wait, then screw her. You don't need her."

"Yeah, I know. My mom used to warn me, 'Don't be like a bee and fly from flower to flower, you'll end up in the weeds.' "

"Well umm, bees are awesome. I don't know what that's supposed to mean."

"Try not to go from girl to girl. Save yourself for the special one. It's just I've been thinking Janine is that one."

"That's awesome, man. If she is 'the one' then you two will be able to make it work. If she's not, better to know now. No harm no foul. Either way you win."

"Last night bugged. It's hard to explain. Before Monterrey everything clicked between us perfect. For the first time ever we were out of joint. And for me to be conflicted is weird. I love fires. Getting called away again after just coming home last night really throws a wrench in the relationship. That's not going to help get back on track."

"Haha, I love you talking "relationship" now. She cast a spell for sure. Like I said, if you're meant to be together, you two will work it out. Stop thinking and tripping, man. You're gonna drive yourself crazy."

"I know. I know. Everybody tells me that. Finding something special you didn't even know was possible, you want to hold it close, not fly a thousand miles away."

"Everyone goes through this. Fire season is tough on relationships. It's not easy, but what's the old saying? Absence makes the heart grow fonder. When we get back, you'll see. I totally believe that."

"Thanks, Cracker."

A weight lifted. I did feel better. Something about Janine from the first moment, I knew. Whether chemical, magnetic or who knows how to describe the attraction, she had "it."

All the thinking about her and obsessing could drive me crazy, like those masochistic romantic shepherd poets we studied. I surrendered to the notion if we were meant to be, torturing myself would not change anything. Once the vise grip stopped clenching, the worries fluttered away. J.C. wasn't the first person to tell me I thought too much. They were probably right.

Feeling better, I looked around, taking in the airport scene. A commercial jet whined in its approach, landing on the main runway in the distance. The powerful jet engines blared in contrast with the single prop Cessnas and Pipers that populated the small airport. The pilot taxied to the right of the terminal and came to a stop. The ground crew scrambled to place the portable metal stairway for passengers to disembark. Two smaller planes rolled to the head of the runway and waited for the tower to radio okay their take off..

A tan 707 with a green stripe down the side flew in from the east, landed softly for such a large plane, taxied and stopped near our location. We gathered together and hiked across the tarmac with wind blowing and jets roaring. The scene felt like being in a movie. I allowed myself to enjoy the adventure. Excitement and anticipation of the impending journey filled me. Stepping up the rolling stairway, we filed on board. Firefighters decked in clean bright yellow nomex shirts were seated across the front rows. We grabbed open seats behind them in the spartan cabin. Without flight attendants there would be no beverage nor snack service.

This charter plane would not sport inflight treats of movie screens, pretzels or salted peanuts.

After we loaded in, buckled safety belts and took off, the flight was uneventful. We landed in Missoula several hours later. Stepping from the open door and onto a new rolling stairway, the wide open Montana sky greeted us.

"Welcome to God's country." Corndog said from behind me.

"You from near here, Coney Island?" Wadlow asked.

"That's right. My folks' place is a couple hours north."

The town spread across the valley below framed in every direction by jagged mountains and the brilliant crystal blue sky. Why people referred to Montana as "big sky country" was obvious. The world stretched far and wide, sharp and defined as if you could reach across the distance and touch the rocky peaks miles away. Two yellow school buses waited outside the terminal. We grabbed gear unloaded from the plane and filed on board.

"Hey Wadlow, I think you're supposed to ride on the short bus."

"Screw you, Boon. You big f-ing ape."

Sitting with J.C. reminded me of traveling to an away game in high school. Guys practically bounced on the bench seats, full of anticipation. Older one and two story residences with wood frame construction in a western Americana style filled the town. Beautiful, mature trees lined the streets and neighborhoods of this nice respectable Rocky Mountain community. We drove through traffic, past the population center and headed west to the Lolo National Forest. Once out of Missoula, the road straightened and passed through flat wide croplands full of sheep ranches and dark fields of alfalfa and grains.

"After a week or so, them sheep are going to start looking better and better, boys." B.D. immediately revived a recurring Montana theme from two summers ago.

"Montana- where men are men and sheep are nervous."

"You know why they love those big welly boots, right?"

Flocks of sheep gathered throughout the fields. Little lambs in soft wooly coats looked super cute. Maybe the talk was only a big joke. If that were the case, why was the topic so common? Hopefully "where there's smoke..." didn't apply.

The school bus chugged along the wandering highway, steadily gaining elevation into thick forest lands, heavy woods full with timber. The road narrowed and turned into two lanes that curved and wound like a snake, following the rugged terrain at the base of the mountains and mirroring the path of a twisted river below. Douglas Fir dominated. Thick Ponderosa and tall Lodgepole Pines also made up the forest. Sporadic clear cut sections from logging were visible, but mostly the impressive trees stretched like carpet across steep hillsides. The change in elevation from sea level coupled with the winding road made me lightheaded. To avoid getting carsick, I focused on the scenery outside the window. We arrived at the destination in early evening, exited the buses and were able to stretch legs and shake the kinks out. We would eat here and hike to the fireline in the morning.

One aspect of flying meant without our crew trucks life went on without the usual comforts we took for granted. Our own sleeping bags, tents, Thermo-rests, traveling library of magazines, paperbacks and the boom box were left behind. Paper sleeping bags would have to work for tonight. The forest floor was thick with a layer of pine needles, making the ground soft and comfortable. Sleep wouldn't be a problem.

A green Bronco pulled in. An older man with a pot belly and white hardhat, obviously overhead, delivered large cardboard boxes of sack lunches. My beyond sad sack held a sandwich with gray colored roast beef, a slice of American cheese on dry white bread. Corn chips and the opposite of delicious red apple rounded out the meal. Barely crunchy, that doleful apple lacked flavor and had the consistency of cardboard. Packets of mustard and mayo were at the bottom of the sack. Using a packet as an edge I spread the mustard. Who knew how long the bags sat around with mayo cooking in the heat.

With the sun disappearing behind the range to the west, guys grouped together under the mountain twilight. I hopped onto and sat on a wide fallen Ponderosa log next to Lupe, Boon, Corndog, and Lumpy. In a crooked semi-circle, J.C., Pete and Dempsey stood facing us.

"You hear that? What's that sound?" Boon asked.

"I didn't hear anything." Lupe answered, unsure of the gag.

"Something definitely made a noise. There 'twas again. You hear that, Pete?" Determined to torment him, Boon's sights were locked on Pete,.

"Yep, sounded like a screen door." Corndog knew what was up.

"That's right. A screen door. Who left their back door unlocked and screen door unlatched?"

"There, again. Damn, that screen door's slamming open and shut like nobody's business."

"Blow me, both you." Pete wasn't amused.

"You need to oil that door, Pete. It's liable to make a racket all night. A little WD-40 should do the trick."

"Ah, Pete. Maybe it's not even your place. Someone can check. Let's reach out to Rudy or Poofter to look in on Julie."

"Hey, Rudy. Could you do us a kindness, one small favor and swing by Pete's on your way home after closing the store? Please check everything is a-okay?"

In a raspy lisp Boon said, "Hey there, Pete. Rudy here. Everything is copacetic on this end. No need to worry 'bout a thing. Folks be keeping an eye out for your gal. Looks like she has some company and is doing jus' fine. They're unloading cases of cheap wine an having a little party here. A long, sweet Cadillac is parked behind the house."

"A big purple Cadillac?"

Still using the scratchy voice. "Yep, that's the one. Two tone with gray primer on one fender. Big fuzzy dice hanging from the rear view mirror."

Stoic Pete tried to laugh along. A vein pulsed on his forehead, his stew slowly boiling. Apparently jealousy issues were not uncommon on the road away from home.

Boon kept jabbing, pushing buttons. "Them trash bins be overflowing with empty buckets of fried chicken, for sure. Jules will be having a good ol' time."

Finally more than Pete could abide, he lunged for Boon. "Screw you, Boon. That's not cool." They were inches apart, face to face, Pete's fists clenched by his side.

Dempsey and J.C. were closest and quickly converged on Pete, grabbing his arms, holding him back. Boon sat on the log and chuckled awkwardly, the scar on the side of his face turning pink.

"Relax. What's wrong, Petey? Can't take it?"

"Not cool at all, dude. You're crossing a line."

"Oh, get over yourself. I get more shit than anyone. You don't see me crying. Non-stop fellas calling me baboon and monkey boy."

"Don't mess with me, Boon. I'm warning you."

"Gimme a break. We're gone half a day. You're already freaking about getting backdoor-ed by your gal. That's not on me, that's your problem, man."

"That's enough from both of you," J.C. said.

"Seriously, Cracker. You better tell him to cut it out. I'm not kidding." Pete fumed.

"Whatever, dude. Like I said. No one gets more flack than me. One time you get a little bit, you're crying like a baby. How ridiculous."

"Don't mess with me, Boon." Pete shook Dempsey's hands away and stormed off.

"Well, that was fun. Who's got next?" Corndog laughed.

"That was a riot. When is the next showtime?" Lupe enjoyed the entertainment.

"Nice work, Boon. Way to bring everybody together. Great team effort." Dempsey shook his head.

"Whatever, Dempshit."

"You notice Pete didn't get that upset about his girlfriend cheating until thinking it was a bunch of black guys?"

"Dude's a racist. Sure enough."

"No doubt. No other explanation."

"The idea of their gal with a brother always gets 'em. Don't know what it is."

"You guys are assholes," I said.

Jumping from the log, I wandered to the bed area, found a toothbrush in a side pocket of my backpack and brushed teeth. I did not have toothpaste but enough dried residue on the brush delivered some cleaning action. Impressive trees surrounded us, joined by the vast sky full of stars stretching above. The high elevation and our distance from the lights of town and civilization made the stars literally pop and shimmer across the heavens. The night air had a chill. I settled into the paper sleeping bag and soaked the beauty in, trying to remember the names of constellations.

The next morning we ate the same sad sack lunch sandwiches for breakfast, grabbed tools and packs then started hiking. Stew led the way. I was seven back in line, the first Pulaski. The trail wound and curved through countless switchbacks. The back of Stew's boots marching up the mountain were visible to me whenever we rounded a bend. The unyielding pace powered over the steep incline through countless miles, brutal to maintain. The widely held gospel that his legs were built from powerful steel springs resounded in full force climbing this terrain. On especially steep sections, guys resorted to placing hands on each knee and pressing down in an effort to help straighten their own legs, push off the ground and take a step forward up the vicious slope. Stew's boots pounded on, on and on, uphill without pause. A mental picture formed in my mind of John Henry pounding two sledgehammers repeatedly over and over again.

Hours later we finally arrived at the anchor point where we were to begin cutting line. Miles away, the smoke column rose thick and developed, layers of volume shaded black and gray from heavy burning fuels. How far away we were, I could not gauge. Awe inspiring barely describes the expansive and impressive mountains. Amidst the wide open spaces, distances were deceiving. After traveling across country by airplane, then bus and now miles on foot, without ceremony the Supe gave word to do that voodoo, that we do, so well. Chain saws fired up and we started swinging tools and went to work cutting line through the day, past sunset and until midnight. We sacked out on the line with space blankets for cover and backpacks as pillows and slept on rocky dirt until six the next morning. After a quick breakfast of MREs we started again.

The going was not easy either. Interspersed throughout the mountain were buried small boulders. As we swung Pulaskis into dirt, grass and ground cover, with irregular random swings the tool head struck unforgiving rocks. Stopped suddenly against an immovable object, the sound of metal hitting stone rang out. Normally the give of dirt, wooden stumps or roots cushioned somewhat the blunt force of the swinging tool. Collision force would blow back and rattle through the wooden handle and reverberate, shocking your hands and hurting with the violent action and reaction of a moving body wanting to stay in motion. The law of conservation of energy states energy cannot be created nor destroyed. The power and energy a six foot tall man swinging a three foot tool with power in a full arch would come to a savage stop. That energy had to go somewhere. I'm not certain how to figure out tangental force. Using centrifugal force as a guide we would multiply the tool head mass times the velocity squared divided by the radius. With a two meter radius and a five pound tool, if we guess the Pulaski swings 30 miles an hour that works to 13.4 meters per second. Five pounds equals 2.3 kg x (13.4 m/sec x 13.4 m/sec)/ 2 meters = 206 kg m/ sec. Maybe a physics major can explain how the kilogram times meter per second measurement works. I'm an English literature major. The rock will absorb some and maybe my math is off, but a punishing Newtonian force of energy shot into fingers and palms and bounced around in the bones like evil vibrations. Even strong hands took a beating. I don't normally wear gloves and have thick padded calluses. After half the day, the pummeling from damn Montana rock ripped a callus loose off the palm of my left hand. Too late I pulled on a pair of leather gloves to protect them.

Hands were miserable but God's country sure was wide open and beautiful. Gorgeous green woods spread across rugged peaks with sweeping grand vistas topped by an endless insane blue sky. Occasionally I paused to steal a look around to take in the view. Mostly my nose pointed at the ground. The next week consisted of unending brutal work, the whole day long without relief. To make matters worse, the first two day's line cut on that steep ridge did not hold. From a distance away, we watched as the main fire rolled over the ridge leaping and rushing forward. In minutes spot fires jumped ahead and over the line carried by embers in the wind. The first wisp of smoke from a spot rose fifty feet on the lee side of the ridge past the fireline, a solitary stream of white faint amongst the trees. We watched as the smoke trail gained volume, width and expanded. Then other trails appeared nearby and also grew. Soon numerous spots expanded, melded together and become one orange and yellow fire spreading through the green. Flames dashed apart any hope for containment and made a deliberate, steady, but slow run downhill. Burning pine cones and falling branches rolled downward, spreading more fire. Standing quietly a distance away we watched the ridge become engulfed. All the pain and everything we worked for was smack in the middle of burning woods and for nothing.

The next morning we started a new line two ridges over. The Supe could not abide by the folly of our efforts. Frustrated he searched maps trying to figure a suitable logging road or natural barrier we could use to backfire from. Unfortunately the tactics and strategy used in Monterey were not in the cards. We kept going day in and day out, cutting line as best we could. Having earned a nice reprieve from the mesquite and chaparral of the Los Padres, the sawyers' roles consisted of cutting down trees too close to the fire line. After the grind of navigating thick walls of brush, falling massive Ponderosa Pine and Douglas Fir answered the sawyer's dreams. Every sawyer fancies himself a lumberjack. That's why Kingman wore those suspenders. It was definitely not a SoCal beach town thing. In the middle of a heavy duty Rocky Mountain Dry-Mesic Montane mixed Conifer forest, (seriously, look it up) they enjoyed a rare opportunity to cut loose. Each swing of a tool punished us scrapers. The sawyers were dropping trees, having a helluva time.

Gus yelled for attention. We stopped and climbed to a safe zone, super careful in case the holding wood was not cut evenly or another mistake made. If the back cut came at the wrong angle, a falling tree might drift in the wrong direction. You did not risk thinking you could scramble out of the way.

That's how people died. A two hundred foot tree with a three foot radius would demolish a person. Numerous firefighters are tragically struck by falling trees and snags. Our trainings focused on those fatality situations as well. Proper safety procedures were pounded into my head. That said, everyone enjoyed watching a giant tree drop, there being something primal in the event. With Kingman's final back cut complete, Gus pounded wedges to help shift the massive weight forward to lean into the open front pie cut and start the long fall downhill. The remaining holding wood controlled and steered the direction intended for the falling tree. Seeing we were safely out of the way and uphill from their location, Gus pounded one last wedge. Like a cliche he yelled, "Timber." The tip top of the tree began to descend, the movement barely perceptible in slow motion. With the certainty of a second hand on a timekeeper's watch, gravity sucks. Falling forward, the huge tree built momentum and accelerated. The tree's volume made a whooshing sound, creating a sucking wind, moving through the air. The falling giant crashed through surrounding woods, crushing branches and smaller trees in the path, clearing its own way until finally colliding with the ground. Mammoth weight and power expressed tremendous force and violence through a momentous wallop and smashing sounds. Depending on one's proximity to the impact, the fall reverberated in the ground below your feet, waves carrying through the earth.

Sections of the jagged ridge contained innumerable submerged rocks. Guys kept breaking Pulaski heads striking them so hard, something we had not encountered before.

The first time was blamed on the tool's welding. Again and again more broke. Word spread to be careful. A reserve of replacement tools did not live around the corner. Without hand tools we weren't much use to anybody. The metacarpal, phalanx and a mess of other bones in my hands ached from abuse of the past weeks. I grasped the handle loosely, hesitant with each swing to strike the ground with my usual force. Tiredness did not lead to alligator arms but rather leeriness and a desire to minimize pain each time the grub head struck rock.

Except for random moments of excitement watching giant trees fall and strike the ground, cutting line defined wretched. Days ran together in a blur. I choked down MREs or pathetic deli sandwiches on white bread. Even dousing MREs with Tabasco sauce to drown the flavor did not help nor make them more palatable. The so called "meals" were revolting. The worst part was what they did to your system. After two weeks of this grind, I actually daydreamed about canned peaches and drinking the rich, viscous syrup straight from a tin can. Then my thoughts turned to fried chicken. Salt from greasy chicken coated the tongue. Paired with ripe summer watermelon, the juice could run down my chin. I would not even care. Yeah, how pathetic to daydream about food. That's how it was. I found in a side pocket of the backpack a forgotten packet of Beechnut, several months old and far from fresh. I chewed the leaf tobacco anyway and took some comfort for a couple days.

CHAPTER

20

Memories of Janine were my main comfort, long hours spent reliving moments and time together. I'd replay whole days and conversations in my mind.

"I saw you last year. Months before we met."

"Oh yeah. Where?"

"You were at that big park on the Embarcadero across from IV market. A band was playing in the daytime."

"Sunday afternoons bands will play there. That's the Anisq' Oyo park."

"A bunch of tie-dyed hippies were around. One dude with a crazy orange beard and cut-off shorts, twirling around those glass balls they swing around. He had a set in both hands. You were dancing."

"Really? Me dancing in the park. I don't remember. Usually there's some deadhead cover band playing. A bunch of my friends love those guys. I think it's a requirement that you're either high or on L to like the Dead. 'Fire, fire on the mountain.' You'd think I would at least like that song. "

"Definitely it was you. And you were dancing. With cropped short hair and Bermuda shorts, I pointed you out to Elaine. We were up for the day. A reggae band was playing a cover of a Jimi Hendricks song."

"Let me stand next to your fire! I remember that now. I was dancing. They were good."

"Does fire need to be the theme in all your favorite songs?"

"No, but it doesn't hurt. Ha ha. There sure are a lot of fantastic fire songs. "

"I spotted you and thought, he's handsome. The night we first met, I knew it was you."

"Why didn't you say something. Or tell me before?"

"No way. And have you think I'm a stalker, following you? That would not do."

The mischief in her eyes and smile only added to my desire. These feelings were all encompassing and like nothing ever experienced before. Everything inside my core felt fulfilled without strain or effort. I lied on the ground ready for sleep, bones in my hands aching, eyes closed but picturing her and dreaming about the way she looked at me.

CHAPTER

21

The second line did not hold either. Another fire to the south merged with our fire. We were now on an infamous hyphenated fire. Initially named the "Dove Fire," after the "Stovetop Fire" burned through and joined from the south, the two became the "Dove- Stovetop Incident." When merged with yet another fire, which appeared imminent since the whole of western Montana seemed ablaze, we would be renamed the "Dove- Complex." Right now assigned to the two names with hyphen fire, we were encircled by flames on three sides. Grabbing the gear, we marched down the mountain to a safety zone miles away where we paused while the overhead figured a plan for this conflagration mess.

The "Dove- Stovetop Fire" and about twenty others were completely out of control. Some heavy duty brain trusts strategized how to marshal the various resources and contain the worsening situation. Thousands of firefighters spread across the state. Managing the troops and apparatus of the various agencies for that many incidences took organization. We'd been on the line for either eighteen or nineteen straight days, I lost track. A federal law or policy prohibits working twenty-one days without a break. The powers that be decided instead of placing us somewhere only to pull us out a couple days later, we would get two days of R & R now. After a well deserved break they'd deploy us elsewhere.

We staged in the safety zone of a flat marshy meadow. A wide shallow creek ran through the center with black burnt forest surrounding on three sides. Days before the fire burned to the meadow's edge, and still crept slowly around the wet grasses, with faint traces of smoke rising lazily. They picked this spot because the surrounding area burned already and made a perfect safety zone. If the entire forest went to hell and into flames, we could have camped there safely indefinitely with no problem and waited it out.

Late that afternoon the heavy chop chop chop of helicopter rotors came from the east. The welcome sight of a big Chinook helicopter came slowly flying low through the valley. The dull army green blended with the trees blanketing the mountains. When close above, it looked like a large smudge against the crisp blue of Montana sky. The Chinook is a giant helicopter and recognizable by the double rotors. We rolled down long sleeves, raised collars on shirts, pulled down hard hat chinstraps and placed foam ear plugs, finally ready to board the massive aircraft. After weeks in the woods with nothing but hand tools, trees and each other, the powerful army helicopter impressed. Being isolated in wilderness and away from civilization lends itself to a certain frame of mind, mainly being with nature. We worked for the United States Forest Service, a branch of the Federal government. At that moment feeling part of something bigger than ourselves, on our country's team felt pretty cool. I wrote a paper in high school about President Eisenhower's farewell speech warning of the dangers of the military industrial complex. Our excellent teacher Mr. Douthright gave the assignment for government. Some obscene percentage (fifty cents on every dollar) of our taxes fund military spending. Imposing as hell, the Chinook epitomized the strength of our country. After almost three weeks in Somewhere, MT. we were ecstatic to ride out on that fine, powerful aircraft.

The Chinook hovered and took plenty of time to position itself before landing on the creek bed littered with enumerable small, round stones. The rotor wash was savage. Wind gusts buffeted us. The crush of air from two heavy rotors lifted masses of tiny, smooth rocks from the ground. They flew in every direction wildly whizzing by our faces and bodies, striking everyone. The crew ducked heads and shielded faces from the onslaught. Skipping stones rocketed through the air with velocity and hit guys on their sides and legs. We were on the receiving end of a wild rock fight. The strikes definitely smarted. In no hurry either, the Chinook pilot slowly inched downward before finally settling to earth.

After taking a painful shot to the ribs, I exclaimed, "C'mon, dude. Hurry your shit up."

Thankfully the rocks did not seriously injure anyone. The massive helicopter finally settled on four solid rubber wheels, a narrow side door opened and a foldout step ladder rolled down. With tools firmly in hand, leaning forward against the forceful wind and ducking to avoid the heavy rotor whack- whacking, ominous and serious overhead, we filed aboard, scurrying onto the airship. A bench seat lined each side of the helicopter facing each other. We settled on a bench and prepared to lift away. I unslung my pack, placing it on the floor between boots and Pulaski then leaned against the cabin interior. However long the ride, I would be comfortable.

With the cabin doors secure, the Chinook smoothly lifted. If not positioned near a porthole with a view outside, I would never have realized we were airborne, the airship smoothly stable and take off subtle. For a minute I admired the view but then closed both eyes and let myself relax. Physically exhausted, sitting was a rare luxury. With the throbbing thump thump thump of dual rotors as hypnotic symphony, I fell asleep in the seat, head pressed against the side of the cabin and slept through the ride.

CHAPTER

22

Lumpy woke me, shaking my shoulder. I stood without thinking, filed behind the others down the steps, back to safe ground. A painted tin sign on a chain link fence welcomed us to the Helena Regional Airport. The skies glowed eerily, masked by pervasive orange haze. An atmospheric fishbowl, the valley brimmed with gray smoke from countless fires in the surrounding mountains.

The thick air was more warm than comfortable. A chartered school bus soon arrived and drove us to the Harvest Inn motel on the other side of town. Thankfully, the bus carried our travel bags with gear and spare clothes. After almost three weeks in the same clothes, we were downright unmentionable. Even after washing I doubt the socks and underwear would be salvageable. A fresh pack of each was definitely included on the shopping list for the weekend.

Before exiting the bus, the Supe made an announcement.

"Today is Thursday. We are leaving here Saturday morning at oh eight hundred. I repeat, zero eight hundred. That's eight a.m. sharp Saturday morning for the slow ones who don't understand military time. I'm talking to you, Lightning. R & R stands for rest and relaxation. Get some rest and stay out of trouble. No one's gonna come rescue you or search for anyone fool enough to land in the local jail. We're leaving here at oh eight hundred Saturday. If you don't make the bus, as sure as the sun will shine, you can find your own damn way home. Now get out of here. Ya-ta hey."

I shared a room with B.D. on the ground floor of the two story L shaped motel. Although nothing fancy, compared to sleeping on rocks and dirt, the two lumpy twin beds looked like heaven. A television, small table, two chairs filled the room with cheap prints decorating the walls. The bed covers were a hideous pattern of red, orange splashed across purple. The carpet was a comparable matching rust orange. Yellowing beige walls used to be pale. Except for the plain generic ugliness of the room, the worst distinguishing characteristic was a residue and awful smell of cigarette smoke. I surveyed the room, dumped the pack and travel bag to the side of the nearest bed, hustled into the bathroom and turned on the shower.

"Snooze, you lose, Beady!"

The heavenly hot shower had great water pressure. I lathered everywhere. Soon rivulets of brown dirt and grime streaked the white tub. The last haircut more than two months ago, my usually short hair was matted down, tangled, greasy and filthy from eighteen days without a wash. The first dollop from the motel size shampoo container barely produced suds. I rewashed again for good measure. When finished I opened the door and wiped the fogged mirror with a hand towel to shave. My cheeks were gaunt. I looked haggard with eyes sunken in and did not exactly recognize myself with full scruffy black beard. With lighter eyes and longer hair I would have had a Renaissance Jesus look or maybe the dude on the Zig-Zag rolling papers package. Either way, that was not me. I lathered with shaving cream and went to work. Showering first gave the beard a chance to soften. Still painful, two rounds were required to shave clean.

"C'mon Lightning. I got to go."

"No problem, bud." I exited the bathroom with a towel wrapped around my waist. "That was exactly what the doctor ordered."

While B.D. showered I dressed in a pair of Levi's, a Santa Barbara Surf Shop t-shirt, clean socks and the White's boots. I'd have killed for a pair of flip flops or Vans deck shoes and would remind myself to pack some when next we got home. The Whites are awesome and holding strong after the abuse of miles. My poor feet would have appreciated a break from heavy boots.

"Look at you, ready to tear it up? Lumpy and I are in the room next to you."

Pete still wore his greens but carried a twelve pack of Budweiser cans under one arm. A chair propped open the front door to help the cigarette smell dissipate. He grinned and handed over a cold can.

"Come see what else I got."

I followed him outside. Parked in a spot to the left was a plain white four door economy car.

"You rented a car?"

"You know it. We're here two days. Got to roll in style, now. Want to split it with me?"

"Sure. Hell yeah. Pete, that is a smooth move."

"All right then. We have to fill up the gas before turning it in and can work out the money then."

Cold beer carbonation bubbles popped like a breeze on my nostrils. That Bud went down too easy.

"While you clean up, gimme another beer and the keys. Ya-ta hey, now. Let's get out of here. The smell of this fleabag is killing me."

"Okay. No problem," he said, tossing the keys. I pulled another can from the cardboard container and jumped into the driver's seat. A generic domestic sedan would work a heck of a lot better than taking the bus or a taxi if Helena even had them. Helena may not be the biggest city in the world, but having a car opened opportunities for exploration.

With the beer safely between my legs I started the engine, pulled away from the motel lot and turned left onto the street. With no particular place to go, I drove in a big circle, making sure to not get turned around and lose my sense of direction. Keeping the road soda low profile, I checked the sights. Finally spotting a stand alone phone booth in front of a corner liquor store, I pulled in and parked. I was prepared with over two dollars in quarters. Pulling my wallet from the back pocket, I found Janine's number written on the folded tide chart. Standing in Helena, the valley socked with haze, surrounded by barely visible, distant jagged mountains, an ocean tide chart seemed foreign and out of place. We were landlocked. I realized how far from home we were.

Of course, no one was home. The machine Steve's voice answered. I left a fairly long message, explaining that we had been in the backcountry, isolated and nowhere near a phone but were now in town. I would call back again. Not knowing who would hear the message, I did not say everything I'd have liked. Those kind of things are best said in person anyway. After disconnecting the phone, I went into the store and grabbed two twelve packs of Coors Light cans from the cold box and some beef jerky from a plastic container near the register. Wide cut from solid strips of thick beef, the jerky was sweet teriyaki flavored. Jumping back into the rental, I zig-zagged around to get a lay of the town and where the action was. Then I headed to the motel and found some guys in and around Pete's room, some stretched across Lumpy's bed watching the television, others standing around drinking the last of the Buds.

My fresh case of beer elicited a chorus of cheers. Lumpy, Boon, B.D., Corndog, J.C. and Dempsey swooped in, grabbing cold ones. Pete's twelver was dust. They would promptly do a number on my beer too. I figured as much and bought the full case knowing it worked out in the end. Except for Dempsey who conveniently never had any money on him and displayed alligator arms whenever the time came to chip in, the guys were more than generous. We shared everything we had.

For probably the twentieth time again, Pete told everyone about the brawl at the Cold Spring, laughing about what the hell came over me that night. Lumpy chimed in to add detail or affirm a point, giving the story definition. The two gave a pretty fair breakdown of the action as far as I remembered.

"You never said what the hell came over you, Lightning. Did you know those town guys?" Boon asked.

J.C. did not laugh as heartily as everyone else, but looked at me expectantly, waiting for the answer to the question.

"No, I didn't know those dudes. But I did not like them. I especially didn't appreciate them disrespecting Pete. Some people need a little straightening out is all, I guess."

"Well, if you decide to go off like that again, please give some warning. Especially in these hill-billy bars around here."

"I'll be sure to let you know. The world's a tempest. There's a good chance somebody gonna get hit by lightning, right?"

Their expressions looked at me like I was speaking gibberish. Nobody answered.

When finished with the beers, we sauntered over to the diner attached to the motel lobby and ordered dinner. We could look for better food tomorrow. Today this worked fine. A credit on the rooms from a Forest Service account meant we did not have to worry about paying. I had a double bacon cheeseburger, an order of chili fries and a chocolate shake. The meal was far from gourmet. I could go all food critic and expound upon the thinness of the shake and the spongy, weak bun on the burger. In reality that food was light years better than what we'd been choking down the past month. The myth is that death row convicts supposedly order a steak dinner for their "last meal" before the execution. Cheeseburgers are actually the top choice, which makes perfect sense to me. Something about a burger, even from this crappy motel diner, hits the spot.

When finished Wadlow, Boon, Pete, Lumpy and I squeezed into the rental car and hit the town. I called shotgun. Wadlow and Boon are both over six feet. Lumpy naturally got the short stick and had to sit between them. Those three packed into the tight rear seat with knees practically touching their chins was comical. Pete cruised the town looking for a good spot. After a couple songs on the radio Wadlow and Boon begged him to hurry. Circulation in their legs was getting cut off. He pulled into the next tavern parking lot that we saw.

Still daylight out a handful of rummies were sitting inside the dark bar. You knew those men were likely at the same spots each and every day. We rolled in. Everyone in the room paused and subtly both inspected and appeared to ignore us. Boon offered since Pete was smart enough to rent the car, he would buy the first round, undoubtedly a peace offering after their blowup weeks ago. The screen door theme was a common punchline on the road. Since then Boon eased up and did not rip on Pete as much as he could have. Pete proved to be more sensitive than you'd expect. The exposed vulnerability was a revelation. Tough as anyone I've met Pete was not someone to mess with. He lifted weights and could bench press a hundred pounds more than he weighed. Though not huge, he was powerful for his size and no slouch. As brutal and cold blooded as guys could be, there was a fine line and a dance between goodnatured needling and vicious, straight up mean. That line was not frequently crossed.

We stayed at the tavern for several rounds until Wadlow suggested we find someplace more alive. There was a pool table and the jukebox played some decent selections. But a layer of dust covered the interior. Dank air was marked by the smell of stale beer. More significantly, besides the bartender and rummies clutching thin glasses of draft beer and well drinks, we were the only life in the joint. Even if this was Montana, some women had to be breathing somewhere in this town. We settled the bill, piled into the rental and went in search of better spot.

Good thing too. About a mile down the way, we found a large neon sign signaling The Copper King and a much more happening bar with a wide full parking lot of cars and a pack of motorcycles in front. The far livelier crowd inside was a mix of bikers and what looked like genuine cowboys. When we rumbled in, a wave of energy welcomed. The bartender picked us out as firefighters immediately and ringing an old railroad bell behind the bar said the first round was on the house. We each took down a shot of Yukon Jack. I don't know whose brilliant idea that was. One hundred proof, sickly, sweet Canadian whiskey is nothing but a recipe for trouble. A beer chaser to follow the shot was surely the right call though. Fuzzy state MT. was calling. We were helped along by the enumerable grateful Copper King patrons buying rounds. Quickly my sense of time and place jumbled together. With fires burning across the state, the positive reception and response to our being firefighters was unanimous. The whole heroes' welcome thing was pretty darn cool, I will admit.

I grabbed a spot at a curve on the bar with my back to the wall and a view of the whole bustling scene. Stuffed buffalo heads and impressive elk were mounted on the walls along with numerous vintage Colt pistols and Winchester goldboy carbines. Vintage photos, posters and a number of large framed oil copies of Remington and Charles M. Russell paintings covered every corner. At one end of the room a fully stuffed grizzly bear posed in a fierce stance staring at the room belligerently. Interspersed across the heavy wooden beams of the ceiling were solid steel bear and other hunting traps along with several pairs of snowshoes and ancient wooden skis. The bar itself was fifty feet wide and built of heavy dark wood and probably over a hundred years old but well preserved. An antique mirror on the wall behind the bartender reflected the whole room with a slight haze from years of use. The best part, this place was clean and didn't reek of cigarette smoke and desperation. Well, maybe second best. The best thing was there were women here and plenty of them. Cowgirls, biker chicks and regular gals and a lot of them, every one seeming to bounce around festively. Loud honky-tonk music played. The drinks flowed and the hours passed. I sat in one comfortable spot enjoying the scenery and people in fine fettle, talking and friendly. I got nicely soused, thank you very much.

A five piece country bar band set up and began playing music with a roadhouse rocker sensibility. Music I'd describe as having a solid honky tonk, Dwight Yoakam vibe. To the right of the big open room people sat in wooden chairs circled around small round tables enjoying themselves with a view of the shiny dance floor built from smooth, wide wooden planks. People danced and crowded the floor. In the very center thick of the mix bopping about, Wadlow towered over a group of three gals. I hoped no locals got upset with him cause it was not his fault. He could not help that women loved him so much. Thankfully nobody's girlfriend did anything to cause trouble. We were happy to be "one of those California firefighters" and that be a positive. The last thing anyone needed was to deal with an angry bunch of pissed off, heavy duty bikers.

You had to love Wadlow too. He knew from experience that too much of a good thing could be trouble. From across the room he motioned to Boon and pointed in my direction. Boon grabbed and dragged me, working his way through the crowd onto the dance floor with them. So I danced with those two and three local girls. The band played that quick tempo country music. I am by no stretch of imagination even a middling "two stepper." No one cared. We danced song after song. Dancing helped work the booze through the system too, clearing my head. Sloppy enough to not worry about being such a lousy dancer, I had fun. Lean, fit and a foot shorter than me, my partner had shoulder length, straight brown hair and glittering, hazel eyes. Her attractive freckled face had a fun smile with wide, red lips and straight white teeth. She wore a checkered shirt, faded blue jeans and bright red cowboy boots. An excellent dancer she took both my hands in hers and expertly steered and directed me through the moves and smoothly made it appear as if I were leading and semi-knew what I was doing. The opposite was true. I focused on my partner, whose name was Lisa, and tried to keep pace with the different moves and constant spins. Boon and his new friend were grooving along. He had a big chimpanzee smile on his face, clearly having a blast.

Lisa and I danced through the whole set until the band announced they were taking a break. Sitting down at an open table, we caught our breath. Wadlow disappeared somewhere with his date. Boon and his dance partner joined us. We flagged down a cocktail server and ordered a round of beers. Boon's gal Tara was attractive too, and athletic looking. For the first time we were able to actually hold a conversation. They were both in the army and stationed at a base about a hundred miles north.

"I had no idea the army recruited such smoking hot babes." Boon-dog going for the close early.

"Well, the Forest Service ain't too shabby from where we're sitting either." Tara was game.

"Is there some height requirement with you guys?" Lisa asked me. "The three of you are at least six three, six four. What's up with that?"

"We do have a bunch of tall dudes on the crew. It's just a coincidence."

"Maybe there's something in the water in California. Or could be the orange juice."

"Could be." I smiled, sipping my beer.

We danced when the band started again after the break. Hours later the crowd started to thin out. I realized the rest of the guys vanished and left us there. Lisa said not to worry, it'd be no problem to give us a ride to the motel. We agreed to grab breakfast first. Heading outside to the parking lot and their little import, the four of us drove around Helena looking for an all night diner. I sat in back with Lisa. Boon fiddled with the radio searching for some decent music and finally found George Strait's "The Fireman". I never heard the song before. Boon and the two girls apparently loved it. Together they sang the lyrics. Of course, I enjoyed the firefighting angle and will admit it was catchy. Being a beach kid, the whole country western thing is lost on me. I sat next to Lisa and watched them three sing and bop in their seats, enjoying the moment. The mantra about when in Rome fit this situation plenty.

A little after two a.m. we finally found a well-lit twenty-four hour diner and crowded into a cozy booth with red Naugahyde seats and ordered a fine midnight feast. I had a double chili cheeseburger with chili fries, a chocolate shake and a chocolate sundae with a brownie. The girls each ordered a stack of pancakes. Boon had eggs with french toast. Tara also ordered a large appetizer to share of Idaho style finger steaks, deep fried beef strips served with ranch dressing. Dancing up a storm helped clear the head, but I was still a little sloshed. The finger steaks came out sizzling hot and delectable. A steady diet of them would surely lead to a heart attack. Nothing works like a solid dose of sizzling grease to help absorb alcohol in the system and set you straight. They laughed at my double chocolate program. After weeks of horrible meals ready to eat, I was treating myself.

"I bet you've seen some crazy fires. What's the hairiest scene you've been in?" asked Lisa.

"Yeah, tell us a good story," said Tara.

"Heck yeah, we have seen a ton of fire. But I've never been worried. Our Supe keeps us out of trouble, no question." I poured milk and sugar into a cup of coffee turning it light brown.

"What about the Canyon Creek fire?" Boon asked. "Weren't you all 'running to the meadow'? "

"That's just B.D. popping off. We did not run anywhere." Then speaking to the girls, "That fire was a couple years ago, the season before Boon joined the crew. It was north of here, actually not far away."

"What was special about Canyon Creek?"

"You're familiar with how the jet stream works? TV weather newscasts always show graphics on their reports. It's the major air flow that pushes weather systems east. The stream is a powerful current, something like a hundred miles wide and three miles tall. Have you ever flown back east? You know how flying to the east coast is an hour shorter than flying from east to west? The airline pilots ride the current east and get a boost from the flow. The jet stream is a big river of air flowing across the country high in the atmosphere."

Boon gave me a look to hurry with the meteorology lesson.

"On this Canyon Creek fire, the jet stream that is normally four to seven miles high in the atmosphere touched down smack in the middle of our fire. A gigantic God sized bellows blew on the forest fire. It just freaking went off."

"Like a tornado?"

"Not exactly, but kind of. The jet stream's high velocity air current blew volumes of oxygen rich air, stoking the embers and flames to remarkable levels. The fire was already fifty or so thousand burning acres and absolutely blew up. The weather forecasts predicted the jet stream touching down way ahead of time. We hiked out and were fine in the safety zone but were airlifted out. The view from the helicopter was like nothing I've ever seen."

I'm normally not the biggest talker and took a sip of coffee to catch a breath.

"We were evac-ed out on a Puma helicopter. That was one bitchen 'copter. Powerful and cool looking. We piled in general admission style without real seats. I was by the porthole and the view was something out of Milton's *Paradise Lost*. Two hundred foot flame lengths were leaping above two hundred and three hundred foot tall trees. The whole valley, across miles and miles as far as you could see, was burning. Flaming gas balls ignited in the sky, literally combusting from oxygen in the air, bursting into flames. Fire traveled and burned more than twenty-one miles in five hours. We had a view of an entire valley wide with trees, covering acres and acres of forest, fully involved orange and like a scene from a movie. That was something. The fire burned one hundred and seventeen thousand acres in under a day."

The three of them looked at me as I searched for words to describe the destruction. The numbers were hard to register.

"The Canyon Creek fire. You can look it up."

"There was not any 'run to the meadow' ?"

"No way. Can you imagine the Supe putting us in that situation, with that nonsense? We were safe the whole time. And thankfully, I don't think anybody, firefighter or civilians were hurt on the fire either. Which is amazing because that was some crazy shit. Three, four hundred foot flames leaping to the sky. Talk about insane."

We pulled into the motel after four. Boon invited the girls to join us in the room for one more frosty. I had stashed some beers under a towel on ice in the bathtub. They were game. Everything super smooth and easy, until I opened the door with B.D. sleeping there, snoring away. The whole thing fell apart. Looking around, the motel lights were all off and rooms quiet. We were the last awake, still partying.

"We can kick him out. It's cool. He can go to my room." Both women looked at Boon then each other and simultaneously shook their heads.

"I don't think so. We have to get back to the base. It's over an hour drive."

Tara took Boon by the hands and reversed, walking him to the car. They kissed there, standing and leaning against the driver's side door.

Lisa smiled sweetly. "You are really nice. Tonight was a blast. I had a great time."

Out of practice, I shuffled in place, unsure what to do. If I wanted to hook up, telling Lisa I had a girlfriend probably wasn't the sharpest move. At the diner, she asked the question and I told her about Janine. I've never been a liar and didn't see a reason to be less than honest. Janine was still my girl, even if a thousand miles away and we were "separated" like Boon helpfully volunteered. Lisa was super cool and had a rocket body. I would have loved to roll around with her. Trust me, I'm not exactly Joe Puritan with a rock in a shoe for my sins. If we could have rousted B.D. and settled in that hideous room with matching twin beds, I would not have hesitated. Those bed springs would have made beautiful music. We'd have enjoyed ourselves very much. But I would not be dishonest in order to make that happen.

"You be careful out there, Mr. Fireman," Lisa said, bouncing up to give me a hug. She smelled nice. Not more than a hundred and fifteen pounds, Lisa felt sturdy and lithe in my arms. I squeezed her back.

"You be careful too, soldier girl."

The two women drove away, leaving Boon and me standing in the thick gray of false dawn. We silently watched as their car rounded the corner, rear lights fading from our line of sight and leaving us. We looked at each other. Boon shook his head.

"Damn B.D., Brain Dead, D.B. Dirt Bag. Cramping our style. That Tara was smoking hot. I've half a mind to throw his ass in the pool right now for messing our action up."

As much as that appealed to me and sounded like a good idea, I reconsidered. "We're good, Boon. Let's go to bed."

He nodded and did not say anything in return but walked to his room. I did not bother turning on the light but simply undressed in the dark and pulled aside the purple plaid covers and jumped between the cool, clean sheets of the lumpy bed. Pleased with how the night went down, I rolled onto one side and could faintly smell Lisa's perfume on the inside of one arm from holding her at the end. I thought about the night, replaying every moment, trying not to forget the details.

CHAPTER

23

I slept until almost noon and laid around the tiny pool in the center of the courtyard for a couple hours, swimming some and soaking in needed vitamin D onto this scary, white-boy body. I hardly recognized my reflection in the mirror. The guys commandeered the deep end of the pool and enjoyed cold beers while hanging around. A quick benefit, the shampoo effect delivered a nice daytime buzz in the noon hour. When Pete arrived with the car, I jumped in and we ran a couple errands. First we found a bank machine for cash. Then shopping at a corner five and dime department store, I bought a package of cotton tube socks as well as a value pack of five boxer shorts. Restocking undies was crucial. Mine from the first weeks in Montana were beyond redemption and probably against the law in several states. I threw the dirty ones away, burying them deep in the trash hamper like evidence from a crime scene.

At seemingly every intersection Pete would yank the "e" brake and pull a power slide, turning the corner like we were driving an ATV quad, getting sideways. Our good luck held. When a police cruiser finally stopped us, the road sodas were finished and the empties just tossed. Pulling into the motel parking lot, Johnny Law looked us over the way cops do. He gave Pete a warning and said to be careful and watch out.

That night we went out again. This time was more steady and under control than the night before. I called Janine from a payphone outside the restaurant where we had dinner and was ecstatic when her voice answered the phone. A little buzzed but super happy to finally get her on the line, effusive me stumbled describing how happy I felt to speak with her. After weeks without talking, the conversation ran into some bumps. Several patches of silence interrupted with neither of us knowing what to say next. She did not understand why I did not call sooner and could not grasp the idea there simply were no phones in the middle of the forest. Janine wondered aloud why I did not make a better effort to find one and call her. That we were surrounded by nothing except miles and miles of trees and not near a phone for weeks on end did not compute. Although Janine never accused me of lying, I had the distinct impression she did not believe me. My conscience was clear about partying with Lisa the night before. I wondered if Janine, like most girls, could be part witch and sense through her female paranormal extra-sensory perception something was up. But nothing was up, so that did not make sense. If she were part witch, wouldn't the ESP powers tell her nothing happened? Who knew. A sense of relief arrived for both ends of the phone line when I ran out of change and time ran out. We had to end the call.

Everything would be better when I got home, I promised and believed it too. I forgot to mention speaking with the Supe about my plans to enroll in the fall quarter of school. Fire season would be over for me shortly. A week earlier at a particularly low point when really miserable, I confirmed with the Supe what we discussed in Big Sur driving for that cortisone shot. One hundred percent supportive he judged returning to college unequivocally the right call. Not to worry, they would save a spot for me next year, no question. That made me feel good. As much as the idea bothered me to be running out on the guys, I needed to get serious about my studies. Heading back to Janine was an added bonus. The plan was not about her, I lied to myself.

We found the way back to the Copper King. The bar bustled like before with more of the crew joining in. We rallied hard and started right where we left off. But the scene lost a little luster, missing some of last night's magic, at least for me. Maybe not being three sheets to the wind played a part in my now sober mentality. The room of animated faces, abuzz with loud music, resembled watching a rerun of a television show already seen. Of course light years better than being stuck, spiked out on the fireline, the Copper King lacked last night's sense of unexpected adventure and excitement, as if we'd heard this song before.

I sat with J.C. in the corner of the bar. We nursed drinks and quietly took in the rambunctious crowd.

"Damn, you fellas were on fire last night. Those gals you pulled out of here were the goods." The bartender nodded appreciatively.

"They were pretty cute, huh." I said, brightening.

"That's an understatement. Those two wouldn't have anything to do with anyone until you guys came in. I was impressed."

"Look at you, Lightning. You said they weren't bad. Didn't realize you were playing all cool."

"Cracker, please. You should know 'not bad' really means 'pretty damn smoking hot'."

And with that I signaled for a round of Yukon Jack shots and beer chasers. We joined the mix. Too much thinking should be outlawed, bucket head, I told myself. Snapping into shape, nothing would stop us from taking full advantage of and enjoying the last night of R & R.

CHAPTER

24

Everyone made the bus on time. Chipper and all smiles, the Supe hoped we were able to call home and tell our girlfriends how much we missed them. Red eyes and quiet demeanors were prevalent, everyone more than a bit ragged. Once the bus pulled away from the motel, heads either leaned on the seat in front or against the window to the side. Within minutes most everyone was back asleep. We were veterans of going for hours without rest. The ability to quickly grab moments of shut eye whenever possible proved a necessary and valuable skill, particularly when dragging like this morning.

I slept most of the trip but awoke as we rolled into the major fire camp set in a low valley at the base of mountains in the Flathead National Forest. Literally thousands and thousands of firefighters were deployed to a portable city with tents upon tents organized to house and feed the masses. Army vehicles rumbled by transporting crews with exhaust pipes belching gross diesel fumes. The camp even posted cardboard signs with "street" names and arrows pointing directions to the mess tent, showers and other points of interest. It was one major clusterf@*k of a tent city. Port-o-potty's and diesel smudge pots were spaced around everywhere. I even noticed a bank of portable telephones in a row at one corner location. At least we'll be able to call home.

Stumbling from the bus, the pleasant surprise of our friendly old crew buggies greeted us. Masses of green Forest Service vehicles were everywhere, parked throughout the camp. I immediately recognized these special rigs by the telltale LP crest logo on the sides and rear and Crew Four markings on the bumpers. They were shipped from Santa Barbara on a lowboy diesel big-rig. Seeing the boombox on a seat in the rear cab, I realized for the first time how much our music and soundtrack tunes had been missing.

We marched to the mess tent for lunch. Even in the middle of day people packed the camp. The lines were huge. Who is fighting the fire? I thought to myself. Waiting I took a gander at the other firefighters around and was surprised how many American Indian crews there were. The Native Americans were universally lean and athletic looking with dark angular features and black straight hair. One crew captain or squad boss carried himself like a boss duck. Endowed with a huge belly, he stuck out from the others who looked like marathon cross country runners. Each person grabbed a sack lunch and must have been heading for the fireline. The big one grasped three bags from the box and kept going. I heard a guffaw and something about a three lunch belly from the group of Native Americans behind us in the chow line. They laughed heartily. I caught the eye of one who looked about my age and height and nodded. He returned my smile and we shared in the joke.

Behind us were firefighters from somewhere in the South discussing whether or not there'd be grits in camp. They went on and on about the grits and would not stop. The line took forever. I have never had grits and don't know if they are good or bad. The way the southerners went on and on, they better be worth the fuss. After thirty minutes, we could not get the hell away from fire camp, people and back into the woods fast enough for me.

Fish, fish I got my wish. At four a.m. we were rousted from sleep and assigned to structure protection on a group of houses bordering the northern edge of the forest. We rolled from sleeping bags, shaking sleep away and loaded into our comfy rigs in nothing flat. With engines idling, we sat in the dark waiting to get going. Corndog found a Talking Heads cassette and played "Burning Down the House", probably not the most sensitive song to blast considering the circumstances. Hopefully no one worried about losing their home and life's possessions heard. In fire camp, at four o' dark thirty, the tune worked to get everyone charged up and ready to go.

301

We cleared brush around several houses that day. I have no idea if our efforts saved those homes or not. I would sure like to think so. The next day we headed back to the remote back country. We drove for hours, parked the rigs in a shallow, rock covered stream and started hiking. I've talked about hiking and believe I have explained how much we hiked. That day was something else. It was as if Stew was pissed at the world or had something to prove. He powered through at the most epic death march pace I ever witnessed. After the first couple miles, when guys started to realize that we were far from our destination, resignation gripped everyone. We were in for it. People breathed deeply as if on a hard training run, something you did not often hear. The mountain gained elevation. The trail followed the ridge line and kept going and going for eternity. Remarkable forests surrounded us in four directions, majestic, rugged country visible as far as the eye could see. No one gave the scenery a second thought. We were either looking down at the boots of the guy in front or focused on his backpack rocking with each step, trying to put the pain in legs and lungs out of mind.

"Boom, boom, long time." B.D. piped in. B.D. stood for brain dead. One funny character with great comic timing, he was absolutely hilarious. He intended to take his own mind off the hurt by distracting everyone from the pain we all felt, but quickly grew short on breath and could not continue the monologue. It was the thought that counted.

Finally after an agony we arrived at the destination. Waiting for us was an old salty, prospector looking man with a long bushy gray beard, wearing a wide flat brimmed cowboy hat. Mounted on a tall handsome black horse, he led a team of a dozen mules. The mules carried packs loaded with plastic wrapped packages of explosives that looked like fifty foot lengths of big orange sausage coiled in a tight roll. They were an inch and a half in diameter and made from a water gel emulsion called Fire Line Explosive. Imagine a semi-pliable dynamite that was stable, could be stretched out across various types of terrain, then connected together. Each roll weighed about thirty-five pounds. Our job was take over for the mules and unwind the F.L.E. where we wanted fireline. The old timer connected pieces together by the ends with special tape. When one half mile was joined as one and stretched across the target line, he attached exploding bridge wires that were safe around radios. We covered up a safe distance away, shielded from falling rocks and debris. Salty triggered the ignition and blew the whole thing away. The explosion ripped through and tore apart the landscape disrupting roots, grass and flammable material across the path. The momentary blast was so much more productive than struggling by hand through the brutal rocky Montana landscape. With this relatively safe and pliable explosive we blew away fire line faster than anything possible with hand tools. We successfully exploded miles and miles of line in a single day.

The next few days were incredible. We traveled through some of the most rugged country imaginable, unrolling the fire line explosive as we went. Standing on the ridge, beautiful and majestic forests surrounded us for hundreds of miles in every direction, not a person or sign of civilization visible as far as you could see. At one point we were on the edge of a cliff, staring down a sheer rock face. It reminded me of a scene from the movie *Butch Cassidy and the Sundance Kid*. Surrounded by a posse of lawmen, they need to jump from a cliff into a river to escape. Sundance is hesitant and finally admits he can't swim. The Paul Newman character laughs. It's the fall that's gonna kill you. Lugging the package down the sheer embankment, unrolling the orange F.L.E. sausage with one hand, I grasped the rocky outcrop with all my might and inched down the steep incline a little at a time like a stink bug. Although happy to avoid pain and brutality against my hands swinging the Super P into rocks like a work camp prisoner, vertigo was no picnic either. I momentarily questioned the wisdom of our path.

We finally stretched out almost a mile of explosive. The order came to duck down, grab cover and protect ourselves. The old timer wired in the blasting caps and detonated the lengthy line. The explosive went off, sending dirt and rock flying in the air like a gaseous earthen cloud in a mile long curtain. The percussion wave hit with a clamor. The force of the explosion knocked on my chest. Earlier I wrote about the kick from watching mammoth trees get cut down. The destruction from these explosions took that primal feeling to a new level. We loved watching stuff blown to smithereens. Killer was in high heaven. While not a demolition specialist back in the military, he sure had the aptitude and propensity for it.

Days went by in a blur. The fire grew exponentially as more and other fires merged together. The whole complex became shaped like a giant Kraken with tentacles branching in multiple directions, compounding the difficulties of containing the massive blaze. We were assigned to a different area and went back to cutting line by hand. The unending labor wore on like purgatory. A couple guys grew sick. Looking around at everyone, it was easy to see why. We were plumb worn out. Eyes were sunken in and cheeks haggard. The flight weights printed on the brim of each person's hardhat were easily ten to fifteen pounds more than our current weight.

I started to feel ill too and loaded myself with non-drowsy Alka Seltzer cold medicine mixed in a quart canteen. Getting ready that morning, J.C. said I looked like hell, to take it easy and stay with the crew buggies for the day. I shook the notion off and stumbled along, taking my usual position in line and hiked with everyone. Swinging a tool, I was pitifully weak and more gravity flow candidate than ever in my history. I powered on though and did not stop. An extra dose of cold medicine made my heart race. Returning to camp that night, I bundled in the sleeping bag and slept through dinner.

Thankfully I felt marginally better the next day. Although weaker than my normal self, the worst was past. I never tapped out nor sat a day. One morning a week later hiking to the line, the Killer's radio crackled. He stopped and we paused en masse. The volume was on low. From fifteen feet away I heard the Supe across the airwaves say my name.

"Curt," the Killer proclaimed. "Today's your lucky day. There's a truck waiting back at camp to take you to town so you can catch an airplane ride to Santa Barbara. You're headed home. Ya-ta-hey, better git now and hightail back ASAP."

Voices murmured, but I didn't grasp his message, the words not sinking in.

"F me. Why's he get to go?"

"Lucky duck."

"Have one for me when you get to town, bro."

"That sucks. Adios, cock sucker."

"Try and learn something in school, you stupid bastard."

The news sunk in. I was going home. Like sunlight parting clouds in my head, Killer's words finally made sense. Better git now and hightail back ASAP. The notion the plane might leave without me on board set off inner alarm bells. On one heal I reversed direction and started towards camp walking past the fourteen guys in line behind me. About thirty feet beyond the last of the crew, I stopped and paused, turning around.   Everyone remained standing there, silently watching me walk away.

"Hey fellas." Twenty faces looked at me expectantly. I did not say anything else, but dropped the Super P's tool head to the ground. Stepping on the metal hoe end with one boot to keep the wooden handle vertical, I raised both free hands chest high and gave everyone the bird. Two birds rather. Double middle fingers. I don't know why that seemed an appropriate and fitting salute, but that's what I did.

"Fuck you too, buddy," Robbie Wadlow said laughing.

"Yeah, fuck you very much, Lightning," Pete said.

"You see how fast he was moving? Didn't think he had it in him."

"Slow ass molasses bastard. Better get going, you're gonna miss that plane."

J.C. did not say anything but gave me the hang loose symbol in return. With that I turned again, started downhill and hiked to camp by my lonesome. The morning had a chill in the air, the warming sun still low in the huge sky. Days were getting shorter. Supposedly a snowstorm might actually be on the horizon soon, welcome talk since the common belief was we would be stuck here forever. This fire would not be completely extinguished until there was snow on the ground. But not me. I was headed home.

CHAPTER

25

When I made camp no one was there. The driver arrived a half hour later carrying another firefighter. I loaded my travel gear into the pickup bed and joined them in the cab. We drove for hours to the Missoula airport sitting three across the front bench seat. I lost any sense of place a long time ago and have no idea where we were, but sat silently looking out the window. We drove over narrow bridges and down a windy, curving road that followed a thin, blue river through thick green forests. I marveled to be on the way, going home. For a while a voice in the back of my head said school would be starting shortly, but did not put two and two together. In fact, school was starting next week. Since the driver informed me today was Thursday, leaving now made complete sense.

The driver dropped us at the airport and pointed to an operations manager who showed where to wait. After the hurry and rush to return to camp, predictably we waited around most of the day until late that afternoon when we were joined by another group of firefighters. The six of us flew to Redding, California on a ten seat turbo prop airplane. The flight was bumpy, particularly right after take off. Momentarily claustrophobic, I wondered about our oxygen in the cabin. How safe could we be in this narrow tube hurtling through the air? In Redding the others caught another plane to their home base. The flight to Santa Barbara would not leave until ten o'clock the next morning. The Forest Service reserved a motel for me in town. I caught a ride there via a shuttle van, checked in and walked the stairs to a single room on the second floor. Opening the door, the room smelled of Lysol and bleach. The curtains were open. The evening sun shined through the window and bathed the plain room in soft yellow light. I threw the travel bag on the floor, rolled onto the single bed and barely exerted enough energy to unlace the boots and kick them off. Pulling the covers to my chin still dressed in shirt, pants and socks, I closed both eyes and went right to sleep.

I slept for almost twelve hours and woke at six-thirty in the morning. It was gray out the window and quiet. Completely alone for the first time in months, no snoring or grunting hotshots were nearby. With no cursing nor laughing, the silence boomed different and strange. I laid in bed soaking in the stillness. Rolling over onto both feet, I took off socks and dirty clothes and jumped into the shower. Standing under the hot water for probably twenty minutes, I scrubbed and lathered my entire body, from the soles of the feet to my matted down long hair. First thing after breakfast would be to find a barber. Get a haircut and get down to business.

I dressed in the cleanest clothes I could find in the travel bag, packed again and went out for breakfast. After a lumberjack special of a thick slice of ham, three eggs, toast, grilled potatoes and coffee, I wandered the neighborhood on foot until finding an old school barber shop with a cream colored linoleum floor and two vintage green, barber chairs. On one wall hung a framed Winchester poster with an actual round attached of every rifle and handgun cartridge ever produced. The barber in his late sixties with a severe gray crewcut looked capable. A faded green tattoo of an anchor adorned his forearm. Plus, four bucks was a good deal. I asked for a forward brush cut. Short but don't make me look like a jarhead. Sure enough, the buzzers quickly worked their magic. I did not look at the reflection in the mirror when he was done, but simply ran fingers through the scalp and over the head, happy with the cropped, tennis ball fuzzy outcome.

I made the airport with over an hour to spare and waited patiently until they directed me to a little four-seater prop plane. Just me, the pilot and the non-stop hum of the engine, the flight lasted three hours. We cruised along through the central valley most of the way. Riding that little plane was like floating along like a leaf in the breeze. After the deep rich greens of Montana timber forests, I marveled at the barren dry, dun and brown grasslands below. Even the sky seemed less vibrant and bleached of color. We headed west and crossed over the Caliente range and then the San Rafael mountains. The motor whined louder gaining in elevation. When the choppy blue of the Pacific came into view through the haze in the distance, I knew we were almost home. The pilot spoke via the radio with the control tower. The whole of the University and the jumble of Isla Vista were spread below like little rectangular models. We cruised right in, gliding through the air, approached the runway and touched down with two soft bumps. When the plane came to a stop, I extracted myself from the harness, climbed onto the ladder and stepped to firm ground. After almost two months on the road, I was finally home in Santa Barbara.

A lady from the regional office waited in a green Blazer to drive me to the ranger station and hotshot barracks. Rolling down familiar roads and over the pass was strangely surreal. That feeling became pronounced after she dropped me at the flag pole in front of the office. Standing there with travel bag at my feet, the still dry air possessed weight. Echoes of quiet were broken by the buzz of countless insects. Pickups and vehicles filled the parking lot, patiently waiting for the guys. The buildings in the hotshot compound possessed sharp edges and a strange deserted quality like walking through a ghost town. I half expected someone to be in the Supe's office or working in the tool bay. There was no one around. I was alone.

The GPZ clicked and started without hesitation. I could not get away from the empty hotshot compound fast enough and was soon cruising down the road, over the pass and homeward. It felt like cheating and wrong to be home early without everyone else. Although pleased to be home, something was not one hundred percent right. My conscience twinged with guilt and maybe a touch of regret. Singing a couple lines from "The Boys are Back in Town" to myself, the words rang tinny and hollow.

Without a cloud in the sky, the motorcycle purred and was my company tearing down the road. Under the harsh glare of sunlight the landscape and buildings looked washed out and bleached. Soon I rode through campus, the little section of "S" turns, past the on-campus dorms and into town. The energy in the air was a welcome greeting entering Isla Vista. The student ghetto bustled with people unloading cars of clothes and furniture, carrying possessions upstairs and down the street, moving into apartments. People were riding bikes, walking about, and cruising by on skateboards. The population must have quadrupled since I was last home. The positive exuberance and optimism from the influx of new and returning students looking forward to the new year was a tonic and helped clear away the mental phantoms of the crew I was missing.

Ben, Chris and Marco gave me an uplifting greeting. Marco is short and gregarious, built like a stocky bear. I had not seen him since May. He gave me a huge hug and high five. Thankfully the ridiculous remnants and notions of regret at leaving the crew were officially and effectively banished. They evaporated away.

"Everybody's here. This is cause for celebration," Ben proclaimed. "I say we get some beers and fire the barbecue. I'm for cooking a feast."

"That is music to my ears," I replied. "I have to head downtown for a little bit, but can I give you money to buy whatever you need? I haven't had a decent meal in seems like forever."

"You going to see Jaybird?" Chris asked.

""Oh yeah. I thought I'd surprise her at that store she's working at."

"She came around a couple times when you were first gone. We haven't seen her in a while."

"Did you see some crazy stuff?" Marco asked. "You burn down some forests?"

"Those fires in Montana were all over the news. We looked for you whenever they came on."

"Yeah, we saw some fire. Nothing too crazy through. We spiked out in the back country, probably a hundred miles from a news crew. We did demolish a bunch of line with fire line explosives. That was cool."

"Ha, not content with being a regular pyro, now you're blowing stuff up too?" Marco was a transplant from near New York somewhere and a computer major. He thought I was half crazy.

A constant stream of people rode by on bicycles or walking. A large group of coeds were playing volleyball in the park. The sound of the ball getting smacked and spiked carried across the street. The players whooped and hollered whenever there was a good rally. From an open window of the apartment complex down the street, a stereo loudly blasted new modern music. The song had a catchy melody with a driving chorus. I immediately liked it. Hearing a great new song the first time is the best. As much as I appreciate the classics and all genres, today's music is current and relevant right now. The song was probably a big hit the past summer and I was late to the party, Montana fireline not exactly the hub for modern music.

I showered again washing away any residual grime from dusty clothes. The last of the Montana dirt and trail dust circled down the drain. I was clean and refreshed. With the exception of both forearms which were deep tan, the torso and even my legs were frighteningly pale. Instead of cargo shorts I pulled on a pair of jeans and a short sleeve collared red and gold plaid shirt. I was pleased with the haircut from this morning. It was basic short and not the hippest cut. Admiring the reflection in the mirror staring back at me, I cleaned up pretty good. A healthy dose of aftershave slapped onto both cheeks guaranteed I'd smell nice too.

Smooth could only describe the twenty-six minute ride downtown. I zoomed easily in and out of the fast lane, riding the highway stripe, slipping past cars and traffic. Nothing would delay me from seeing my girl. I parked the cycle in a parking structure a half block from State Street and sauntered down the sidewalk to the woman's clothing store where she worked.   My heart fluttered like a bird, the anticipation building to a crescendo. Like a river time flowed steadily forward. On the surface I rushed onward.   When I opened the door and walked into the store, everything paused a beat and went into slow motion. I felt weightless like a jumper after deploying a parachute, each moment a frame of a photo frozen and extracted from a motion picture film.   No customers were inside the boutique.   Janine sat behind the counter peacefully flipping through a magazine. Techno house music played softly in the background.   I soaked her in for delicious seconds before she raised her eyes and looked at me. A moment passed before reality sank in. Then she recognized that it truly was me. The expression on her face brightened and shifted, in a split second ran a range of emotions from joy to surprise and confusion. I casually floated towards the counter, watching her face the whole time.

"Oh. You're here."

She stood and glided around the counter towards me.   A skydiver's peaceful descent through the air cannot last. Suddenly the ground comes rushing in.   We hugged, her body warm and right in my arms. I squeezed tight.

"Hey, you. I'm home now for keeps. My fire season is over."

"That's great. When did you get home?"

"Earlier today. I flew special delivery. The Supe arranged travel so I can start school next week."

"Very cool. I'm glad you're home."

"Me too. I came here first thing. I missed you."

"I missed you too. You were gone a long time."

"No doubt. Too long. You look good. Good enough to eat." And she did. Janine wore an electric blue top and white shorts made from a light and flowing fabric. The modern decor of the shop was spare and clean. The boutique struck me as very high-end. She looked to fit in perfectly. Her face was beautiful with defined cheekbones and full lips, her makeup subtle, but well done. The gold flecks in her eyes flashed. The blue irises looked purple, different than the color I memorized and thought about so much.

"What time do you get off? We're gonna barbecue. Ben's fixing a feast."

"We close at seven."

"You should come by then."

"Um. I can probably swing by for a little while." Two women entered the shop. Her eyes looked to the door and then met mine again. She was so pretty I found it hard to think.

"Okay. We'll see you after 7:00, about 7:30 or so?"

"For sure. At least for a little while. I'm not really supposed to have friends here and should get to work now," she said in a low voice.

"I'll see you later then." I backed out and walked to the door. Janine greeted the two women with a casual, friendly professionalism. I stopped at a rack on the way out and read the price tag of a top similar to Janine's. The narrow tag read two hundred dollars in neat script.

"Holy moly." I thought.

When I arrived back at the apartment, Ben and Marco were gone to the market. Chris sprawled on the front yard couch reading a magazine. He sat up when I rolled in and parked under the covered awning.

"There's an early North wind swell coming through. You want to head out and catch some surf?"

"That is about the best idea I've heard in forever. "

I scrambled out of clothes and pulled my three-two Bodyglove wetsuit to the waist, the torso and sleeves hanging from the sides. Also soon ready Chris jumped on his banger strand cruiser. We peddled to Sands beach, each with a surfboard comfortable under one arm. Our place is two blocks from the edge of town. The pavement ends at the boundary to the undeveloped open space of Coal Oil Point Reserve and Deveraux Foundation and turns into a dirt path of packed clay, lined and ridged with ruts from last year's rains. The fat bicycles tires navigated smoothly over the hard pack. We cruised through, bumping along the way. With the ocean on our left, the Channel Islands were visible to the south. The path meanders through open land near the bluffs and jutting hills that frame the water. Seagulls and pelicans squawked and circled about in the hazy sky. Thick sounds of rolling waves crashing against the base of eroded dirt and ice-plant covered cliffs signaled the building power held within the swell. Warm against my bare chest, hopefully the sun's rays would impart some color on the embarrassingly pale skin. We were quiet but both our smiles were wide as the sky. Nothing is as fun, healthy, soulful or productive as surfing. Skiing and riding mountain bikes can be a blast. But in my book surfing wins. You can ride a bike downhill any time. Surfing requires nature's blessing. Winds can blow out the waves or minus a swell, the ocean can be flat as a lake. How many times have we shown up early hoping to surf, only be skunked and disappointed. The Power of No is strong. When you can't have something, of course that makes you want it more. That's why when there is surf, you have to enjoy the moment. It had been too long since I caught real waves. Chris had a gleam in his eye, clearly thinking along the same lines.

The path leads southwest until hitting Devereaux Point, then veers and turns sharply right and follows the coast. Sands beach is a prototypical west facing sandy beach break. We locked the bikes against a gated chain link fence near where I sunbathed with Janine ages ago. Devereaux Point is a long, slow right point break that can be fun and handle big, heavy surf if the direction of the swell is correct. With high tide and the swell from the wrong direction, today did not look appealing. Sands was pumping nicely though. Along the long stretch of beach were several different peaks to choose from. We chose a peak a hundred feet down with only three other guys in the water. I will always choose surf with fewer people at a less consistent spot than deal with a crowded lineup and bigger or technically cleaner waves. The head high waves were a revelation compared with the ankle slappers from summer. We paddled out. I've never liked turtle-diving, so usually hold on with one arm and submerge the nine foot longboard into the on-coming wave as best as possible. Not too cold, the salt water felt incredible and revitalizing on my face. Foamy whitewater from a set wave dragged me backwards. I pulled back onto the board and scratched hard to paddle out of the impact zone. When through, I sat upright on the board and caught my breath, waiting for the next set. Chris pulled alongside me.

"So good you're home, brother."

A band of haze across the horizon outlined the chromatic sky. A row of oil derricks were perched in the distance. Compared with the expansive Montana skies, our visibility here seemed less by a third. To the north a pod of dolphins appeared and then disappeared amongst an expanse of kelp and seaweed floating near the marine blue and green surface. The pale yellow sun looked like a huge pill in the sky. With a brief pang of guilt I wondered what the hotshots were doing right then. Feeling conflicted did not last more than a flicker of time. This was too awesome. I was beyond happy to be here right now. The juxtaposition of this moment with the misery of Montana did not compute.

I spotted a large set emerging on the horizon, the line of the wave's face pushing upward.

"You got this one, bro. Woo hoo."

The crest of the wave began to break. I paddled hard and scrambled to get into position. The steep wave quickly started barreling. Not the most maneuverable board, the thick nine foot noserider sure qualified as a wave catcher. The wide board sliced through the water as the face of the wave pitched upward. I rapidly gained speed and jumped up to make the take off. I am goofy footed which means my stance is with the right foot forward. The wave broke to the left, ideal for me since I could face the wave and ride frontside. After making the drop in, I smoothly carved across the bottom to the top and then down the face, setting up in the powerful heart of the breaking section. The fat lip crashed behind me with a rushing noise. I rode across the face again and down as the wave opened and developed in front of me. I surfed the wave to the very end, until it finally closed out. The white water pushed me farther and straight to shore. Then I fell backward into the water like the Nestea plunge. Grabbing the board, I pushed myself back on again and paddled straight out, pulling hard through and over the oncoming set waves, beyond the impact zone.

We surfed for a couple hours and caught more than our share of waves. Sets would roll though every twelve or fifteen minutes.

"I've been worried about Ben."

"Why, what's up?"

"He's been acting different. While you were gone he smoked out three times a day. It's changing him."

"How so?"

"It's hard to describe. Like we'll be talking and all of a sudden his words seem to have a totally different meaning. The conversation will shift and be about something else. Then after a while he'll revert back to normal like nothing happened. At first I thought it was my imagination. It's really weird."

"He seemed normal, but I'll see if I notice anything ."

"That'd be great. There's this dude Bobby that he's been hanging with. The guy always has bud."

"Ben always smoked a lot."

"Yeah, but this is different. His stuff is richter. It's way strong. I'm serious. Ben's been acting strange. Hopefully you and Marco being home will help."

"I think I know the Bobby guy you're talking about. He always wears flannel shirts and an SF ball cap. And drives a red Falcon? He kind of gives me the creeps."

"Yeah. That's him. Me too."

"I'll keep an eye on Ben."

"Cool."

At the apartment, doors and windows were wide open with music blasting loudly. Ben had gone to town at the market. Groceries scattered across the kitchen with a cookbook open on the table. He chopped furiously, prepping vegetables and the ingredients for an exotic spice sauce. The dude should seriously forgo studying chemistry and instead become a chef and open his own restaurant. A natural with no formal training Ben could whip up a dish.

Chris and I entered the room, salt water dripping from the wetsuits. Ben looked up from his activity.

"You're right on time. Marco started the coals. They should be ready soon. You guys are in for a treat!"

"All right!"

"Hey Curt, Janine called looking for you. I invited her to our feast. She can stop by, but only for a little while. Something about an uncle in town, going to see him."

That sucks, but we'll get some quality time tomorrow, I assured myself. Rinsing off in my third shower that day, for the first time in months, I felt cleansed. The soot, dust and grime in the sinuses and cobwebs clogging my head were finally gone. The three showers helped of course, but the ocean water purified and revitalized my body and soul.

Even better than advertised and delicious, we devoured the feast as soon as Ben served the meal onto our miss-matched colored plates. Murmurs of appreciation filled the silence. No one breathed until the meals were finished. Ben devoted time shopping for ingredients and preparing the food. After such patient work and attention, we wiped out the meal itself in nothing flat. The trick was he enjoyed the process. It wasn't about the end result. He relished the creativity, nuances and details of cooking. The sensory pleasure of eating the actual meal provided an added bonus. No matter if I reminded myself to slow down and enjoy the experience. That would not happen anytime soon. After too many hungry days and waiting in painfully slow chow lines, the habit of eating like a hungry wolf was hard to break.

We stayed around the kitchen table and drank beers. Marco told a litany of funny stories about back east this past summer. I stood to buss the table and went to work cleaning the kitchen mess. Washing pots and dishes, I listened to the talk and interjected a little about the summer fires. Twenty-four hours ago I inhabited a parallel universe. Already Montana began to seem like a dream.

Janine finally showed at eight-thirty. She changed from the nice work outfit, but looked smoking hot in a burgundy t-shirt and white jeans. The way her jeans fit reminded me of a song lyric about a girl with a tiger in her hips. Chris stood and offered a beer from the fridge. Smiling yet shaking her head, Janine said she could not stay long. Finished with the dishes, I dried both hands on the dish towel and walked outside with her to the couch in the front.

A buzz of energy filled the night air. Several songs were audible, carrying from multiple directions, drowning out and playing over each other. A hum and rumble of countless people talking mingled through open windows across the yard and space around. Crowds walked, biked and skated by. The increase in foot traffic from the summer was dramatic. The entire student population had arrived back in town, ready to start another school year. In comparison with the sounds of the woods and the company of twenty hotshots, Isla Vista clamored with a crush of humanity.

I sat on the edge of the couch. Janine stood in front of me, hands on her hips.

"That was some surprise seeing you today at the shop. I didn't recognize you at first. That a new haircut?"

"You like it?"

"Yes, you look handsome." Her eyes were steady in mine. "I'm sorry we can't hang out. My uncle came to town and I'm supposed to meet with him."

"Maybe we can hook up later."

"Oh, I don't think that will work."

"Maybe tomorrow then?"

"Yeah, okay. That should be good. I'm working and close the shop at seven. Why don't I call you then."

"I can come by your place, when you get off if that's better."

"How about I call you after we close up. We'll figure it out then. Okay?"

"Sure, I guess. I mean. No. Not really. I haven't seen you in forever and don't understand what's going on."

"What do you mean, what's going on?"

"Well, you're acting weird. Like something is up."

"There's nothing up. That's not true." With that she moved in closer and kissed me. Her lips were soft and cool. I closed my eyes. She smelled exactly how I remembered. The scent like a tray of ripe strawberries filled the air. Then she took a step away backward.

"That's nice. I missed you."

"I missed you too. So much."

"You were gone a long time and never called. My girlfriends, nobody understood."

"That's not fair. I told you."

"Never hearing from you was the worst. I worried and didn't know what to think."

"You knew we'd be okay. Nothing was going to happen to us."

"There's no way to know that. It sucks to have zero idea about what's happening. For weeks and weeks with no word. I wasn't going to stay home every day and wait for your call that never came. I have a life, you know."

"We went over this. I called you every chance possible. There weren't any phones in the boondocks."

"Yeah, you said that. But things are a little different now. That's all. Let's talk tomorrow. I am sorry and have to go."

Sitting motionless, I looked at her. She held my head in both her hands, rubbed my hair and kissed me on the forehead.

"No need for the sad puppy dog look. I'll call you tomorrow after work. Okay, Butch?"

She turned and walked across the lawn to the parked white pickup. I stood and watched as she started the engine, switched on the headlights, pulled from the curb and drove away. The pickup rounded the corner before I fully realized she was gone. Talk about getting hit by the white tornado. How many hours and days had I obsessed and spent thinking about her. The promise of Janine's touch helped me carry on when exhausted beyond words, my bones ached and I would have paid good money to simply lie down and sleep. The presence of her in my memory and the very idea of her being gave me comfort. Needless to say, this was the opposite of the homecoming I imagined. I sat back on the couch, watched the crowds pass on the street and tried to square my expectations with the reality of the situation.

"Hey, what are you doing? Jaybird leave already?" Chris stood under the awning after walking out to check on us. Face dark in the shadows, his frame was outlined by the light coming through the open door from the kitchen.

"Hey bro. Yeah, she had to take off."

"That's kind of messed up. You've been gone all this time."

"She didn't know I'd be back today. Her uncle is in town. I get it."

"Well, if you're cool, that's what matters. C'mon in, we're celebrating."

"Okay. I hear that." Explaining to Chris helped square the situation in my mind.

We listened to music, drank and hung out. After a couple hours with the beer gone, I volunteered to head to the store and buy more, my treat. One tangible benefit of returning from the road, waiting for me were a stack of U.S Treasury envelopes with fat paychecks inside.

"I'll come with," Ben said.

We jumped on bikes and peddled down D.P. to the market. Twelvers of Milwaukee's Best were on special. As the long recognized connoisseur's choice amongst the multitude of low budget brands, I grabbed two twelve packs. Just because I was flush wouldn't stop me from being a value shopper. The wall clock read eleven fifty-one. The market would close in nine minutes. Behind the cashier at the register were single cigarettes for sale a nickel apiece. With no Camel straights, Ben bought one filtered Camel. Deciding to hang out a while, we set the beer in the bike baskets but sat on the cement wall to the right outside the market. Ben ripped the filter from the cigarette with two strong fingers and littered it in a nearby bush. Holding the stubby remainder, he scratched fire against the cover of the matchbook with one hand and held the flame underneath. When lit, Ben took a long drag, holding in the smoke and then silently handed me the cancer stick.

The taste of tobacco was strong. I held the smoke in as well, like we were smoking a jay, then passed it back to him. We sat on the wall and shared the now unfiltered Camel, watching as random bicyclists roared in and stormed the store trying to beat the clock and enter before they closed for the night. The manager walked out and emptied a round trash can into the large side bins. He dragged the standup metal newspaper rack into the store and looking at the second hand move across the face of his watch, placed the "Closed" sign inside the door. At exactly midnight, he pulled down the drawstring blind and turned the deadbolt lock. Inside people stood in line waiting to pay. The manager unlocked the door and let the customers exit one at a time. Nobody new would be let in. At midnight IV Market closed for the night.

Two guys on bikes rushed up and seeing the closed sign, stopped and knocked on the glass door.

"Hey man. " they pantomimed to the store manager, motioning to their wrist watches. "It's not midnight yet."

The manager looked at them through the window, shrugged his shoulders and shook his head.

"Sorry." He mouthed through the glass. His expression cordial, he didn't seem that sorry.

Another group of bicyclists rolled to the door and made their entreaties, each one gesticulating to the manager. Again he shrugged his apologies through the glass. Two girls stood and waited at the door to plead in person. When the man with the keys to the shop opened the door to let out the last of legal shoppers, they applied their charms to convince him to let them in. He shook his head. "No. Sorry, guys."

Ben and I sat on the wall and passed the cigarette back and forth, watching the scene play out in front of us. We were content and well stocked with our beers. Obviously these people should have planned ahead better. At thirteen after we jumped from the wall, ready to leave. A lone bicyclist came tearing in and swung off the seat with the bicycle still rolling. He landed on both feet, shuffling and bouncing in a dance to stay upright. He pushed off, aiming his bike towards the other bikes near the front door. It rolled there in a ghost run, barely wavering, crashing into the bike rack with a loud clamor. The guy's forward momentum pushed him onward. He mirrored the bike and progressed in a straight line until practically smashing into the closed door.

"What the hell?" he asked loudly to no one in particular upon discovering the locked door. The "Closed" sign apparently needed to be more orange or maybe the printed word a larger font. Ben and I watched as he wandered back to the bike which barely missed crashing into ours. He positioned himself on the saddle and started off in a lazy, wavering pattern like a snake. Climbing aboard our own bikes, we followed in the same direction. We were twenty feet behind when his wavering advance come to a sudden halt. His bike folded. He crashed hard to the pavement. I don't know if he turned the front tire too far to one side and got crossed over or what. It is rare to see someone completely endo on flat ground, out of the blue, all by their lonesome. Ben and I snickered at his hurt pride after confirming he was essentially okay. Lucky thing for him, drunks bounce well. Concrete is unforgiving. The crash must have smarted something fierce. His body would ache tomorrow, but he could have been in worse shape. Two policemen on bicycles from the IV Foot Patrol rolled in from the left. They dismounted and checked him out in quick fashion. I've heard of people busted for drunk driving while on bicycles. This was a first to actually witness an arrest. I always figured you had to be a complete spaz to be too drunk to ride a bike. Seeing this bozo go down in a heap did not change that opinion. We stopped and watched as the cops gave the poor fool a field sobriety test. He promptly failed. What rotten luck.

"You know, Curt. Think I'm gonna go check in on a friend."

"Midnight booty call, huh?"

"It's early yet. Almost forgot we planned for me to stop by."

"Okay, bro. We'll see you tomorrow."

"No doubt. Let's surf in the morning. I'm glad you're home, Curt."

"Thanks, Ben. Me too. Sounds good."

Ben made a u-turn and peddled back towards campus. I took a right to avoid going too close to the cops who were in the process of handcuffing the drunken cyclist and headed in a roundabout not the most direct way towards our place. Ben had seemed normal enough to me. Talking about upcoming classes, at one point he did get momentarily paranoid. Then he snapped out of it. I'll remember to keep an eye on him, I told myself.

The night was winding down but there were still plenty of people peddling about and walking. I enjoyed being in civilization and rode around, checking out the town. There were scattered parties and music coming from open windows. I peddled first down Trigo road and then turned right on a side street. Then I made a left onto Sueno. The apartments on Sueno were newer and not stacked on top of each other as badly as other streets. I liked these bigger lots with more elbow room. Humming a Dramarama song to myself, I cruised along in my head. That's when I thought I recognized a white pickup on the side of the road, a little Nissan like Janine's. I did a u-turn in the street and circled back. A familiar Progressive surfboard sticker decorated the right corner of the rear window. I did not remember if she had that exact one. The pickup sure looked like Janine's, but I could not swear for one hundred percent certain. I gazed at the apartments on both sides of the road. In a two story building two houses down, a handful of people sat in a well lit living room visible through a wide glass front window. The apartment set back thirty feet from the street. An ornamental maple in the front yard partly blocked the view. The people were watching television. Flashing moving images reflected across their faces in their wide sofa and chairs. There were three guys and two girls. I rested on the seat of the bike and narrowed both eyes to focus on the girls. No mistake, one of them was Janine. She wore the burgundy top and sat on the edge of the sofa, leaning practically on top of a guy next to her. My heart felt like a brick. The nearest street lamp sixty feet away I sat deep in shadow on the Super Duty, trying to clear the fog in my head and figure out what was happening. The show must have finished because everyone stood and milled about, packing in for the night. With the room brightly lit, someone looking in my direction would have seen their own reflection in the glass and not me in the darkness. Janine stood. The guy next to her reached over and took her by the hand. They walked from the room together and to the rear of the house not visible from the street. The others filed out of the front room as well. The lights went off. Two rooms on the second floor were still lit. Within minutes one after another they went dark too. I took a deep breath. The muscles of my chest constricted, making it hard to breathe. Kicked in the head, I had trouble thinking.

I needed to shake away and extricate myself from the chaos and noise surrounding and clogging my brain. The guy with his arm around Janine's shoulder was near my age and not much how you would imagine an uncle would look.

I reached into the cardboard twelve pack, opened a can and drank the whole thing in a handful of long slugs with a peculiar Best aluminum taste. Carbonation bubbles fizzed my nostrils. Everything hurt. My head spun in circles. I wanted it to stop and opened and drank a second beer down. In my old hometown there is a popular yet unorthodox "Ironman" race where contestants paddle a surfboard one mile, run on soft sand another mile and then drink a six-pack of beer. If you throw up, you're disqualified. The race takes place every year on the Fourth of July. I've always been fighting fires and have never been able to participate. The way these Best went down would be pretty competitive during the beer portion. I finished the second can and opened a third. Soon also dust, I threw the empties one after another into the bed of the white pickup, stood for another minute or maybe an hour, then peddled away and towards home. Ben's bike was gone and the house dark when I pulled in. Chris and Marco were asleep. I sat in the living room without turning on the lights and opened another beer. The suffocating apartment walls pressed on me. I tried not to think what Janine was doing at that moment. Being alone in this room with my cruel imagination would drive me crazy. I grabbed the keys to the GPZ and headed into the night.

I rode through town towards the highway where I could crank open the throttle. The rush of wind would help. The cool night blew past in a blur. Initially I drove past the airport, cheered by the blue lights lining the runway. The lights were bright and blurred from the water in my eyes. I headed north away from Goleta where there were less people, wanting to fly as fast as possible to be free and not sweat a speeding ticket. Then the thought hit me. I'm not sure why the possibility didn't occur to me earlier. Maybe this could be a mistake. Perhaps that wasn't Janine or her little pickup after all. How could I be sure? Turning off at the next exit, I looped around and headed south towards S.B. If I found the Nissan parked at her house on the Mesa that would prove I'd been mistaken. Hoping for the possibility of being wrong brought a sliver of relief. I wished I'd thought this through earlier. With barely any cars on the road I made great time to downtown and the exit to her neighborhood. The GPZ's engine sounded like a big metallic cat's purr. Tension enveloped my brain. Full with excitement rounding the corner to Janine's block, I looked for her white pickup parked on the street, hopeful to dispel these crazy thoughts in my head. Are you going to believe me or your own lying eyes, I asked myself. Approaching the apartment, no white pickups were visible. I circled the block. The Nissan was nowhere to be seen and the house dark. Her roommates were apparently asleep. Having a hard time breathing, I pulled the cycle to the curb and tried to think. My chest muscles constricted and lungs struggled to expand against the pressure. The stars above and blackness of space crashed down on my head. Pealing away, I headed downtown. A jumble of screaming attacked my head from the inside. I needed to numb and shut the ruckus down. Please grant me a reprieve from the blare and pain of thoughts.

I pulled onto State Street and found an open parking spot a block from the boutique where I saw her earlier today. How many hours ago did I wake in Redding? It seemed a million years. I walked down the street to the world famous and always dependable Joe's Cafe. Thankfully they were still serving. A dozen people surrounded the bar. The Hispanic bartender with a thin, neatly trimmed mustache greeted me like an old friend. He was dressed in a neatly pressed black golf shirt and said they'd be announcing last call in a couple minutes. His welcoming demeanor was the kind of positive energy I dearly needed right then. Joe's is legendary for the strongest drinks in town. I was confused what to order. A beer was out of the question and a shot seemed a waste too. I decided on a tequila and tonic. The bartender looked at me like that was a new one but nodded and said, coming right up. People drink gin and tonics. Why wouldn't tequila and tonic work? Quiet, the bartender smiled wide with perfect white teeth while mixing the drink. A normal drink has an ounce and a half to two ounces of booze. There must have been close to four ounces of tequila, barely a splash of tonic in the tall glass, and three small wedges of lime. I squeezed the limes between two fingers releasing the juice into the drink and promptly gulped the clear liquid down. Cold, wet and yes, the taste of tequila was strong. The carbonation of tonic and citrus from the lime combined to make one stiff thirst quencher of a beverage. Both eyes watered. A flush crossed my face as I signaled to the bartender.

"Otra mas, please."

"Wow. You were thirsty."

I took my time with the second drink and checked out the dozen stragglers standing around. At its peak earlier that night the long bar probably served five times that many people. Boisterous laughter and too loud voices echoed against the walls of the emptying bar. The acoustics of this Santa Barbara institution told the story. Noisy and pumping an hour earlier, the room now rang hollow and empty. The bartender announced last call, truly winding down the night.

I finished the drink, left a twenty and stumbled, walking for the door. The alcohol finally started to kick in and do its job. Now suitably numb, I was not obsessing about things that I did not want to think about. An upstanding place, Joe's set the main wall clock fast by ten minutes to avoid trouble with law enforcement and shut down at 1 a.m. The Silver Fox around the corner and a block away from State Street was an old school drinking saloon. They served until 1:30. When I bounced through the narrow front door, six older rummies sat hunched over drinks at the bar. The desperation was not as palpable as in that sad joint we stumbled across in Helena before finding the Copper King. The Silver Fox shared that same smell of dank air, rich with fumes from hard alcohol, stale beer and the noxious stench of cigarettes. Sharing that smoke with Ben earlier was a rare occasion and gave a nice rush. The cloud of second hand fumes permeating this bar revolted me. The bartender was an overweight bald man in a plaid short sleeve shirt with buttons straining to stay in place. He looked at me dully when I ordered a shot of Yukon Jack after spotting the bottle in a far corner. Baldy dutifully poured a shot and stood waiting with his hand resting on the bottle in front of me. The label was faded and peeling away, years old. The bartender knew I would slam the shot down and order another. He was conserving energy, not stepping away. Taking the cue, I downed the shot of Yukon and choked down the sickly sweet honey with the rough awful bite. Blinking both eyes and making a grimace, I motioned for another. He poured another shot into the same thick glass.

"That'll be eight bucks."

I rummaged in the left pocket and pulling out a ten, pushed it towards him.

"Okay, you all. Last call for reals this time." He sidled down the bar and fetched the rest another of whatever they were drinking. When he made his way back to me, I looked at him through blurry eyes. "How about a Coors."

He reached into the refrigerator, opened the bottle with a flat, iron opener, showed me three fingers signifying three bucks.

"You've got five minutes, Yukon Cornelius."

I pulled a five from my wallet and left it on the bar top, grabbed the beer and for the first time walked around and inspected the bar interior. Several ragged and stained LA Rams and other NFL team banners hung from the rafters. Faded tin Budweiser beer signs and an assortment of beer company posters of buxom babes in bikinis filled the rest of the walls. The images of long haired beer promo chicks stared boldly from the posters. They're probably the closest thing to a woman this place had seen in a forever, I thought to myself. The dump gave me the creeps. Carrying the full bottle of beer, I walked out the front door without looking back.

I hoofed it down the street in the direction of the GPZ and looked around at the now darkened and shuttered store front businesses. There were barely any cars on the streets and only a scattering of random pedestrians out and about. A bearded, homeless man sat on a wall near the corner with a border collie mix sitting obediently with him. A blue bandana was wrapped around the dog's collar. On the ground next to them, a handwritten cardboard sign asked help for a veteran. I stopped and speaking low to the dog, found a crumpled dollar in one pocket and tossed it into the open guitar case in front of them. The homeless dude nodded appreciatively, but gave me a sage look.

"You aught to finish that beer, bud. They'll ticket you real fast round here."

"Thanks." I mumbled. I'd forgotten about the beer and took a long pull from the bottle and offered the rest to him.

"No thanks, man. I've been clean and sober five years now."

"Ghoul for you," I responded and took several more gulps, finishing the last off.

"I'll take the empty though."

"Kelp yourself." I said, tossing the bottle underhanded. He caught with both hands, careful it didn't drop and break on the ground.   The avalanche of drinks hit, negatively impacting and confounding my coordination. I swayed while standing in one place. I started moving again and walked down the empty sidewalk, veering like a rudderless boat, on the verge of stumbling and falling flat on my face with each step.   Suddenly very unbalanced, I felt like a wispy tree buffeted in a windstorm. The miles and miles of hiking the summer long were a savior as muscle memory kicked in. The legs and feet went into death march mode and pushed me forward, ignoring the confused directions from the inebriated control tower brain. In a smashup of disarray, I leaned into the storm tossing me about and strode through the chaos with purpose, and finally made the way several blocks back to the GPZ.

I rested on the motorcycle's saddle, breathing deeply, getting my bearings. Ratcheting on the helmet, I started the cycle and pulled away from the curb and onto the darkened road. I turned in the opposite direction from State Street. There would be less cops in that direction. Johnny Law was the last person I needed to run into.

"You are leery hammered, Curt." The words spoken aloud were slurred and indecipherable. Downtown Santa Barbara is criss-crossed with one way streets. This one headed in the correct direction towards Goleta, back to the apartment and safety. There were not many stop signs and I made excellent progress. Alas, the cycle kept veering back and forth from the right lane and into the oncoming left lane and not because I was doing that on purpose. "Dummy, you have to crocus."

The visor of the helmet opened for ventilation. Leaning forward with both arms hugging and resting on top of the gas tank for support, I clenched the hand grips. As much as I tried to ride a straight line, I could not. For a half mile I swerved in and out of the two lanes like a slalom skier maneuvering invisible gates. The irregular movements were far from intentional. As much as I tried to straighten the cycle, we kept on a crooked path. Thankfully I realized this was a horrible idea. At the next intersection I pulled into a darkened parking lot of a gas station that appeared closed for the night. I stopped the GPZ at the side of the building, shut off the engine, put the kickstand down and pulled the helmet off.

"That was the opposite of smart."

I breathed heavily. Not yet spinning in circles, the world jumbled and rushed at me. Everything looked like a tangled patchwork quilt with tunnel vision. I could see the unlit and darkened orange symbol for the Union 76 gasoline company. Intricate bushes lined the street. Whenever I looked at one object the rest of the world disappeared out of focus. The brain could not process the world traveling towards me at mach speed. Objects rushed upon me before I realized they were there. With a flood of relief I registered salvation in the form of a pay phone booth on the street corner. If I called the house, one of my roommates could come get me. I stumbled towards the booth. Walking I swerved as badly as the GPZ slaloming down the road. Not able to keep a straight line, I finally arrived. Pulling the door closed, an overhead light inside the booth shined like a spotlight. I rummaged in pockets for change and plugged a coin in the slot. Ready to dial the number, I stopped, realizing I had no idea where I was. Sheez. Placing the receiver back, I took a deep breath and forced myself to the corner intersection to try and read the street signs. Holding myself upright, hanging onto the pole with two hands, I read and reread the letters of the sign and sounded out the Spanish words to myself aloud. I'd never been in this neighborhood before, but the street names were familiar. I repeated them several times to not forget. With no concept of time or how long this process took, I veered walking back to the phone booth saying the names over and over. A black and white sheriff's patrol car pulled into the parking lot and stopped diagonally in front of me.

A woman sheriff with her hair tied in a bun and a short sleeved uniform tight over muscular arms and thick body stepped from the cruiser. She slid a billy club into the ring on her Sam Browne belt.

"Please step over to the vehicle and place your hands on your head."

"I wasn't doing anything."

"Please step to the vehicle, sir.".

"I was trying to call my friends to come get me," I explained. She wasn't listening but walked closer, glowering at me.

"Please follow my directions, sir. You don't want any trouble."

"What are you talking about, trouble. I'm just trying to go home."

It was hopeless. I placed both hands on my head, locking the fingers together. She walked behind, patted me down, grabbed the left hand and pulled it behind my back with force and placed a cuff around the wrist, locking in place. Then she grabbed the right hand and bent the arm back and attached the metal bracelets to the right wrist. The hand cuffs were tight and bit into the skin. The lady deputy opened the rear door of the patrol car. With one hand she steered me into the back seat to avoid banging my head on the frame of the vehicle. The windows were rolled up and the doors locked. A thick metal grate separated the front from the rear area now imprisoning me.

"What did I do? What is wrong with you. I didn't do anything."

I could not move hands or arms. Claustrophobia and an uncontrollable anxiety kicked in. Feeling trapped and helpless overwhelmed me in a red flood of alarm. Crying, real tears rolled from both eyes and down the cheeks. I was locked with both hands behind my back in the caged rear seat of the patrol car. Hyperventilating, I could not breathe. My heart pounded. I thought it would explode. A wave of hysteria and panic coursed through me.

"Fuck you, I don't deserve this. What'd I do? You bitch. I wasn't bothering, hurting anybody. I'm a good person. What the fuck. I try an help people, be a good guy. What's your problem? Why are you doing this to me? You're fucked, that's what. You're all fucked."

Tears poured down my face. The lady sheriff did not say anything while driving. I ran out of gas, grew quiet and tried to calm myself to not completely lose my mind, my breaths still struggling to get oxygen. We drove through darkened neighborhoods to the county jail. By the time we pulled into the concrete facility, I pulled it together. She helped me from the patrol car in reverse order of how she got me into the back seat, and escorted me into a bright booking room.

Fluorescent bulbs glared incessantly. The panic adrenalin overload helped clear the drunken jumble. Aware of the handcuffs coming off, I felt ashamed and could barely look at the sheriff as she went about taking sets of fingerprints.

"I'm sorry about calling you those names."

Silent she steered me to a different room for mugshots. When the lady took the front view photo, out of habit I smiled, the kind of "say cheese" you do when taking school portraits. I then waited in a holding pen until two other police entered, leading a handcuffed man with them. They left him in the holding pen with me. We stood with our backs against the thick wire mesh. I nodded "what's up" to the guy in his mid-thirties, dressed in a striped red and white shirt with short, light brown tangled hair. His face was burned from the sun. The dude's eyes had a strange light in them like staring directly into a fading bulb from a flashlight. He looked at me without blinking and took a half step in my direction. We were a couple feet apart.

"Don't fuck with me."

"We're cool man.. not fucking with anyone."

Even though both hands were locked and cuffed behind his back, the pure venom and raw demented look caught me off guard. My stomach lurched and tightened. I've never been good with the crazy. An invisible cloud of noxious electricity surrounded the guy. Two police returned to the holding pen and led him away. The lady deputy steered me to a jail cell down the hallway full with eight other men. She deposited me there. The heavy door locked into place and closed with a baleful and hard metallic finality. A couple drunks looked over with glassy, red eyes, dully inspecting me. The rest stayed slumped over and did not move, either sleeping or trying to sleep on the hard floor or leaning against the walls. I did not say a word to anyone but found an open corner, sat down, wrapped both arms around and on top of bent knees and rested my head on them. The cellmates were a mix of younger and older Hispanics, two skinny looking black guys and two older white men. I discreetly checked out everyone, trying to anticipate other potential hassles. No one seemed obviously troublesome. They were most likely unlucky drunks like me, content to sleep it off. If anyone was a hardcore criminal, I could not tell. After a while some yelling broke out from the holding area. The two cops dragged in the crazy guy doing the screaming. They were in his grill about shutting up. He ignored them and kept loudly mouthing off. The cops dragged him into the empty cell adjacent to ours. I don't know what he did, but the two cops started pounding on him. One had a billy club and whacked him across the torso and legs. The other cop wrestled the crazy dude onto the floor and had a knee in his back holding him down. A whole bunch of sheriffs ran in. They piled on until crazy dude stopped struggling, each one getting a number of solid licks and kicks on him. When the pile of cops finally untangled off the dude, blood rushed down the side of his head. The color red covered his face. He looked a mess. His hands were cuffed behind his back the whole time. I don't know what he was thinking but obviously nothing too straight. Our cell sat quietly watching the fairly one sided beat down. When they picked the guy up and dragged him to the holding area, everyone returned to trying to sleep. No one said a word. A puddle of dark red blood glistened on the shiny, waxed linoleum floor of the adjacent cell. They would take the crazy guy to the hospital to check out the cut on his head. Fine with me. Take that force of negative energy somewhere else.

By now, my shitfaceddrunk had worn away. Replaced by a painful ache, with both eyes closed, I rested my head on forearms, and tried to sleep. The cold cell floor made me shiver. Air conditioning blew freezing air direct from an overhead vent. No matter how miserable, I can usually grab sleep when given the opportunity. That said, I sat on the hard ground for some time and could not still the wild scenes and pictures jumbled in my mind. I don't remember finally nodding out.

I awoke curled on the floor, lying on one side with both hands between the legs and balled together in the fetal position. A deputy stood over me repeating my name. I looked at his polished, black tactical boots. Blinking I realized where we were, last night happened for real and was not a bad dream. He said they were releasing me. We walked to the original booking room. The clerk behind the partition slid over a paper bag holding my wallet, keys and a form to sign. A round wall clock read five minutes after seven. Fluorescent lights buzzed on the ceiling. There were no windows. Without that clock, you could not tell whether it was day or night. Surprisingly the receipt for my property was the only paperwork to sign. There were no charges. The deputy sheriff walked me to the exit door, kicked it open with the side of his boot and let me go. I stepped into the bright light of morning, free again. My head pounded. The nauseous empty feeling that went down through my core was shame.   I walked south towards the frontage road that parallels the highway, turned right and kept walking until finding a pay phone in front of a boarded up fruit stand one block away. The deputy offered that I could use their phone and call from the station and wait there for a ride. No thanks. Hanging out didn't really appeal to me. Once released from the cell, I wanted as far away, as fast as possible.

Dialing the apartment from a phone booth, Chris' scratchy voice answered after the third ring.

"Hate to wake you, bro. I need you to come pick me up."

"Hey Curt. No problem. Where are you?"

"I'm in front of that fruit stand near the county jail. Right off the highway."

"Near the jail. What are you doing there? Did you get picked up last night?"

"It's a long story. I'll tell you when you get here."

"Okay bud. No worries. I'm leaving right now. Be there soon."

Bright sunlight washed edges out like an overdeveloped photograph. I kicked myself for not asking Chris to grab my sunglasses. The harsh morning felt worse from the empty feeling in my stomach. A part of me inside was either missing or broken. I wasn't a bad guy, but something went horribly wrong. Standing and ashamed with a guilty conscience, waiting for my friend to arrive took an eternity.

Cars rounded the corner. Most came to a complete stop. Several barely slowed, then rolled right through. I watched them drive by and tried to be patient. Finally Chris' black FourRunner came into sight. Relief like the cavalry arrived, saving me from isolation, myself and poisonous thoughts. We drove straight home and were mostly silent. My friend's presence was good medicine. Arriving at the apartment, I grabbed a beer from the fridge. Hair of the dog might help the hurt in my head. Chris raised an eyebrow, but did not say anything. I felt bad enough without judgment from anyone, especially my friend. I laid on the couch and tried not to think behind closed eyes. Chris made breakfast for himself. He asked if I wanted anything. Lacking an appetite, I shook my head and said thanks but I was good. Two Excedrin and the beer helped. The headache slowly faded. Finally I fell asleep and slept stretched on the couch until noon.

When I awoke alone in the apartment. Looking around, I deduced my friends had gone surfing. Not wanting to be alone, I jumped into the wetsuit still damp from yesterday. I peddled down D.P. and the path to Sands beach, then parked near Ben and Chris' bikes locked to the fence. I searched the lineup from shore but could not make out their silhouettes. Less consistent than yesterday and more crowded, I paddled out and caught a couple waves. Dealing with more people required a more aggressive mentality. Dropping in on a guy by accident once, I waved "sorry" but wasn't really. That was a fun ride. The purifying salt water worked like medicine. After a nice long left, I recognized both Ben and Chris way farther down the shore. I paddled across to them. Seeing me, they both yelled hello. We surfed together and my spirits brightened. The ocean is a crucial, pure elixir. The nap helped and definitely did me right. The surf acted as a cure, without which I'd have been walking wounded the whole day. The waves and salt water were a soulful, healthy tonic. My reserves were close to one hundred percent. Except for the void and aching pit in my core.

In between sets, I told them a little about last night, but not everything.

"Why were you riding your cycle downtown anyway?" Ben asked. "Especially after watching that dude get the 502 on his bike. Talk about rolling the dice, tempting fate."

"You are lucky you didn't get a 502, Curt. Where did you park your GPZ?"

350

"Near a service station downtown. Can you give me a ride there after?"

"Sure deal, amigo. No problem."

I made no mention of Janine. Sharing that info would force me to face the truth. I could not deal right now. No getting around it, as much as I knew what I saw, that would not stop me from trying to ignore the situation. Humans can only focus on one thing at once. We cannot be happy and unhappy at the same time. Repeating that as my mantra, I threw myself into the surfing and caught more waves. The exhilaration of free feeling, dropping in on a surging wave seemed like flying. The action and exercise helped. Beating in my chest, the heart pumped healthy oxygen throughout the bloodstream. My strategy involved using the Jedi mind trick to convince myself to simply enjoy this beautiful slice of the natural world. God's amazing ocean delivered life to the planet and peace to me. Bury the hurt somewhere and you won't feel it. Riding waves, the trick worked.

After a couple hours the tide dropped and with it our surf. We each caught a last wave to shore, navigated soft sand to avoid globs of tar, unlocked and jumped onto the bikes and peddled home with boards secure in our arms. After a quick sandwich, Chris drove me downtown for the motorcycle. We found the 76 station from last night. The GPZ was barely visible from the street, safely parked in the back. Chris kept the FourRunner in gear and pulled away after I slammed the door shut. Before heading home, I entered the attached convenience store for a soda and a pack of gum. The Hispanic clerk in his sixties had a wide face, blotchy complexion and wild gray hair. He greeted me as if we were old friends.

"Hey, there you are. How you doing, buddy? Good, huh. Your motorcycle is safe in back behind my van."

"Do I.. do I know you?" I asked.

"Sure. We tried to help you out last night. You don't remember? Well no wonder, you were blitzed. And all over the place. Ojola. Haven't seen anyone that smashed in a while. Me and my partner tried to get you to crash in the back of the van to sleep it off. You kept repeating you needed to get going, and would try to take off. We finally convinced you to chill in the van where you'd be safe. There's new carpet. It's nice and comfortable with a mattress too. You must have crawled out 'cause when I checked early this morning, you were gone."

"Well. Thanks, I guess."

"You were going on and on and did not want to lay down. I worried you'd get rolled or picked up by the law for sure."

"I appreciate your looking out for me."

"Not a problem. Everybody needs a helping hand sometime. Didn't want to see you end up trouble. You were in rough shape to be roaming around. We've all hit the juice too hard before, for sure. Although it's been a while for me. Ha."

Thanks again, I said sheepishly and waved goodbye. I sat on the cycle, opened and took a drink from the root beer, absorbing the old man's story. I finished the soda, thinking through why none of the words registered. Strapping on the helmet, I started the GPZ and looked around at the service station, the van in back and the phone booth not far down the street. As much as I tried to piece together his story, I did not remember seeing the man before. The whole thing was a mess and brought back that rock in the stomach feeling. Opening the pack of gum, I popped in a piece, stuffed the wrapper into the empty soda can and tossed them together into a nearby trash bin.

On the way home I stopped by the campus bookstore and purchased books for the coming quarter. Reviewing the schedule of classes, the mix worked for me. Besides two English courses and Spanish which fulfilled a mandatory language requirement, I signed up for physics and an ethics class. Meant for kicks, physics would keep my math brain sharp. I looked forward the most to ethics. Philosophy seemed the highest form of studious pursuit. Up until the last twenty-four hours my personal code worked for me. We'll see if studying the masters would make me adjust my theories of the world.

I rode home, planted onto the front couch and kicked my feet up. Leafing through a novel from literature of the American South, the phone rang.

"Hi. How are you?" Janine.

I did not respond but stood frozen, phone receiver pressed against the side of my head. Hard and lifeless, the plastic left a mark on skin. A lightness carried in her voice. My stomach tightened with the sensation of wanting to throw up.

"Hello... Curt?"

"What's up?" I finally answered.

"Hey there, hotshot. I'm on break and thought to give you a call."

"Oh yeah?"

"Yes. So I actually get off work at six tonight. Why don't I come over then, right after work."

My insides were in knots. I wanted to scream, but answered, "Okay."

Immobile and helpless, the desire to see her face overwhelmed me. I hoped to look into those eyes and make sense of this. I wanted her to hold me and explain the big mistake. Everything was all right. We were going to be fine. With trouble breathing, I finally responded.

"I'll see you then, then."

"Okie dokie, Smokey."

After placing the phone onto the receiver, I gagged a little, bile rising in my throat. Stomach muscles clenched into a fist and burned with acid, the pain physical like a stab wound from a thick, dull knife stabbing unprotected flesh. I collapsed on the couch. When able to breath again, I attempted to return to the book but could not concentrate. Giving up I walked to my bedroom, arranged the new books neatly on a corner shelf, then lied down on top of the bed. Closing both eyes, I tried to shut out daylight, quiet the brain and find some solace. Sleep mercifully arrived, the black a relief and welcome escape from the hurt.

Chris pulled me from the deep, his voice saying Janine was here. Her being had been a constant presence throughout the slumber. Initially hearing the name, I couldn't tell if this were real or an extended dream. I stared without recognition at my friend's figure in the doorway. She squeezed past him and entered the room, my room, sitting on the edge of the bed at my shoulder, looking down on me. I rolled both legs over the side and sat upright. Janine leaned in to give a kiss. Reflexively I flinched and unintentionally pulled back a few inches. Surprise filled her eyes.

"What's that all about?"

"How's your uncle?" I asked.

"My what... What about my uncle? Where'd this tone come from?"

"Please tell me what's going on."

"I don't know what you mean."

"I think you do. Why'd you do it? You must think I'm an idiot."

"No, I don't. What are you talking about? You're being mean."

"Please just tell me the truth. About last night."

"What are you talking about?"

"Don't lie. Lying only makes it worse. I don't want to hate you."

"Hate me.. What in blazes is going on? Where is this coming from? Why are you fighting with me?"

"I'm not picking a fight."

"You've been gone such a long time. This is crazy. I missed you so much."

"Really. You pick a funny way to show it."

"I don't understand you...why you're so angry. What's wrong? You don't know how hard it was."

"I told you I loved you. And, and, and that's what you do?"

"What are you talking about? You left me a drunk message on the answering machine. No one wants to hear that for the first time like that, and you were drunk."

"I said I love you, and the whole time you're sleeping with someone else?"

"What? Where are you getting that?"

"I saw you last night. Don't fucking lie. I thought you were with your uncle."

The expressions crossing her face were like a scarf caught in a breeze, the material shifting and flowing. Her eyes flickered like an animal caught in a net. The wheels in her head spun, trying to figure out what I knew or didn't, and a plausible excuse or an angle to escape.

"I never lied to you. Last night I had dinner with my uncle. Then I met with some friends. Where did you see me? I must have been with friends."

"Who was the guy?"

"That was Mark. We're friends."

"Oh yeah? Friends."

"Yes. Friends."

She looked at me steadily. Her eyes were always the color of deep cold water speckled with flecks of gold like fire and alive, full of life. Tonight they were simply ice blue and cold. I stared into them futilely, trying to figure out what to do. I needed a map for direction to find meaning in the world. She was a blank slate, however. I could not read anything, except that maybe an absence of empathy in her eyes held the truth.

Do you have any idea how much I wanted to believe her? A million times I've heard that peace comes from within, giving in and letting be. I wanted peace so badly, I could kill for it. By whatever means necessary, I would gladly pay the price, to release, blow the bad dream away, make everything better and stop hurting so much. There had to be something to cure this pain. I would forget the whole thing and be with her. That is all I could think of.

"I'm so glad you're here. I just wanted to be with you. The whole time we were gone, all I could think about was you."

"Me too. I wished so much you didn't go away."

"I'm truly happy when I'm with you. I just want to be with you."

"I like being with you too."

"No, you don't understand. I'm only truly happy, at peace when I'm with you."

"That's not healthy. You have to be happy with yourself. Within yourself."

"Really? What about you?" I asked.

"Me too. I'm working on it. You are a great guy, you really are."

"Aagh please don't say that. I hate that phrase. It's the worst."

"Why? It's true. I've always thought you are such a special guy."

"What about your friend? Is he special too?"

"It's not like that. I told you. We're friends."

"Okay." And even though I believed her, the thread broke. That delicate silk strand severed, and the ends flapped apart. The thing we had, at that moment, went away.

"I think I should go," she said looking down at her wrist and the bulky man's diver watch. Her eyes were full of life again and not empty. I looked into them resigned.

"Okay. I'll see you out."

She stood and walked through and out the apartment with me two paces behind. I soaked in everything about the way her body moved, the way clothes hung from the lithe frame, the distinctive soft scent from her hair that trailed in the air and was unmistakeable. Smell is the most closely tied sense to memory. Walking through the narrow hallway, I remembered that same fragrance from the first night riding her on the handlebars of the Super Duty. Our random meeting that night a lifetime ago, but perfect.

I stood at the curb as she climbed into the pickup, then followed her to the driver's side. She rolled the window down. I bent my knees so we were the same height and at face level. I smiled bravely.

"I'll see you later."

"Okay. I'll talk to you later. Later dater." She raised her face to me. This time I leaned in and kissed her on the lips with light pressure. Her lips were soft and nicely moist. I breathed through the nose to soak everything in. The sweet long kiss done, I stepped back to the curb. She pulled the little pickup onto the street, made a right at the stop sign and drove away. Glued to the passenger side cabin was the distinctive Progressive surfboards decal that I always remembered and had recognized the whole time.

CHAPTER

26

The next afternoon being Sunday I decided to check out the bands in the park. For some reason I rode my bike down Trigo road, which isn't the most direct way. When I peddled past the Holy Trinity parish church, twelve o'clock mass just ended. The congregation were streaming out, gathering around the priest in white robes, shaking hands. We went to church sporadically with my grandmother. I haven't been in years. On a whim I looped around, parked the Super Duty and decided to go inside. The building was empty except for a lone usher collecting hymnals scattered amongst the rows of pews.

I chose an open pew towards the front and sat down heavily on the wooden bench. Built in the seventies and the size of a four bedroom house, the church consisted of one open, fairly modest room. A large plain wood cross commanded the front area. The reddish wood shown with polish like mahogany. A sculpture of Jesus stood to the left where worshippers could kneel and light candles. Sunlight cascaded through brightly colored stained glass windows that lined the walls. With everyone outside, quiet filled the room.

I've always been a fan of Jesus. If you study the man's actual words and works, He was amazing. Surfer, carpenter, winemaker, teacher. "See the lilies, how they grow. They neither toil nor spin". That is how we're supposed to be. Stop thinking so much. Just be. My relationship with God was more complicated. While I appreciate the incredible majesty and beauty of our world and universe He created, His plan has not always been benevolent. I have a difficult time separating God from the horrible deeds done in his name. Atrocities through the ages have occurred because of religion. Far more harm than good has been done as a result of God. Pain, suffering and outrages even today. Worst are the plague of pedophiles who abused their authority and position to physically and emotionally violate countless vulnerable youths and their families who trusted and looked to them for guidance and security. And the Church, at the highest levels, permitted and enabled this horror to continue, then attacked and shamed the victims instead of holding their own corruption accountable. I can't imagine a more awful abdication of their moral and sacred responsibility. But this wasn't what I thought about while I sat in the quiet house of worship.

A stained glass window of a white dove struck me with its simplicity. I admired the vivid purple, green and white colors and beautiful artistry. Sunlight shined through, making the white dove appear brilliant. For some reason the vision reminded me of a Saturday afternoon with my mom when I was eleven. It was before she got sick and one of her good days. Good in the sense that she was coherent and not drinking. I had scored two goals that morning and was telling her about the soccer game.

363

"I'm sorry I missed it, Curt. I'm so happy for you though. You must have had a ton of energy. Remember to eat a peanut butter and jelly on flour tortilla before all your games. Your blood sugars were dialed perfect for a superior athletic performance."

We were out of bread for sandwiches. She improvised with the tortilla.

"Your dad loved tortillas with everything. Soup, rice, beans of course, chili. You name it. Any kind of meat, he'd make into a little sandwich. Even when there weren't tortillas, at dinner his left hand would be clenched at the side of his plate with the thumb up. At any moment he looked like he'd sop up the meal with an invisible tortilla. Or worse I worried he'd use his thumb to scoop or push the food. I was always on him about manners. He was the sweetest man, but table manners are very important. People pay attention and will judge you."

She brightened with the memory. Too soon her eyes clouded again. Sorrow was never far away and weighed heavy on her.

"You know it was my fault, their accident. We'd been arguing. I didn't want him to leave on that hunting trip. I never cared for his friend Roger. He was a drinker, still single and not a good influence. Always finding trouble. Your dad called from a bar, a little ways from the cabin. They planned to stay one more night. I gave him a hard time. They were gone a week already. Snow had started with a larger storm front moving in. If they got stuck at the cabin, he might not make home for another week. Of course, your dad relented. He'd do anything I asked him. Always. I knew too. They would drive home that night through the storm."

My mom had such a beautiful face. Her eyes were brilliant and skin clear. Though the drinking later took a toll, her cheeks had a glow like roses. She had me at nineteen and was only thirty when we had this conversation.

"I had a horrible feeling as soon as we hung up the phone. Immediately I thought about calling him back, but didn't remember the name of the bar or have the number. You have to trust your instincts, Curt, always. That voice inside your head, please listen to it. When the phone rang later that night, I knew the news was horrible, even before answering. The state police said it was an accident. But I knew it was my fault. Driving that broken down old pickup, they shouldn't have been on the road. They could have stayed the night. It was too dangerous and all my fault."

Her voice broke then. The last bit of light remaining in her eyes darkened completely. I tried to argue their actions wasn't her mistake.

"He was a grown man, mom. They drove those winter roads all the time. Sometimes accidents happen. Dad always told me about being safe. No matter what, 'provide for safety first' he used to say. He jumped out of 'perfectly good' airplanes, he'd say and wasn't afraid of anything. That doesn't mean they were reckless."

She was not listening.

"They swerved to avoid the deer and lost control. It was an accident."

"No. It was because of me. Don't you see. The roads were treacherous and icy. They could've waited out the night, except I made him come home. It's all my fault."

The blame she placed on herself grew corrosive and lingered for years. That's the reason I always believed she brought the sickness upon herself. Guilt, sadness and depression consumed and stole her life. My mom's weakness was never being able to forgive herself. Heartache and grief racked her body. The terminal illness that took her life resulted from self-directed toxic feelings. My characterizing her pain as selfish was not fair. She felt culpably responsible and believed her own actions directly led to my dad's death. Sitting in the tranquil church, for the first time since her death, I understood and had empathy for her. Mom died of a broken heart disguised as a blood disease. The failure wasn't of not loving me enough. My mom loved my pops too much. She never gave up on me. She loved me.

Alone with my thoughts in a church, I don't know if that would be considered prayer. Remembering this forgotten exchange brought a welcome sense of calm. Maybe the holy spirit gave me this gift, because I felt uniquely at peace. A weight lifted. Perhaps a divine force helped me. Who knows. For this reason, when they talk about the Holy Trinity, the Holy Spirit is my favorite.

I took a deep breath, admired the brilliant stained glass white dove for a few more moments, rose and walked out into the sunshine and jumped onto the Super Duty. Three blocks away at the park a reggae band was playing.

CHAPTER

27

School started on Monday. I threw myself into the studies and for the first time in a couple years actually read every assignment and finished the books we were supposed to complete. I had morning classes twice a week. The other days I would rise early and surf before school. After class I headed to a quiet section on the fourth floor of the library to read and do homework. Invisible clouds of dust from the stacks hovered around, keeping me company. The temperature in the library always seemed five degrees warmer than comfortable. I'd drink gallons of coffee to keep awake and not fall asleep at the desk, reading the dry books. Coffee worked but also brought a sharp edge. To release and work off the manic energy from beaucoup caffeine, I went through packs and packs of bubble gum, constantly chewing and blowing bubbles while studying.

Surfing proved my salvation and helped keep me sane. Forced to live in the moment while paddling and catching waves was my self-medication. Thick fast waves required me to focus on the right now. Escaping into books helped too. I will admit to sometimes having trouble concentrating, and would become distracted and lose my place. Wherever I went and no matter what I did, a nagging, dull pain of an inner emptiness accompanied me. A hypochondriac would have self diagnosed cancer. I knew better.

Janine and I spoke a couple times on the phone. I don't remember if I called her or she called me. The details don't really matter. Funny how there's conversations you can remember every single word, even years later. I can honestly say I have no idea what we talked about. The words were halting and superficial. We were over. That was it.

Ben, Chris and Marco were as awesome roommates that anyone could ask for. We had good times, listening to music, hanging out and partying. Chris surfed with me mostly. I'd often go on my own too. The ocean turned colder with the change in seasons and north swells rolling in. I bought a new four-three wetsuit to keep warm. The thrill and rush of dropping in on big waves worked to purify and help me feel alive and whole again. The action and movement kept blood pumping in the heart. Salt water cleansed the sinuses and washed away the cobwebs. When on dry land, the sick feeling slowly creeped back and nibbled at my insides. The brain was the real enemy. The phrase "you think too much" could not have been more appropriate. If someone described a straw man, running on empty, only going through the motions, I would resemble that remark. Or hollow like that hangman scratched into the paint of the payphone at the burger joint near the airport.

In Spanish class a girl name Erin purposely sat next to me. She was drop dead, gorgeous with clear skin, long flowing hair and an incredible body with long legs that never ended. We spoke often in class and paired together for an assignment. One morning she brought me a maple bar. For an essay I translated into Spanish a song lyric about there being a lack of sweetness in my life. She proclaimed this was the baker's cure-all for what ailed me.

The majority of enrolled students in Santa Barbara are women. Go Gauchos! Of this abundance, there is no shortage of good looking girls. A monk or hopeless, blind squirrel could luck into hooking up. Erin was stunning and one of the most beautiful girls I'd ever met. On the spur of a moment, I even found the way to her place at midnight one night. She greeted me with a smile, was game and invited me to hang out. Settled comfortably on her bed, Erin looked at me with incredible deep, oval brown eyes. All systems were clear and lights green for go. I paused and stopped before going the whole way. Feeling like an observer and detached from the moment, I did not make the move for sex. Surprise and confusion crossed her face. Given that rare opportunity who would have hesitated? We snuggled and talked about our worlds and fell asleep without anything physical happening. The next morning, I said how great I thought she was, then made myself scarce. The moment passed. I felt like damaged goods. Erin deserved more than I was offering, better than my rebound material. We were still always friendly and spoke often in class. She was a truly nice girl. Maybe she thought I was gay. No matter, the opportunity for our ship together sailed away.

Halloween is a big deal in Santa Barbara. The holiday came and went. I have a vision of Ben standing in the front room holding an industrial size ziploc bag with one pound of magic mushrooms. Rachel and Michele were over. There was tremendous whooping and hollering. The whole week was an epic, wild kaleidoscope blur. Thousands of costumed students from across the state converged on our little town. The massed jumble of superheroes, goblins, witches, breakfast cereal cartoon characters and whatever other outfits the active, addled imaginations of brilliant college students could dream up swarmed the street in front of the apartment. The walls of wildly dressed people parading by were only slightly more crazy because of the volume of natural hallucinogenics ingested.

Wearing a Walkman, I jammed along with Peter Tosh while riding the Super Duty on the shore of the beach. I peddled along wet sand near the water where it was hard and firm enough to support the path I carved. The songs and moments went on forever. Then somehow the night was almost over. With the sun not yet peaking over the horizon, the sky turned soft pink and orange over the mountains in the east. The deep grape jelly sky transitioned to a crisp, sharp electric blue. Alone in the world of music, the movement of air kissed the skin on my face. Riding the bicycle at speed, the heartbreaking beauty of colors across the sky reflected against salt water pooling along the shore. The world struck me as a magical place, full of wonder and mysteries. Even then I wondered about Janine. I thought about sitting with her at my kitchen table and how badly I wanted to prepare for us slices of oranges and watermelon. The natural sugars in the fruit would surely make me whole again and healthy. How much I wished to show her this special place in the universe, a morning so majestic she would never believe her eyes. I would give anything to share it with her. She was likely asleep, who knows where.

Arriving home, my pant legs were wet from the ocean. I rode in the low tide of water a foot deep. Because of the perfect functionality and utility of the bicycle fenders salt water did not spray across my back. The peddles and feet submerged under water more than once though, soaking my shoes and making the corduroy pants stick to my body. I pealed them away, carefully stepping out from each pants' legs while simultaneously pouring myself a giant glass of orange juice. Standing in the kitchen in boxer shorts, drenched pants on the linoleum floor, sunshine and the glass of perfect juice made me feel whole. I retreated to the bedroom to finally grab some sleep. In bed with Marco was some gal I did not recognize. Careful to not wake them or disturb their sleep, I crashed out within seconds of my head hitting the pillow. I slept through the day and finally rose for an hour to watch the sun go down. With my head on a different plane, half the brain worked properly. I missed the entire day. After the sunset I went back to bed and slept again. When I arose the next morning only a faint echo of something weird remained. Even that shifted back to normal the next day.

I went to the Store after school one Thursday in November a week before the official end of fire season. My timing was excellent because the shots had just returned from Tennessee of all places. I was able to see everyone before they disbanded for the season and went in twenty different directions and their own separate ways. Everybody enjoyed treating me like a long lost piñata. They ganged up, calling me a no good wanker, ripping me for quitting and leaving them in a lurch. Of course, I bought a case of beer and probably owed more than that for every fire I missed. Sitting on the wall hearing the stories made me happy. But something felt minutely different and slightly off. As terrific as it was to be around the crew, I felt like an observer now and not a one hundred percent part of the unit. B.D. told a story about taking a taxi to the next county over to purchase beers for everybody. Of all the crazy luck they were stuck in a "dry county." I did not realize such a thing existed. Something was horribly wrong with this picture. How positively un-American that there were actual places in this great country where a grown man can not simply walk into his friendly neighborhood package store and buy a cold beer without judgment. Brave grandfathers died on the beaches of Normandy for our freedom. This could be worse than Communism. Who were these people trampling on our rights. Were we living in the nineties or Prohibition time?

B.D.'s delivery made everything seem funny. I usually knew every story by heart, but did not make the Tennessee trip and missed out, solidifying that separate feeling.

With the time change darkness came early. Waving goodbye, I rode home with a nice beer buzz going, nothing too serious. I learned that lesson, and had promised myself never to make that mistake again.

Thanksgiving came and went. When school broke for Christmas, most students went home to their families. IV grew quiet again, a nice shift from the crush of people. I surfed every day and enjoyed the break. This was my first real vacation not having to work or study for school. Ben and Chris brought three girls home one Thursday night. We made apple-pie shots from a gallon jar of apple juice with cheap vodka in a coffee cup with a dash of cinnamon. I'd been taking it easy on the drinking, being good too, but let loose this night. Sitting in a circle passing the ceramic cup around, I mixed the drinks together and played bartender. Looking at my friends laughing, I enjoyed the scene. This was fun. We played albums and danced in a group together in the front room. The mix of music covered old sixties and seventies soul to more rocking modern grunge music. The apple pie shots made me warm inside with a nice hazy glow. Dancing to some eighties funk I caught my reflection in the window twisting and shaking my body without abandon and came to a realization. For the first time in forever I was not running from the memory of Janine or trying to bury the idea of her deep inside. She loved music and would have enjoyed this. Thinking about her brought a smile and didn't hurt. The pain was gone.

I kept dancing until the song ended, then picked another album and stared as the record spun around on the turntable. The flash of an idea came to me. I walked into the kitchen, grabbed a light blue highlight marker and on a clean sheet of white paper wrote, "Thanks alive, I be cured!"

With a black ballpoint, I outlined the thick blue letters. The words possessed a three dimensional effect. Using two pieces of scotch tape I affixed the page to the wall in my room above the bed. I'm clearly no poet, but the words resonated with me. I could read the phrase as a mantra and remind myself every morning just in case I forgot. We kept dancing and ended piling into Chris' FourRunner to drive downtown to a club for a real dance scene. Feeling free and easy, a page turned. Time for a new chapter to be written. The girls were pleasant and fun to be around. Their silliness made me laugh. We danced until closing time in the dark club with flashing colored lights and throbbing music. The smell of clove cigarettes filled the dark club. Finding a stick of bubblegum in a back pocket, I popped the piece into my mouth. The empty wrapper read "Carefree" and resonated with special meaning. The world was speaking to me.

A major result to burying myself in books were straight A's and an A minus on the report card. Definitely a first. Forever I have been cursed with B pluses, that grade driving me crazy as not good enough and an obstacle to break through. After finally breaking the B plus barrier, surprisingly it did not seem a big deal. When things click into place, they are meant to be, natural and not an accident. On a roll, I nailed winter quarter as well. I called the Supe to let him know I would finish the school year but hoped to join the hotshots in early June, if that was okay. The crew would form in April to start trail work. Supe said not to worry, he would work something out. They could not leave an open spot once fire season started, but he would make sure there was a place for me. I thanked him.

"Curt, you keep those A's coming. That's outstanding, son. Straight A's. You can write your own damn golden ticket. Get you wherever you want to go."

"Thanks again, Supe. You should know how much I appreciate everything you've done for me."

CHAPTER

28

We were in the kitchen. I'd volunteered to cook. Still top chef, Ben kept a watchful eye, often offering helpful advice or feedback. Recently I've been stepping up in the kitchen to pull my share. Am proud to say a couple of my "go to" dishes are pretty decent. The shake 'n bake chicken is salty and all right. If anyone is confused, all right means, all~ everything~ is right~ correct ~ the opposite of wrong. All right has a declarative, positive definition and doesn't mean okay. Words have meaning, people. My chicken and beef tacos are tasty too. I cook the soft tortillas in sizzling oil one at a time in the trusty heavy iron skillet making them nice and crunchy. We were spread across the front room and kitchen celebrating Friday evening and the end of week. The menu tonight called for spaghetti with meat sauce. From scratch the sauce had been simmering for hours. The rich smell of ground beef, sausages and spices marrying together filled the apartment.

Marco told us about some lady he heard on the radio that morning. On the third of May, the KJEE disc jockeys were getting ready for the weekend, methodically taking shots of tequila to test how quickly alcohol impaired their faculties. As a public service a deputy sheriff administered a breathalyzer test to everyone in the studio several times over the course of the morning. I wondered if the deputy was anyone I'd recognize.

"This lady said Cinco de Mayo is really Jose Cuervo's birthday. That's why we celebrate the day."

"No. That's not true." I said. "It's something to do with a battle the Mexicans fought against the French. We learned about it in Spanish."

"Well, that's what they were saying on the radio. I don't think they can say stuff if it's not true. The sheriff was there and everything."

"You're from New York city. What do you know, Marco?"

"Cinco has been co-opted and is a corporate Hallmark holiday now, intended to sell margaritas and get people to eat chips and guacamole. Originally the day celebrated this battle they won. That lady was probably some liquor rep. Cinco de Mayo is definitely not Jose Cuervo's birthday."

"Whatever, dude. They were hilarious. Morning radio is the best for comedy. It's great laughing in the morning."

"Laughing is crucial the whole day long, Marco. You're a goof."

Incredulous, I threw a noodle against the wall to check if the pasta was ready. The test noodle stuck to the wall signifying it was done. I directed the three to grab their plates and line up to be served. Using two tattered potholders I carried the large pot to the sink to drain the boiling water. A solid chunk of Parmesan cheese lay on the counter to grate over the pasta. Ben would never let us use that green cylinder stuff. Mismatched plates and silverware were stacked ready to go. With two hands I poured boiling water into the strainer in the sink, catching the noodles. Turning my face away to avoid steam rising, I looked through the window to the street.

Chris' Toyota rested in its usual spot on the grass in the front yard. Visible past the black vehicle on the left and parked at the curb, a white Nissan pickup truck looked familiar. Music from the latest Social Distortion album boomed over the speakers. I set my sights on the pickup momentarily, then scanned and looked to the right. Standing on the porch, Janine peered through the smudged glass of the window, undecided about whether or not to knock on the door. She had watched our scene in the kitchen while steeling nerves, deciding her mind. I froze in place at the sink and stared at her. Our eyes locked in place. The sliding glass door was open.   A breeze from the park rustled leaves on the tree outside and carried into the room.   The screen mesh separated us. We were barely nine feet apart. I did not say a word but fixed on those entrancing eyes. A mirage of clear blue water with gold flashes like slivers of stars radiated from space, piercing me. I did not move.

Made in the USA
Middletown, DE
24 February 2018